Content Warning

This novel addresses topics that may be sensitive to some readers such as mental illness, depression, and suicide.

The Paths Between the Stars

From Layla Dog Press
an imprint of Blank Slate Communications, LLC
Tucson, AZ 85719

The Paths Between the Stars
Book One of the MANY SKIES series

YOUNG ADULT FICTION
SCIENCE FICTION / FANTASY

Publisher's Note: This book is a work of the imagination. Names, characters, places, organizations, and incidents either are products of the author's imagination or are used fictitiously. While some of the characters, organizations, and incidents portrayed here can be found in historical accounts, they have been altered and rearranged by the author to suit the strict purposes of storytelling. The book should be read solely as a work of fiction.

Cover design by James Egan and Kira Rubenthaler at Bookfly Design.

Library of Congress Control Number: 2023932959
ISBN 9780998425955
Printed in the U.S.A.

Amira K. Makansi

The Paths Between the Stars

Book One
of the
Many Skies
Series

Layla Dog Press | Tucson, AZ

"There are more things in heaven and earth, Horatio,
Than are dreamt of in your philosophy."
—William Shakespeare, *Hamlet*, Act I Scene V

C8H18

"Octane is an alkane with the chemical formula C8H18. It has 18 isomers. It is an important constituent of gasoline. Less dense than water and insoluble in water. Hence floats on water. Produces irritating vapor. Flammable." —The Open Chemistry Database, "Octane," National Center for Biotechnology Information

Petrol. Chemical. The sweet scent of gasoline that burns the back of your throat. Slick on my skin like a silken dress. Shimmering multicolors dancing across my body in the afternoon sun. It is the smell of power. But also of fear.

I press the match to paper; pause. Hesitate. Once I strike, there's no going back. I close my eyes and breathe a sigh of relief, relishing my last moments.

"Let it work," I whisper, my words floating out on the flammable wind, the vapors already evaporating off my body, chilling me. A silent prayer to whatever gods or ancestors may or may not be watching.

It won't, comes the haunting voice of doubt in the back of my head. Nothing has changed. Just like every other time, I'll fail. I grit my teeth and shake my head. It *will* work this time.

It has to.

I let out a deep breath. Only one way to find out. I strike the match.

Heat and flame erupt around me. God, it's beautiful! I smile as the gasoline ignites and is carried off in front of me on the spring breeze like the unfurling of a flag. The orange, red, and white tendrils lick at my hair and skin. No, they *are* my hair, my skin, my fingertips. The chill in the air is gone. I stretch out my fingers and marvel at the way the flames caress me. They are warm and welcoming, like an embrace from an old friend.

But there's no pain.

Is this what death feels like?

Worry bites, and my happiness evaporates like the gasoline off my skin. No, god, no, it's not working, there's no pain, nothing's happening. The fire does nothing. It's supposed to *burn*, like wood, like buildings, like humans when their bodies are immolated after death, but to me the flames are gentle, welcoming, and powerless. I cry out in anger and clench my fists. I bite my lip hard and again feel no pain. Nor does my skin blacken and turn to ash. As the fire burns out, its energy exhausted and with nothing else to feed on, I bite my tongue and choke out a sob.

Why? Why doesn't it work?

The flames are gone. I blink back tears and look down at my skin for traces of a burn, for blood, for anything. But there's nothing. I am unblemished. I am clean. I am alive.

I stare around the little copse of wood I'd chosen, the pine trees nearby and the lush, damp floor of pine needles. Before I started, I set a ring of stones around me to contain the flames. I didn't want to start any forest fires. I'm not trying to destroy the world. Just myself. I look down at the scorched ground beneath me, wondering at how everything around me seems capable of death.

Everything but me.

Suddenly angry, I pick up one of the stones in the circle and throw it viciously at a nearby tree. It misses, and my rage only ignites further, like the striking of the match. In a fit, stumbling over my own limbs, I step out of the circle and pull my underwear back on. Uncoordinated and foul, I trip over myself as I pull on my pants. I throw my tee shirt over my head and spit on the ground, cursing every vile force of nature that for some godforsaken reason refuses to allow me to leave this world on my own terms.

A dose of the familiar shocks me out of my anger: black spots freckling my vision, crinkling like the static on my father's old television. Renewed fear floods through me. I am alone, and they will find me here. The shadows. The energy from the fire, from my hope and my anger, surely will have drawn them to me. Vertigo washes over me. As blackness crowds out my vision, browns and greens and spring flowers disappear, replaced by swallowing, empty darkness. I stumble and throw my hand out, catching my palm on the rough bark of a nearby pine, trying to clear my head, trying to fight them off.

It's gone.

I straighten. My vision clears almost instantly. The forest around me reappears. My breathing, ragged, slows.

"Noomi?"

I whirl, my heart pounding. The sleek black hair and gentle green eyes of my younger sister, Ada. I rush toward her, pulling her into my arms. With her, I'm safe. With her, no one can hurt me.

"Are you okay?" she asks.

I scoop her up into my arms—though she's almost too big for me to do so—and plant a kiss on her forehead. "Now that you're here."

"What were you doing?"

I plop her down on her feet again, and she stares suspiciously at the circle of stones a few feet away, and the charred earth inside. Even Ada, as young as she is, has learned over the years not to trust me alone.

"Teaching myself to build a fire," I lie.

"Oh." She stares at the blackened dirt. Then she looks at me, smiling. Maybe she believes me. Or maybe she decided it doesn't matter. She slips her hand in mine, pulling me back toward our house. "Mom said lunch is ready."

"Let's go, little Peach."

I let her lead, pulling me through the pines and the mossy carpet of leaves and needles and around to our house. When Kuri starts barking, my sister drops my hand and dashes toward the house, where the little dachshund is waiting impatiently inside his invisible electric fence. She scoops him into her arms and carries him up the porch stairs and through the sliding glass door, as he licks at her ear the whole way.

Inside, my mother is frying balls of falafel, and my sister is already at the table with Kuri, named for the chestnut color of his hair, sitting on her lap. The kitchen is steamy and warm and smells of fresh bread and toasted cumin.

"Noomi, where have you been?" my mother asks as she sets a plate with warmed pita in front of me. There's restraint in her tone. She wants to say more. I know she's trying not to be too impatient, too demanding. Her short hair bobs around her chin as she moves. She sprinkles fresh-cut scallions over a bowl of *baba ghanouj* and crosses her arms to watch me.

"Outside," I say. "Practicing building a fire and setting up my stove. For our overnighter in a few weeks. The counselors said it would be good to practice. They taught us last weekend."

"Really? Is that what you were doing out there?" It's a good thing I hid the gasoline canister in a blackberry bramble so thorny no one but me could wrangle it without a full hazmat suit. I know she'll be out there later. Like Ada, she doesn't trust me. She doesn't believe me. But I don't blame her. After ten suicide attempts—now eleven—in my sixteen years of life, my mother has a right to be suspicious.

"Yes, Mama."

You don't need to worry anymore, I want to say, my thoughts solidifying, crystallizing. This afternoon's failure has finally proven that my attempts at self-destruction are useless. Worse than useless, as the energy from the attempts will draw the shadows to me. They'll find me, like they did today. It's impossible for me to hurt myself, so I won't try anymore. Instead of fleeing the things that haunt me, I must finally acknowledge the truth I've been running from for the last eight years: I am here to stay, and so are they.

I shiver. I don't want to feel the emptiness anymore. But escape is impossible.

I laugh as Ada pushes Kuri's muzzle away from her plate while he begs. I relish the warm spices on my tongue the way I relished the flames lapping lovingly at my skin. The cool tingle of the fork against my lips, the delicate pull of the pita against my teeth, the softness of my mother's eyes as she looks at me—

I don't want to leave these things behind. I never have. All I want is to escape the shadows, and death seemed the easiest way.

It's time to find another path.

SUBLIMATION

"Sublimation is the conversion between the solid and the gaseous phases of matter, with no intermediate liquid stage… sublimation is most often used to describe the process of snow and ice changing into water vapor in the air without first melting into water." —United States Geological Survey, "Sublimation and the Water Cycle"

Flakes of snow curl around me like yesterday's flames. They're as puffy as clouds, as wet as Kuri's tongue licking at my cheeks. They drip from the sky in great empty breaths. I brush them out of my hair and hold my bare fingers in front of me. They are purple and pink against the vast, empty whiteness. My hands are cold. But it doesn't hurt. It never does.

I glance down at my feet, sunk almost a half-foot deep in the snow, bend and scoop up a handful of the stuff, bring it to my mouth like a sacred offering. I take a bite and savor the sweet cool taste of mountain snow as it melts in my mouth. It reminds me of honey. Sky honey. This emptiness, out here in the snow, surrounded by firs, is different from the blackness I've been fleeing. This emptiness is cleansing, purifying. Maybe it's not even emptiness I feel here, but fullness: full of simplicity and elegance and awareness.

"Noomi! Are you trying to get yourself killed?"

It's Paul. He's trying to catch up to me, trudging ahead of the rest of the group.

"Generally speaking, Paul," I shout back, "it's not a good idea to joke about killing yourself with a girl who's been clinically diagnosed as suicidal."

I wait as he catches up to me. He stares at his feet, stomping them on the ground as a pretext for his embarrassment. He's nearly a foot taller than me, but right now he looks like a lonely duckling.

"Don't tell Leah I said that," he mumbles.

I laugh. "You know that's why I like you. Because you're not like Leah."

"I need this job, okay?"

"I won't tell her."

He huffs. Paul is the youngest counselor in my wilderness therapy group. He's not very good at his job—he's only doing it because it's a part of the requirements for his doctorate program. He doesn't want to go into counseling, so he's not interested in talking about our feelings or what he calls "psychobabble," and he's told me a few times he's going to get himself fired if he's not more careful about what he says. Of all my counselors, I like him the best. He doesn't ask me to try to be someone I'm not. He says things to me he wouldn't be allowed to say to the other students, and in exchange, I give him high ratings when they pass around the surveys.

A quarter mile behind, the other members of my adventure therapy group trudge through the snow, along with two older counselors. I stare out at the vast spread of the valley while they catch up to us. It's so green down there, so wondrously green, and yet so white here. In the throes of spring, the world below is blossoming. But here on the mountaintop, winter reigns. I close my eyes and tilt my head to the sky. Crystalline flakes land on my face and melt down my cheeks. The droplets burrow into my scarf, chilling me, rinsing me clean.

"Noomi," Leah chastises when she finally catches up, "you need to stay with the group."

"I know."

"Well, stay with us this time, please. The tree wells can be treacherous up here. And you need to stay warm."

The cold can't hurt me. But I nod anyway.

"We're almost at the top," Leah says to the whole group. "Once we're there we'll break for lunch and do a meditation—" Paul rolls his eyes, and I fight back a laugh "—and then head back down."

This time, I stay with the group as Leah and Paul lead us to the summit. In a month or two, this peak will be crawling with day hikers come to enjoy the wildflowers and picnic with their families while taking in the view. But for now, we have it to ourselves. I like it that way.

"Peanuts?" A boy next to me holds out a handful of nuts. He's new. Today's his first outing with us. I shook his hand earlier in the week when he showed up at the therapy meeting, noting the dark, mossy-green color of his eyes. But now his name escapes me.

After lunch, I sit next to Paul while Leah leads a twenty-minute mindfulness meditation. Adventure therapy was something I only agreed to at my psychologist's insistence and to pacify my mother. The "therapy" part doesn't interest me in the least. Two years ago, when I first started, I thought that doing dangerous activities like whitewater kayaking, mountain climbing, and extended backpacking trips would give me the opportunity to kill myself and make it look like an accident. An easy route into danger. But I gave up after I tried to drown myself last year on a whitewater rafting excursion. I was underwater for four minutes before I realized the lack of oxygen wasn't going to kill me.

"You should be dead," she said, the counselor who pulled me back into the boat after I spat up a half-gallon of water.

"I know." I stopped seeing the wilderness as a place to die after that. It became, instead, a kind of solace. The mountains are my favorite, especially above the tree line, where the snow never melts. There, the shadows can't find me. The whiteness is protective.

The sun crawls out from behind the clouds, and the mist that surrounds us dissipates. As Leah drones about empathy and self-awareness, I notice the way the sun's rays lounge here and there on the snowfield, warming the air. A thin cloud of water vapor, only visible in the hazy yellow light, rises from the snow. The triple point; when the atmospheric pressure and temperature converge so that a solid substance is able to convert directly to its gas phase.

Sublimation.

We talked about it in chemistry with Mr. Bailey. Chemistry is my favorite class. It's not as hard as math, because all the ideas are concrete. They make sense. They apply to real properties that can be measured and quantified and tested. Last week, we learned about phase changes, and how, under certain conditions, some substances can transition from a gas to a solid without ever becoming a liquid. That's what's happening here. The snow absorbs the heat from the sun and evaporates, turning directly into water vapor. The opposite is possible, too, where energy is released into the system, and a gas transitions into a solid.

I watch, entranced, as the snow vaporizes in the sun, amazed by how warm it is now that the clouds are gone and the sky is clear, despite six inches of snow beneath my feet.

"Noomi?" It's the boy with green eyes. "Why aren't you wearing gloves?" His eyelashes are as long as a butterfly's wings.

Leah has stopped talking and the rest of the group has gotten to their feet.

"I forgot mine at home."

A lie, of course. I don't need gloves. The chill of the snow can't hurt me. The boy extends a hand to help me up, and I notice he isn't wearing gloves either. I let him pull me to my feet. His hands aren't cold in the slightest.

"Why aren't you?" I ask.

"I don't need them. Not in this world."

"In *this* world?"

He smiles, waving his arm at the snowy scenery around us. I nod, my mouth open in a silent aha, and he turns away and says no more. He rejoins the group heading down the trail, and I stare at the wide, white plateau, the flecks of green and brown trees in the distance, and the yellow sun dripping across the landscape.

I replay the moment in my head: his slow smile, green eyes faintly glowing. His arm sweeping out. *Not in this world.* There's something enticing about the way he says it. Like there's something delicious waiting for me, just out of reach.

After a moment, I follow the others down, moving slowly, one foot in front of the other. My legs are tired. It was a strenuous hike up—we climbed almost a thousand feet. Now my belly is full and my body warm from the sunlight against my skin. All around me, the snow is evaporating, plumes of mist rising from the whiteness like the curl of a feather.

Unlike earlier, when I charged ahead of the group, now I lag behind, slow as a sloth and yawning the whole way. A vague sense of danger pulses, but I push it away, sleepy. Pay attention, a voice in my mind says. I open my eyes a little wider and see that I am heading into a patch of trees, tall, dark Douglas firs, and the sun has disappeared behind a cloud. The world has turned monochrome. Like photographs in a darkroom, bathed in a pool of dim red light. The shadows from the trees etch into the ground, treacherous. I straighten, trying to wake up, wishing for company. Where's the rest of the group? How did I get so far behind?

My boots grow heavier with every step. The shadows swell like a vortex, lurking, leaning into me. The happiness

I felt earlier, the freedom, the invulnerability, sloughs off me like the snowflakes I brush from my hair. My feet drag. The green needles on the firs have faded to grey and black. They're growing, I realize. The shadows are here. I'm too tired to be surprised. They dislocate from the trees and rocks that own them and take on a form of their own. Spindly fingers creeping up my shoulders, peeling emotions away from me. I am dissipating. Evaporating. The stain leaches into my eyes and dark ink, impenetrable, spills across my vision. I stagger. I try to claw through it, but I have no energy. No emotion. No fight left in me. Now even the tiredness fades and there is nothing.

Black.

Empty.

Nothing.

"Noomi!"

A voice rips through the inky curtain and a vivid, brilliant green shines through, green like chlorophyll, green like spring grass, and I look for the boy with the butterfly eyelashes, expecting for no reason at all to see his green eyes staring at me.

When my vision returns, blurry, his face is swimming before me. His amber skin and black hair make me think of sun and sand dunes. But when I meet his eyes, they aren't green.

They're *iridescent*. The multicolored shimmering of a rainbow. Vivid oil-slick spectrum of color.

"Oh, God," I gasp, sitting up. I'd fallen. I'm on my back. The heavy branches of pine and fir frame my vision. Yellow sun. Dusky green needles. The boy's maroon hoodie. The shadows are gone, or at least diminished, drawn back to normal. Reattached to their earthly bodies.

"Sublimation point," I say, making sense of it all. I am energy. They want energy. They need me.

The boy cocks his head to the side, looking at me like I've sprouted feathers.

"Phase change," I say. "That's what it felt like was happening. Like the snow." I cough out a laugh as I realize I'm spouting gibberish.

"That's an interesting way to put it," he says, which strikes me as an odd thing to say after you've found one of your fellow therapy members passed out in the snow. The iridescence in his eyes is fading back to the mossy green I saw earlier. The sun is gone now, hidden behind clouds the color of goose down, and there's a chill in the air.

Sublimation. I don't know what it means, but I know what it felt like. There's energy bound up in me that needs to be released. And the shadows, whatever they are, wherever they come from, want that energy.

"What's in your eyes?" I say, stupidly.

"What do you mean?" he asks.

"They're...colorful."

He stares at me for what feels like a long time. He rarely blinks, and I have to fight the temptation to look away. It's unnerving to feel so *seen*. Finally his lips turn up in a small smile. "So are yours. Aren't all eyes colorful?"

"Not like this."

But the iridescence is gone, his irises once again a dark green. The wind is picking up around us, the clouds turning an ominous grey.

"Let's focus on the important stuff. Are you okay?"

"I'm fine." I stand, brushing the snow off me. "I lay down because I was tired and fell asleep for a half second."

Now he grins. "You expect me to believe that? That you lay down to take a nap up here?" I fold my arms and glare at him.

"That's what happened, okay?"

There's a moment of silence as the wind whistles through the trees. Snow dusts our eyes as it falls from the boughs.

"You should get going." He turns to walk away. "I'm glad you're safe," he says over his shoulder as he stomps through the snow.

I watch him go, wondering what just happened.

"Hey," I holler after him. "What's your name?"

But the howling wind swallows my voice, and he doesn't respond.

SURFACE TENSION

"Among the purely physical properties of their materials to which the chemist and the biologist have been compelled to pay an increasing amount of attention during recent years, surface tension undoubtedly occupies the first place. In great measure this is due to the development of colloidal chemistry, which deals with matter in a state of extreme sub-division…so that the properties of surfaces become important, and sometimes decisive, factors in the behaviors of such systems." —Richard Smith Willows, *Surface Tension and Surface Energy and their Influence on Chemical Phenomena*

"You know how much I love you, sugarplum?" I pull up in front of Mr. Arcadio's home, the brick exterior crawling with ivy.

"Tell me how much," Ada says, giggling.

"I love you as much as all the stars in our galaxy. How many stars is that?"

"One hundred billion."

"Yes! Which galaxy do we live in?"

"The Milky Way, duh!" I can hear the eye roll in her voice.

"And what kind of galaxy do we live in?" I pop the handbrake and open the door.

"A spiral! Stop asking easy questions!"

"When did you get so smart?" I jump out of the car, and Ada follows suit. Mr. Arcadio is waiting outside. Ada runs up to him and throws her arms around his waist.

"Ada! I hope you're ready for a game of chess. I have the board set up in the living room."

Malcolm Arcadio, a retired professor from Reed College in Portland, is one of my mother's best friends. They met at the local library when she was picking up a stack of books for me to read. They connected over their mutual love of science fiction novels, and when my father died a year later, Mr. Arcadio was invaluable in helping to look after me and Ada while my mother adjusted to life as a single parent.

"Oh no," Ada sighs, pulling out of the hug. "You always beat me at chess. Can't we play something else?"

"What would you like to play?"

"What about poker?"

"Poker?" Mr. Arcadio stares down at her, feigning shock. "Has someone been teaching you to gamble?"

"Abuela Mariana," Ada says, without a hint of shame. Abuela Mariana is our Dad's mom. When he died, she moved to a house a few blocks from ours to help our mother look after me and Ada. "She says it's her favorite game because it combines luck and skill. And because you can win real money if you're good."

"It seems I'll have to watch my wallet today," Mr. Arcadio says with a smile. "All right, Ada, you win. I think I have a deck of playing cards in a closet somewhere and some pennies we can bet with."

"Pennies?" Ada says, aghast. "Abuela lets us play with whole dollars."

"Ada!" I chastise. "Remember your manners." But Mr. Arcadio is still smiling. Nothing she says can faze him.

"Thank you for watching her," I say, as I always do. He waves me off, as he always does.

"Of course, Noomi. When will you stop calling me Mr. Arcadio and start calling me Mal?"

"When I've forgotten my own manners," I reply with a smile. "I'll pick her up from the library around five-thirty?"

"That'll be just fine."

"Great. See you then!" I turn back to the car.

"Oh, Noomi, I almost forgot," Mr. Arcadio says, walking quickly around me to his own car. He pulls out his keys and unlocks it, reaches into the passenger seat and pulls out a book. "I found this in the stacks the other day and thought you might enjoy it." He hands it to me. *Flatland: A Romance of Many Dimensions.*

"What is this?" I ask. He's been feeding me a steady stream of books on chemistry, physics and biology since I was young, but recently the books have taken a turn from concrete ideas into philosophical approaches.

"A very readable book about math," he says, a twinkle in his dark eyes, grey brows waggling. "You mentioned calculus has been difficult for you this semester, and this may give you new ways to think about the subject. Not to mention, there are some very interesting ideas in there."

"Like what?"

"You'll see," he says, vaguely. "But the most important is that of multidimensionality."

"What does *that* mean?"

"Why don't you open the book and find out?" His lips curl in a smile. "It's due back in a month, but if you need more time, I'm happy to renew it for you."

"Thank you," I say. "I'll take a look."

I walk back to the car and open the door. A weight sinks into my gut. Reluctantly, I release the parking brake and pull from the curb. It's five minutes to my next destination, but I'd rather drive into the ocean.

Every Wednesday at 4 p.m., I have an appointment with Dr. Chase, the latest psychiatrist brave enough to take me as a patient. Five therapists, six different combinations of antidepressant, anti-anxiety, and antischizophrenia medications, and an infinite number of visits in which I "talk about my feelings" in the seven years since my father died.

None of it has made the shadows go away.

If anything, they've gotten worse. The attacks have grown longer, more debilitating. The shadows come more frequently. And when they do, the darkness is complete.

In the first few months after Dad died, it was just a grey haze, like static on Abuela's old TV. My mind would get foggy. I couldn't see clearly. Bright colors faded to grey. It wasn't until a year later that the darkness became total, and even then, the attacks were only once every few weeks.

Now, they come every few days—if I'm lucky. They practically knock me unconscious. They drain all sensation from my body. I'm surprised they haven't killed me yet.

And not one of my therapists has been able to do anything about it.

I park in front of the office, kill the engine, and sit in the car, steeling myself for the endless questions. I crank up the music—RJD2's *Deadringer* has been on constant rotation—sit back and close my eyes, breathing through the song. The airy keyboard dances above the drumbeat, and I wish I could sit here for an hour instead of walking inside. Talking about the shadows isn't fun. Reliving them is almost as painful as experiencing them. Still, I'd do it over and over again if I thought it would help.

But after seven years with no results, I know better.

When the song ends, I grit my teeth and get out of the car. Dr. Chase's personal assistant checks me in, a twenty-something man named Pat with carefully combed blond hair and the beginnings of a mustache. He smiles warmly and says that Dr. Chase is with another client but will be ready in a few moments. I stare at the ficus in the corner until the door opens and another patient, also a teenager, walks out.

Dr. Chase stands at the doorway and beckons me in with a smile.

"Noomi. How are you?"

I follow her in, opting for the plush armchair instead of the leather couch. Dr. Chase has *seating options.* This is a step up from my last therapist, who had only an uncomfortable brown armless couch.

Dr. Chase smiles at me. Instead of meeting her eyes, I stare at the painting on the wall. Swirls of orange and blue mixed with splattered pops of white and green—all overlaid on a placid painting of a sailboat. Some statement about the subversion of traditional art, I presume. I've been staring at this painting for an hour a week for most of the last two years.

It almost makes me miss the aquarium at my last therapist's office.

"How are you liking your new adventure group?"

"I like them fine."

"Made any friends yet?"

"I like Paul, one of the counselors. Well, not, 'like,' like. It's not weird. But he's funny. Leah's a little bit…stiff."

"Stiff?"

"She can be very formal. Follows the rules to a T and all that."

"Do you like talking to her?"

I focus intently on a white-and-green blob of paint.

"Not really. I liked Shana better than Leah. Shana was down to earth. Leah can be patronizing. Like she knows better than us all the time." I watch as Dr. Chase types notes into her iPad, and I can't help but imagine what she's writing. *Complainer. Self-righteous. Too smart for her own good.* I push these thoughts down and try to remind myself she's here to help. "But overall, I like this group better than the last one."

The one I had to be transferred out of when a counselor caught me before I jumped off a cliff.

"We think a different wilderness therapy program, one where she can stay closer to home and under more direct supervision, would be better for your daughter's needs." That's what they said to my mother after the incident. What I heard was: if not for her perfect school attendance and stellar grades, your daughter would be in an institution.

"Leah has mentioned that you don't seem to engage with the meditation sessions." Dr. Chase pauses. When I don't rise to the bait, she pushes. "Do they help you at all?"

"I prefer just being outside," I say. She bides her time, waiting for more. This time I'm the one to give in. "I don't like all the mindfulness stuff. All this talk about self-awareness and consciousness and controlling our breathing—it's tacky."

"Why is it tacky?"

"It's based on Buddhism, but it's not real. I've read about Buddhism. It's a religion. They have gods and spirits and they hang prayer flags. I'm not into religion anyway, but I'm definitely not into this half-assed version."

She purses her lips at my swear word, typing on her iPad, her fingers clattering against the screen. I smile inwardly. I love getting a reaction out of her. It's a game.

She's not looking at me when she responds. "Do you think good things can come out of meditative practice that aren't spiritual?"

"Maybe," I concede. "You can learn to focus, to be more aware."

"What if I told you there are scientifically-proven benefits to meditation?" She stops typing and looks at me. "Would that be helpful?"

I shrug. "If the data hold up."

She smiles. "I'll send you some papers. I know you won't have any problem understanding the studies. Why don't we call that your assignment? We can go over them together next week."

I try not to roll my eyes. Every week, she gives me an "assignment." Some ritual to try, papers to read, some new experiment. I am an experiment to her. One week it was journaling. Another was breathing exercises. One time was running. But like everything, I need to see data to believe. And none of her experiments have done anything to stop the shadows.

Instead of rolling my eyes, I nod in agreement. Reading papers is okay. At least it's not breathing exercises.

"Have you had any more attacks?"

I pause, trying to decide whether I want to answer truthfully. Dr. Chase doesn't believe the shadows are real. She thinks they're anxiety attacks. "Manifestations of your psychological trauma," she said.

Instead of telling her about the incident on the mountain, I choose to lie.

"Not recently." I look away from the painting to meet Dr. Chase's eyes. She raises a blonde eyebrow. I stare back, daring her to challenge me. Her straight, cropped hair seems to defy the laws of physics, hardly moving when she does.

She looks away. "How are things at school?"

I let out a breath I didn't know I was holding. "Good."

"Anything in particular you're learning about?"

"Today we talked about infinite limits in math class. We're getting ready to move onto derivatives pretty soon."

"How is chemistry going?"

"Really well."

"Still at the top of your class?"

"I set the curve on the last exam. Kalifa came in just one point behind me. I did a special project on the physics of surface tension last week for extra credit."

"It sounds like you don't need extra credit."

"It never hurts."

"Tell me about it."

"I worked out a few charts that model how much mass and volume an object would need to break the surface tension of a given body of water based on ambient air pressure and temperature. It explains why some insects can walk on water, or how to design products that let kids float without drowning." I look at the ground. "It's not very useful. Scientists already know all this stuff."

It occurs to me that a much more helpful model would be one that would tell me what words I need to say to break the tension between me and Dr. Chase. But there aren't equations to derive those words. Numbers can't predict human behavior. That's why I stick with chemistry.

"That's okay," Dr. Chase says. "You don't have to be deriving new models at sixteen. I'm sure your dad would be proud."

"My dad was taking college courses at sixteen. He would hardly be impressed that I worked out a few equations scientists have known for centuries."

She ignores my petulance. "We've never really talked about your dad's work. He was a chemist too, right? What was he studying?"

I hesitate before answering. No matter how many years pass, talking about him never gets easier.

"He had this grand idea that he was going to tie quantum physics and chemistry together. We already know that the way electrons behave in an atom has to do with chemical bonds. He was trying to take it further. The last few years before he died, he was researching the relationship between the quantum behavior of electrons, specifically the wavefunction and the Uncertainty Principle, and the chemical concept of entropy, trying to figure out if there was a connection."

"Did he succeed?"

"No," I say, bitterly. "He died too soon."

"Did his graduate students stay on the project? Was he working with someone who could keep moving?"

"I was nine. I hardly keep in touch with them." The words come out with a meanness I regret as soon as they're spoken.

"Do you want to continue the work he started?"

"Yes. It's what I think about every day."

Dr. Chase raises an eyebrow. "You seem excited about this. I'm glad to hear it, but I'm also curious. What sparked this new enthusiasm?"

What can I say? I dumped three gallons of gasoline over my head and struck a match, but I'm still sitting in front of you. After trying and failing to kill myself eleven times, I've finally accepted that it's impossible. But I don't understand why. Nothing makes sense. I only know one thing for sure: the shadows aren't going anywhere, and neither am I. Maybe if I keep looking, keep learning, I'll find an answer.

"I've decided to stop running from the things I'm afraid of," I say at last. "It's time to face my fears."

Dr. Chase leans forward, and I notice the iPad in her lap has gone dark.

"That's wonderful, Noomi. I'm thrilled to hear it." She pauses, and I wait for the *but*. "I have another question for you. What are you so afraid of?"

This isn't the first time she's asked me this question. She asked me once, two years ago, in our first session together.

What are you afraid of, Noomi?

Drowning, I said.

Your mom said you're on the swim team.

I didn't say I'm afraid of water.

The answer I gave her then wasn't the full answer. It wasn't the real answer. I meet her eyes, clear pools of crystal blue.

"Everything," I say.

Quantum Entanglement

"If the two dice were entangled quantum-mechanically then throwing one of them alone...would always unavoidably alter the other." — Jim Al-Khalili, *Quantum: A Guide for the Perplexed*

I throw my pencil down the table. "Finished!" I exclaim. My mother glances up from the sofa, where she's engrossed in a book. "Just in time. Claire should be here any minute."

"Who are you going to see, again?" she asks.

"They're local. You wouldn't know them. They're called L.E.O." I start packing away my papers.

"Ah," she says, as if she understands. "Very cool. Sounds like it'll be fun."

I repress an eyeroll. My mother wouldn't know what to do with herself at a live show. She doesn't listen to anything but classical music, so she certainly wouldn't be familiar with the local music scene. Instead of something snarky, I say, "Yeah, they're one of Claire's favorite bands. She's been talking about this all week."

"Will Kalifa be there, too?"

"The Three Musketeers, together as always."

She chuckles. "I hope you have fun. And remember, no—"

"Drinking, smoking, or sex." This time, I can't hold back the eyeroll. I know her pre-fun speech by heart.

"Exactly," she says. "And if you get into any trouble, call me, *habibti*. I want you to have fun, but I want—"

"—You to be safe, too," I finish for her, again. She presses her lips together and looks down at her book.

Don't push your luck tonight, Noomi.

How I convinced my mother to let me out of the house on a school night to go to a rock and roll concert at an all-ages venue downtown will forever be beyond me. Normally she's as watchful as a hawk, leery of letting me out of her sight even for a moment. I can't blame her, after everything I've put her through—from a constant rotation of therapists to two separate hospitalizations for attempted suicide. I suppose I have Dr. Chase to thank for tonight's freedom. She no doubt reported on my improved "zeal for life" after our last session.

My phone vibrates on the table.

"Claire's here," I say, stuffing the last of my papers in my backpack. I grab my phone and pull my hair out of my messy bun. "See you in the morning!"

"Noomi!" My mother shouts as I dash out the door. "Curfew on a school night is—"

"—Eleven! I'll be back by then, I promise!"

I sling my jacket on and step outside. Claire's 1999 Volvo station wagon—emerald green and inherited from her older brother when he moved to Seattle for college—is idling by the curb. I slide in, reaching across the console to give her a hug. As we pull apart, I look at her. She's wearing a vintage leather motorcycle jacket and blue skinny jeans with black ankle boots. Suddenly I feel almost as uncool as my mother, in ripped jeans, a black zip-up hoodie, and a basic band tee I've had for about five years.

"How are you always so stylish?" I ask.

"What are you talking about?" Claire only has one volume setting: loud. She's a theater student, trained to project her voice at all times. "You look so cute! The LCD Soundsystem shirt is a nice touch. Ohmygosh, I'm so excited!"

She shifts into drive and hits the pedal. I scrunch my face as tires squeal, hoping my mother didn't hear.

"I can't believe we convinced our parents to let us go."

She shrugs, her Cheshire cat grin pasted on her face. "My brother did so much shit in high school, going to a concert on a weeknight is no big deal."

I sigh. "Being the older sibling sucks. I have to break my mom in for everything. By the time Ada is my age, she'll have the keys to the kingdom."

"Not to mention, we'll corrupt her."

"Like we're such troublemakers."

"*You* might be Miss Innocent, Nooms, but I've got tricks up my sleeve." She drops one hand from the wheel and flashes silver metal at me from inside her jacket pocket.

"You brought a flask?"

She laughs. "Don't you want to have fun?"

I shake my head, but I'm smiling, too. "What's Kalifa going to say?" Our best friend—the Athos to Claire's Porthos and my Aramis—is a no-smoking, no-drinking Muslim. She also has killer taste in music. She talked the local university into giving her an hour-long DJ slot on their music channel when not enough college students volunteered. She got so many listeners in her first semester that they bumped her from the 11 p.m. to the 8 p.m. hour every Tuesday.

"What she doesn't know won't hurt her," Claire says.

"Is Basi coming?" I ask. Kalifa's boyfriend, also Muslim, from Ethiopia, is a year older and headed to Stanford next year. He's the only one in his year who got in.

"Of course, he is." Claire rolls her eyes. She spins the wheel and pulls into a parking spot a few blocks from the venue. "They're like conjoined twins. It's gross." She fake vomits. Basi leaves for college in six months, and he and Kalifa are trying to make the most of their time together.

"You're just jealous you don't have a boyfriend."

"Don't poke the bear." She kills the ignition and jumps out. For a moment I'm worried I've pushed too far, but when I emerge from the car, she's still grinning. "You're right. I'm a little jealous. But the lead singer of L.E.O. is super hot—and rumor has it he's single."

If anyone could seduce a hot and locally famous musician, it's Claire. With shoulder-length straight blonde hair, baby-blue eyes, and confidence a Glossier model would kill for, Claire's got more sex appeal than half our town combined. At heart, though, she's a theater kid whose favorite activity is belting out the lyrics to her favorite shows.

She leans against her car and zips up her moto. I follow suit, enjoying the cool evening air, the quiet before we head into the show. Claire pulls out her flask and unscrews the top. She takes a swig. "Hot single musician means I need a little courage. Want some?" She holds it out to me.

"Why not?" I take the flask from her. Then I think twice. "Germs?"

"Oh my god," she says dramatically, rolling her head from side to side. "Nooms, the booze will kill anything that might hurt you. I thought you were good at biology."

I shrug. "The alcohol will kill most things, but not everything, unless it's higher proof than your typical—"

"Oh well, what the hell," Claire interrupts. "If you don't want any, pass it back."

Oh well, what the hell, I repeat in my head. I take a swig—and immediately cough, almost spitting it out. Claire laughs.

"I didn't know it tasted this bad," I say, after I get it down. I've had a few beers at parties before, but this is new.

"Pretty terrible. You get used to it after a while. Kevin says he actually likes how it tastes now, but I'm never sure if he's pulling my leg." She takes the flask back, screws on the top, and puts it in her pocket. "Ready to go in?"

I nod. "Let's do it."

We show our tickets and ID to the bouncer and hold out our wrists to be tagged with the blue wristbands that identify us as minors. The opener is already playing—some rock-folk crossover with a mandolin and acoustic guitar. The sound isn't great, but we thread our way to the floor anyway, hoping to find Kalifa.

"Oh my god, there he is," Claire yells. "The lead singer." I press my hand over my ear where she's probably just ruptured my eardrum but follow her finger to where she's pointing. A tall, lanky man with a denim vest and brown hair that stands on end like he's recently been subjected to electroshock therapy is standing just outside the bar area, chatting with Kalifa and Basi.

"How do you know that's the lead singer?" Out of the corner of my eye, I see a figure that looks familiar, sitting by himself on one of the benches that line the room, hunched over something in his lap. I squint to get a better look, but he's hidden in the shadows.

"I've googled them all," Claire says. Her blonde hair bobs and catches the light as she leans closer so she can talk at a more reasonable volume. "He wears that vest in all his band pictures. His name is James. Isn't that a sexy name?"

I shrug. "I didn't know names could be sexy." I turn away from the familiar figure at the bench. "Well, now's your chance—it looks like Kali's already done the hard work for you." I grab Claire's hand and pull her forward.

"There you are!" Kalifa exclaims when she sees us. She pulls me into a hug, and I relish the silken feel of her hijab against my skin. She hugs Claire while Basi and I kiss cheeks.

"So nice to see you, Noomi," he says, the merest touch of an accent in his voice. "How are you?" Always so polite. A model student and an athlete—he was captain of the tennis team in his junior year of high school. It's no wonder he got into Stanford. It doesn't hurt that he's incredibly good looking.

Kali got a good one. I can understand a piece of Claire's jealousy, although I'm nothing but happy for our friend. Where's my Basi? I ask the universe, not for the first time.

"I'm great. I'm pretty sure my mom only let me out because I told her you'd be here."

He laughs. "I have that effect on parents."

"Noomi," Kalifa says, "this is James. He's the lead singer of L.E.O."

He holds out his hand, and we shake awkwardly. I stare up at him, feeling a bit starstruck.

"I've never met the lead singer of a band before," I say, before I can stop myself.

"Well, now you have," he says, uncreatively. But he's smiling, so I smile back.

"How do you know each other?" Claire asks Kalifa.

"We didn't," he says, turning to Claire. "But I listen to Kalifa's radio show on 92.8 every week. She introduced herself about five minutes ago. We were catching up about Thee Oh Sees."

Claire doesn't miss a beat. "Oh my god, I *love* Thee Oh Sees! They're so wild and ridiculous—they're bringing spirit back to rock and roll."

"Couldn't agree more," James says.

"Do you ever go by Jim?" Claire asks, teasing. "Or Jimmy?"

"Only my brother's allowed to call me that." But he's smiling too. I don't think he's looked away from Claire since they started talking. I check my phone absently, wondering if I should text my mom for a ride after the show. "Hey, I've gotta find my band, but let's catch up after the set?"

"Definitely!" Claire exclaims.

Kalifa meets my eyes and makes a face.

"Rad," James says. "Catch you later." As an afterthought, he smiles and waves at me, Kalifa, and Basi before he walks away.

"What a cool dude," Claire says from cloud nine.

"You talked to him for exactly one second," Kali laughs.

"I can tell he's cool," Claire says. "Let's go listen to this mediocre opener, that way we'll be front and center for the L.E.O. set."

"Yeah, the competition is really stiff for a front-row spot," I say. But Claire ignores me, grabbing my hand and pulling me into the throng, Kali and Basi close behind.

Two hours later, the show is over. We're all sweaty but exhilarated—and sticky from having beer spilled on us by college students.

"That was so much fun," Basi says. "I haven't danced like that in a long time."

"They're like if The Ramones and Foals had a baby," Kalifa says. "I just wish I didn't smell like a frat party."

"Handsome, cool, *and* an incredible singer-songwriter," Claire gushes. "I can't believe you just went up to talk to him."

"It's easier when you're not obviously in love," Kalifa says, leaning into Basi.

"You are obviously in love," I say, feeling a little glum. "Just not with the lead singer of L.E.O." Kalifa has Basi and Claire has a hot musician crush. Where does that leave me?

"That's what I'm saying," Kali says. "That's why it was so easy to introduce myself. Plus, we have music in common. He gave me some new bands to look into."

Claire fake-gasps. "You mean he's handsome, cool, and he introduced *Kalifa* to new artists? This man is a god."

As we come outside, I spot his denim vest. He's standing by the back door and chatting with his drummer.

I point discreetly. "Time to walk the walk, Claire."

She grins. "Catch you in math tomorrow, nerds." Then she's gone, threading through the dispersing crowd to meet him in the alley.

"Isn't she your ride?" Basi asks.

"Yeah, but it's okay. I already texted my mom. She'll be here in about ten minutes."

"Do you want us to wait with you?" Kalifa asks.

A vague, nagging fear tells me not to be alone right now. It's dark, and the streets are full of shadows. They never come when I'm with other people. But if I'm alone, I'm vulnerable. Dr. Chase says this is because when I'm alone, my thoughts grow louder. The anxiety turns up the volume. She says having people around helps keep those dark thoughts at bay.

I push the fear away, telling myself not to keep Kali and Basi up past curfew on my account. "No way. It's late. You should head home."

Kalifa and Basi exchange concerned looks.

"I'll be fine." I push her gently on the shoulder, trying to believe my own words. "Go home and get some sleep."

Then I see him. The familiar figure I'd seen inside. He's sitting on the curb about a half-block down the street, illuminated in the faded white light of a streetlamp. It's the kid from wilderness therapy. The one with iridescent eyes. I recognize the jacket he was wearing the day we hiked—a thick, maroon zip-up hoodie.

"Noomi?" Kalifa says, waving her hand in front of my face. "Are you okay?"

"I'm fine." I start back to attention. "Just tired."

"It's been a long day," Basi says. "Your mom will be here soon?"

"Yes, Dad," I say, feeling calmer now that someone I know is waiting here, too. "Get home safe."

Kali gives me one last hug and then they turn, walking hand-in-hand toward the fire-engine-red BMW her parents bought for her 16th birthday. His car is a beat-up old Honda, so she drives them everywhere. "Do you want us to pay for your college tuition or for a new car?" his mom asked him when he sent in his applications. The answer was obvious.

As soon as they're gone, my attention shifts. I walk over to the boy in the maroon hoodie as casually as I can. As I get closer, I realize the item he's hunched over isn't a phone or a tablet but a sketchbook.

"Hey," I say hesitantly, standing behind him. He looks up at me.

"Noomi," he says. "Did you like the show?" He doesn't sound surprised to see me.

"It was awesome. You like punk rock?"

He shrugs, looking down at his sketchpad. "I know it's cliché, but I like all music as long as it's good."

"For a local band, they're talented. I bet they could make it in Portland."

He nods but says nothing.

"What are you drawing?" I ask, my curiosity getting the better of me.

He doesn't respond, his pen flicking across the sketchpad. I crane my neck to see, but his arm is covering most of the paper. I wonder if it was inappropriate to ask. Self-conscious, I pull out my phone to check my messages.

Mom: *Be there in five.*

I put the phone back in my pocket and try to look everywhere except his sketchpad, but the pull of his movements is magnetic. The motion of his body as he works and the scratching of the pen on paper are the only movements around us. The world is quiet in the dim light of the streetlamp, the air yellowed like parchment. I feel drawn to him, like the gravitational force exerted by his body has grown exponentially. It's impossible not to look. Not to want to see what he's doing.

He pulls his arm away from the paper and tilts the sketch-pad so I can see it better.

"Sorry to be rude," he says. "I wanted to finish it before I showed you."

It's like something out of a surrealist painting, mashed up with wild science fiction art. A series of enormous, mis-matched robots float or walk through a desert landscape littered with bright blue plants, as creatures that look vaguely human herd flocks of smaller robots. Melting clocks adorn a blocky horizon, and small animals leap from the desert sands as freely as fish would from our rivers.

"Wow. Did you do all that just now?"

"No. I've been working on this for a few days."

"Where did you get these ideas?"

He gives me an odd look, a half-smile. "From the places I've been."

"Like art museums?"

"No." He glances back down at the paper. "Okay, I borrowed the clocks from Dali."

Is he joking? It's a strange joke.

"What 'places' then?"

"All kinds of fun worlds," he says. He looks at me like he expects something, and I shake my head. He sits very still, his hand poised over the paper, pen uncapped, as if he's about to begin drawing again. But his eyes are fixed on me. I remember the iridescence, the rainbow of color in his irises on the mountain, and for a moment I can almost see the colors again.

I wonder if I'm dreaming.

"What are you talking about?" I ask.

"You mean you've never..."

"Never what?"

"...Traveled?" He leans toward me, his expression growing more intense.

"Of course, I've traveled." The words come out defensive. I start to wonder if this is some trust fund kid who thinks he's more cultured than the rest of us because he's been to dozens of places when plenty of kids our age have never left Oregon. "I've been to New York, Dubai, Japan, San Francisco, Los Angeles…"

But he's shaking his head as if I'd misunderstood the question. His eyes fix on mine, and I notice there's a kind of brightness coming from his irises, bright chlorophyll green in addition to the mossy hue, and also sunflower yellow and ember orange, as vivid as a summer sunset, and deep blue, and on the edge of his eyes there's a tint of purple. It all bleeds together like the soap bubbles Ada and I blew all last summer, like oil-slick colors against black asphalt, and now I have the sensation that I'm on the edge of a precipice and pitching forward, that I'm about to tip over and fall into them, that the colors are a bottomless pool that I could just—

"Noomi!"

I jerk out of my reverie. My mother's here, her car pulled up in front of us. Ada's in the backseat, her dark bangs and long straight hair hiding her eyes from view as she stares out the window at us.

"One minute!"

"Listen to me, Noomi," the boy says. His voice is low and urgent. I try to shake off the hazy feeling of almost falling, like when you start awake just before you hit the ground in a dream. He scrawls something on the paper before ripping the pen-and-ink drawing from his sketchbook. When he lifts his eyes to mine, they're green again—just green. He hands me the paper. "You can go anywhere you want. Anytime. You just have to find a path."

"Why are you giving this to me?" I marvel at the detail of the pen work, the skill in the perspective, the precision of his lines. "Don't you want to keep it?"

"I don't need a drawing," he says. "I can go anywhere I want, anytime. Just like you."

What are you talking about? I want to scream. Instead, I stuff the paper into my jacket pocket and stand up, jogging to the passenger side of my mom's car and open the door, slamming it behind me. I stare sullenly at the fog descending on the streets.

"How was the show?" Mom asks in Arabic. I glance at the car's digital clock, which says it's 11:15.

"It was great," I reply shortly, in English. "Really fun."

"It doesn't sound like it," she says, sounding hurt.

I close my eyes, shift my tone, and try again.

"Sorry for being short. I'm very tired. The show was really great. Thank you for letting me go. Why did you bring Ada along?"

"Your sister woke up when she heard me leaving and didn't want to be left behind."

I turn back to look at Ada. "Aren't you tired, Peach?"

"Yes." She yawns, as if to prove the point. "But Mom said she was coming to get you, and I wanted to come too."

I smile at her. "That's sweet. Thank you for coming."

"You're both going to be exhausted at school tomorrow," my mother says, sounding weary herself.

While she drives, I pull the drawing from my pocket and unfold it, staring at the giant robots and the sand fish, wondering what strange places this boy has been for him to think this could represent reality. In the darkness, it's hard to see the full image. But as we pull into our driveway and the motion-sensor bathes the car's interior in creamy light, I realize there's something new on the page. Something I didn't see when he held it up to me before. It must be what he added right before he ripped it out and handed it to me.

Silas Voladores.

It must be his name.

I turn the name over in my head. Vola-dores. It reminds me of an old story my abuela used to tell. She said there was a religious ceremony in Mexico called the Danza de los Voladores, where men leap and dance around a pole, suspended by ropes as they soar through the air.

Voladores. The ones who fly.

DUST

"In the sweat of thy face shalt thou eat bread, till thou return unto the ground; for out of it wast thou taken: for dust thou art, and unto dust shalt thou return."
—Genesis 3:19, King James Bible

"H*abibti*, you will have to learn to sleep without the light on sometime."

My mother is hovering at the door, smiling worriedly at me. We've had this conversation a thousand times. Her finger is on the light switch, waiting for my permission to turn it off. Sleeping with the light on doesn't guarantee they won't find me. But it does make my dreams less dark to begin with.

"Another night. Please. I want the lights on tonight."

Just then, Ada pokes her head around the corner of the door frame.

"You can sleep with me, Noomi!"

"Ada!" my mother chides. "You were supposed to be asleep *hours* ago."

"I'm not sleepy." She pouts.

I grin and hop out of bed. Kuri, who was curled up at my feet, looks up at me with round, mournful eyes, but doesn't move. He snuggles in at the foot of my bed every night, even when I'm not there. He glares at me over his long nose, looking offended. I rub his ears as an apology.

"Maybe I will sleep with you tonight," I say to Ada. "We had a good time telling stories last week, didn't we?" Ada's head bobs up and down. I tuck in the sheets on my bed and take her hand in mine.

"Yes, and she was also a nightmare to get out of bed the next morning," Mom reminds me. "It's already late. Promise you won't keep her up all night."

"Believe me, *Ommi*, I'm exhausted too. I won't keep her awake." I pick Ada up under the armpits and swing her onto my hip, and she wraps her arms around me so I can hold her. I flip the light off as I walk out of the room.

"It wasn't so long ago you were so little," my mother says ruefully, in her accented English.

"Hey!" Ada shouts. "I'm not little."

"Of course, you're not." I plant a kiss on her cheek.

"No, you're not," my mother says, slipping into Arabic again. "But you are smaller than the other kids in your class."

"I'm still the best at soccer!"

A smile breaks across my face. She is good at soccer. She's one of the best on her first-grade team.

"I can take her to school in the morning if you'd like." My mother doesn't always like me to take Ada to school—she doesn't like the idea of having a teenager at the helm with Ada in the back. But the hospital is on the other side of town, and I always volunteer. I prefer never to be in the car alone, and Ada hates taking the school bus—she used to cry and scream in the mornings before she had to get on the bus, shouting about how people push and shove and make too much noise. She's so small for her age, it's no surprise she gets pushed around. Most of the time, my mother gives in when I offer.

"Okay," she sighs. "That would make my day a lot easier."

"*Masaa alkhaier, Ommi!*" Ada calls to her over my shoulder. *Good night, Mother!*

I open the door to Ada's room and set her down. She immediately jumps into bed and grabs her stuffed dragon, Kaf. I hesitate for a moment, my hand on the light switch, afraid, as always, of the dark. It's okay, I tell myself. Ada's here. They won't come.

"Tell me the story of the bear and the hare," she says. It's one of her favorites. I made it up when we were younger, and she's been asking for it ever since. Her black hair is flush around her face, her emerald eyes bright with eagerness.

"I can do that." I flip the switch and the room goes dark. I'm safe with her, I tell myself, even as my stomach flips. The panic consumes me for a moment, but I calm myself. I take a few tentative steps in the darkness to the other side of the bed.

"In the northern world where the days are white and clean, and the nights are rainbows of light and color, two friends, a bear and a hare, were traveling from one part of the world to another. They were coming for a great gathering of the animals to celebrate the shortest day of the year, the Winter Solstice." I reach the bed, my eyes wide open for signs of the growing darkness, the empty blackness, shadows within shadows, but there are none. I'm safe with her, I tell myself a second time. I peel back the covers and climb in. Ada's fingers reach for mine.

"Tell me about the other animals," she whispers, and dutifully I tell her about all the other animals, the white winter world, and the gifts the animals gave to each other. As she drifts off, I keep talking, telling her how the bear was getting sleepy, and started to make a cave to rest in, and then I start to get sleepy too, and I think about the long wings of Silas's eyelashes, flapping on a summer breeze above iridescent eyes, and soon I'm quiet and my eyes are closed.

When sleep comes it's drifting, deep and dark like the black spaces between the stars.

I dream.

I dream of a vast bamboo forest. I am barefoot and walking. The ground is soft. It's green all around, as far as the eye can see. I walk between the rows, touching the ridged, wooden plants, letting the cool stalks graze against me. The sky is the color of summer storms, pink and violet with electricity. The bamboo morphs into columns, columns tall enough to touch the sky, so tall they're holding up the clouds. And they're dark now, the color of the clouds, but fiercer, more terrifying, green and grey and orange and slate. The dirt beneath my feet is gone and now I walk on cold marble. My feet are chilled to the bone.

The shadows of the columns grow. They lean and creak like the trees of ancient forests. They groan. They stretch. The shadows grow to twice, three times their size and now the world is nothing but shadows. The columns are gone and all I see are storm clouds and shadows. The clouds are on top of me, heavy, pressing me down. Wind whirls around me, pulling at my hair, tying knots in my soul, twisting me this way and that.

"What are you?" I ask this question every time they find me in my dreams. They have never answered.

I feel myself being emptied. Pulled apart. Torn and fraying.

We are nothing, they respond. They have never replied to me before. *We are everything*, they taunt. I shiver as the wind tears my skin to shreds. It peels off me like a tattered flag.

We are growing stronger, they say.

I try to fight back, to reassemble myself, an archaeologist reconstructing a vessel whose pieces are lost. I am a puzzle begging to be put back together. I am a thousand water droplets in the sky, desperate to condense into rain.

"What do you want from me?" I cry. My vision darkens but I remind myself of the green in Ada's eyes, the chestnut hair on Kuri's back, the purple of my mother's silk robe. Now instead of blackness there is a rainbow in front of me. Like the northern sky in the stories I tell my sister. Like Silas' eyes.

You are our portal. You are our doorway. Once we have used you, you will be nothing. Your world will be destroyed.

"I won't let you."

You have no choice.

"You can't have me."

We are *you.*

The blues, yellows, greens, and oranges fade. Silas's eyes, purple silk, and Kuri's warm body all disappear. Everything stained by an inky, impenetrable black.

Vanishing Point

The point at which something that has been growing smaller or increasingly faint disappears altogether."
— Oxford Languages, "Vanishing Point"

I jerk awake , gasping for air. Sit up straight in bed. Color and light flood back into my vision. A thin sheaf of sunlight is streaming in through the window as dawn breaks, bathing the floor in a delicate glow. I sit for a minute, taking it all in, basking in the renewed experience of sound, color, and sensation. I glance to my side where Ada's lying, eyes open, watching me. She must have turned on the lamp. The slight glow from the shade casts her face in shadow.

A chill runs through my body, leaving gooseflesh in its wake. This is new. They've never come when Ada's here.

They've never spoken to me before.

"The nightmares again?" she asks. I nod. "I thought you said I keep you safe." My heart cracks as she stares at me.

"You do," I croak. "You always keep me safe."

"Not this time. What did I do wrong?"

I lie back on the bed and pull the covers up over our heads together.

"Nothing." I pull her to my chest and hold her there for a long time. "You did nothing wrong."

When I let her go, she pulls back, our breath hot between us, the air trapped underneath the sheets.

"What happened in the dream?"

"I was in a forest," I say. "And then the bamboo turned into columns, and the columns turned into the shadows."

"And then what?" she whispers.

I shake my head, partly out of an unwillingness to frighten her, and partly because it's hard to put in words.

"Everything goes black."

Ada nods, unsmiling and serious, as though she understands.

"Your eyes were black."

"What?"

"When you woke up. They're normal now. Brown like Kuri. But before, your eyes were black."

"Black how?"

"Your irises were the same color as your pupils."

I stare at her. "Was it scary?"

She nods.

Your eyes were black. I think back to the L.E.O. show, sitting on the curb with the artist who wrote his name on the paper. Silas. His eyes so colorful. How I felt like I was going to fall into them, like I could tip over the edge and tumble down.

My phone buzzes, vibrating beneath my pillow. I reach to turn it off. Normally I set at least three alarms in the morning. This is the first time in months I've woken up before the first one goes off.

"Time to get up?" she asks.

"Time to get up, little Peach." Though we have at least an hour before we have to leave, this room feels oppressive and cloistered after the shadows. *Your eyes were black.* The words ring in my head. Ada pushes the covers over her head and sits up. I follow suit, rolling out of bed and putting on my slippers. *Your eyes were black.*

What does it mean?

"What do you want for breakfast?"

"You're going to make breakfast?"

"Why not?" I laugh. "It's not every day I'm up this early. What do you think about...pancakes?" She squeals with delight and I shoo her off to brush her teeth while I head downstairs. Ada loves it when I surprise her with American food, which our mother hates to cook. *So unhealthy,* she proclaims, whenever I bring home donuts or make grilled cheese. But Ada's always delighted.

Three pancakes and an hour and a half later, I'm slamming the brakes as I pull into my parking spot outside the high school. I pull the parking brake and kill the engine in one motion, grateful to have made it to school without a second visit from the shadows.

Kalifa's red BMW drifts in beside my car, The Doors' "Light My Fire" blaring from her speakers.

She kicks open the door in her usual dramatic fashion, leading with a pair of beat-up chucks she's had since freshman year. Chucks are the only thing she and Claire have in common, fashion-wise. But while Kalifa's are faded black, Claire's are shamrock-green, and a perfect color match to the station wagon she inherited from her older brother.

"Hey!" Claire shouts, waving enthusiastically as she pulls up on Kalifa's other side. She leaps out, grabs her backpack, and slams the door behind her. "Did you hear the news?" She's still shouting, despite that I'm right next to her.

"What news?" I ask.

"The lead singer of L.E.O. has a new girlfriend named Claire?" Kalifa says as she joins us. Her golden *hijab* glimmers in the morning sunlight.

Claire rolls her eyes. "No. Turns out, James is kind of boring. He just wanted to go home and go to bed after the show. Lame, right?" Kalifa and I look at each other and shrug. "The next round of college admissions are coming in! Elspeth Williams and Bryce Brown both got their acceptance letters to Washington State yesterday." Claire's mom sits on the school board, so she hears all the teacher gossip before the rest of the students.

Kalifa holds the door open for us. "I'm so glad Basi did early acceptance and we don't have to sit through the latest round of anxiety."

"I wonder if Greg and Georgia Reynolds are going to get in together?" There's a pair of twins in our grade who applied only to Stanford and Harvard.

"The better question is," I say, teasing, "do you think Kalifa's going to get into Stanford?"

"And the answer is an obvious *yes*," Claire says. I glance at Kalifa, waiting for a smart retort, only to find her staring off into space, lips pressed into nervous smile. "No one's ever been more of a shoo-in. With a 4.3 GPA, valedictorian status, and enough extracurriculars to go to the moon and back, have they ever seen a better applicant?"

"What about you, Noomi?" Kalifa asks, changing the subject as she drops her backpack in front of her locker. A few freshmen brush by, applying lip gloss and chatting animatedly. "Have you narrowed down your list?"

The list of colleges I'm considering is about twenty miles long. And with just a few months before we start our applications, I haven't got a clue where I want to start.

It's hard to think about college when the shadows get worse every day.

"I think I'll just apply to them all," I say. "Every one in the country."

Kalifa grins. "That'll only take until our senior year...in college."

"Good!" Claire shouts. "That'll give you enough time to make up your mind."

I pull out my notebooks for the first classes of the day. As I'm trying to remember whether I have math or chemistry in 2nd period, someone jostles me. A crowd of younger boys carrying lacrosse gear push past, ignorant of my presence as they bump me into my locker.

"Rude!" I shout as they pass. Only one looks back. A boy in a maroon hooded sweatshirt with a black backpack slung low over his shoulder and his hands tucked into his front pockets. The hood casts a shadow over his face. He's not carrying lacrosse gear.

It's Silas.

Oil-slick colors, iridescent. Shadows growing. Columns of darkness, blooming.

He turns away, carried along by the crowd of junior varsity lacrosse players. The boys sweep down the hall and he disappears into the mass of students.

"Hey!" I call. Claire and Kalifa glance up, confused. "Hang on," I tell them, walking quickly after him. I can just make out his dark hood in the crowd. He's got a lead on me, walking faster than I am, and the halls are full to bursting. "Silas!" I shout. He ducks around a corner into the biology wing, and I break into a jog to catch him.

But when I round the corner, he's gone.

"Silas?" I say aloud, craning my neck as I glance around the hall. Some of the students are looking at me oddly. I check in the classroom nearest us, but he's not in there. There's no bathroom nearby, not even a closet. Why would he hide? I turn away, disappointed, wondering how he vanished so quickly.

I can't explain why I want to see him again. I'm still angry—he was so condescending, so vague as to be maddening. But in my dream, right before the darkness swallowed me, the last thing I thought of was his eyes. The memory was a lifeline, tethering me to reality, holding just for a moment before the maelstrom devoured me.

It was a moment longer than I've ever had. It was something to cling to.

And I want it back.

Newton's Third Law

"To every action there is always opposed an equal reaction: or the mutual actions of two bodies upon each other are always equal, and directed to contrary parts." —Sir Isaac Newton, *The Mathematical Principles of Natural Philosophy*

"How was school today, little Peach?"

"Good."

"What did you learn?"

"How to spell the word *because*."

"Spell it for me."

"You already know."

"Maybe I do and maybe I don't."

It's pouring outside, rain coming down in droplets the size of my fists, clattering onto the windshield as fast as my wipers can sluice it off. Thunder pounds overhead, a rarity here in Oregon, where we get endless days of grey and rain, but few storms. I put on my blinker and spin the wheel, listening to Ada as she spells out *because*, and then *vegetable*, and then *tomato*—once she gets going, it's hard to get her to stop—while my thoughts drift away, floating into the sky like balloons against the clouds.

∞

a memory

pots and pans clanging

sharp noise like pencils against my skin

run up the stairs

hide in the closet

be invisible

"She's my mother, Saida!" hands over ears don't listen don't listen

shut my eyes

smells bad in here like old people and clothes and dead trees and spider webs but it's better than out there

anything's better than out there

pretend it's a storm

you're not afraid of thunder

or rain

nothing to be afraid of just a storm

papa is just a big thundercloud

it'll pass

it'll pass

he's got a lot of lightning to let out

crash

no no no no no

hands over ears don't listen don't listen

"You're being unreasonable, Esteban, you can't expect me to—"

"You have no idea what I sacrificed to make this relationship work. You insisted on so many things that my family hated, and I fought for them. For you. And now you refuse to do the same for me! Chingate, mi amor."

the sound after is like thunder again and i feel it in the wood in the wall in the floor but i also heard mi amor mi amor mi amor i hear those words i know what they mean he still loves her he still loves me

sacrifice

chingate
relationship
words
wish i had my dictionary i could look them up but it's out there and i'm in here and i'm not moving until the lightning has passed
please don't leave papa
please don't leave

∞

"Noomi!" Ada screeches from the back seat. My eyes unfog and I return abruptly to the moment—where a car has just pulled out in front of us from a lane over. I slam on the brakes and bash the horn as we both jerk forward. The man in the offending car glares and raises his arms, palms up, in an exaggerated gesture of *What?*

"You cut me off!" I shout, though he can't hear me through the glass.

There's a long pause as I press the gas to keep moving forward, and my heartbeat returns to normal.

"Mom says you should drive more carefully," Ada says, with more finesse than a seven-year-old has a right to possess.

"I bet," I mutter through gritted teeth. I shove my father's temper tantrum back into the dustbin of my memory, berating myself for getting lost in thought while driving.

"We're here." I pull into a parking space in front of Ada's dance studio and unlock the child safety locks. She grabs her ballet bag and I grab my book bag. "Do you want me to come in with you?"

"No."

"No, what?"

"No, thank you!"

"Okay. I'll pick you up in an hour." I bend down to kiss her on the cheek. "Bye, Peach."

"Bye, Noomi!" She opens the door and runs inside, and I duck under my hood to stay out of the rain and walk down the street to the local coffee shop.

At the counter, I order my favorite study drink—a white chocolate latte—and look for my usual table in the corner. To my surprise, it's occupied. A skinny man in a black turtleneck and a blue beanie sits with an impressive array of books in front of him. I squint and look closer, recognizing wisps of light brown hair creeping from beneath his cap. He's staring at a textbook, his fingertips at his temples. He glances up as if he can sense someone looking at him. It's Paul. Our eyes meet for an instant. But instead of smiling or waving, he looks back down at his books.

I grab my latte and go over to him.

"This is *my* table," I announce. He can't pretend he didn't see me anymore. He draws himself back in exaggerated surprise, looking up at me comically. But he doesn't look as happy to see me as he usually does.

"Looks like it's my table."

"As the queen of the corner table at Hersey Bros Coffee Shop, I declare your presence to be an invasion and assert dominion over this space."

"A duel, then," he says, pretending to pull a sword from his belt. "To the death." He brandishes the invisible sword at me. But he's still not smiling.

"Or we can work together. I have homework." I set my coffee down and sit opposite him in the booth. But the space is so covered with his notepads and books, there's no room for mine. His expression shifts, his brow furrowing, his thin lips pressed together.

"Noomi. We can't study together. It's not appropriate for, you know, a counselor and a student to—"

"Oh." I stand up as fast as I sat down. My bag clatters against the table as I do, rocking my latte. Creamy coffee sloshes out of the teacup and into the little saucer. Paul goes to steady the saucer at the same moment I reach down to grab it. Our hands collide, and he jerks his back as if shocked.

"Sorry. I'll just...go, then."

"No." He leans forward. "Never mind. Forget I said anything."

"I don't want you to get in trouble."

"Don't worry about it." He waves a hand at the space in front of him. "Sit. I don't want to waste any more caffeine than I already have."

I hesitate, but then sling my bag into the booth and slide in. This time, he reaches across the table to clear a space for me. "Sorry. The perils of being a doctoral student."

"Back problems?" I tease.

"And a backlog of library fines."

"I thought they cut you off after a certain point."

"They do. The trick is to have multiple cards."

I put my hand over my mouth, pretending to be shocked.

"You scammer! I'll report you to the librarians at once."

"So this is how you repay me?" He shakes his head and stares skyward, melancholy. "I break codes of conduct to let you study at your favorite table and you report me to the librarians. Et tu, Brute?"

I laugh and pull my hood up so if anyone sees us, they might not recognize me. Paul shifts in his seat, still uncomfortable, and returns to his book. I consider trying to continue our conversation, but decide I'll look cooler if I act as studious as he is, so I take a sip of my coffee and open my textbook to today's assigned reading.

History.

My least favorite class. Just names and dates and locations. No problems to solve or things to discover. Just memorization. In what year did King Henry lop off his wife's head and why? Who cares? I'll never meet him.

My thoughts dissolve away from the words on the page, and instead of King Henry and his many wives I find myself staring at the person across from me, shaggy blond hair poking out from under his cap, blue eyes lightning-focused on the pages in front of him. A dark edge creeps at the periphery of my vision. At first it could just be my hood blocking the light. But then it grows darker, denser. Deeper. It blooms. Dull surprise registers in the back of my mind: they never come when I'm around people. This has never happened before. I try to keep my breathing normal, but heavy fingers wrap themselves around my heart and squeeze, gently at first, then tighter like a vise. The tiredness comes. The lack of sensation. The blackness reaches outside my hood and into the foreground. I grip my highlighter more tightly, trying to bring feeling back to my body, and look away from Paul, out the window. Sparrows flit from one tree to another, and I focus on them, their movement. Brown bodies and fluttering wings. Like Silas's too-long eyelashes.

Remember, Noomi, you can go anywhere you want. Anytime. You just have to find a path.

I think about his drawing, now sitting on my desk in my room. The floating robots, the leaping fish, the hooded creatures walking in the desert. Brilliant colors, blues and greens and purples, popping off the page. Reaching into my memory, I imagine myself there, hot sand and desert wind blowing against my cheeks. I imagine being wrapped up in robes that breathe, and I call up the clearest sky I can remember.

The blackness clears. The pressure eases off my heartbeat and my pulse returns to normal. The rain has stopped, and birds are playing outside, chasing each other from tree to tree, across the street and back again. I watch them, smiling.

The shadows are gone.

It's never been so easy. Usually I have to wait it out—sit down on the ground, lie in the grass, collapse and let them wash over me, let the terror and emptiness and darkness swallow me until I feel like I must be dead this time. There's no way anyone could be reduced to so much nothing and come back to be something.

Why was it so easy?

But at the same time, it's never happened in public before. Just like with Ada. When I sleep with Ada, they don't come. But last week, for the first time, they did.

They're getting stronger.

But so am I.

"Paul," I say, the curiosity that's been gnawing at me for a week finally getting the better of me. "Do you know where Silas is from?"

He doesn't look up from his notebook.

"Who is Silas?"

"The new kid in our therapy group. Silas Voladores."

This time he glances at me. "What are you talking about?"

Fear grips me. I hesitate. I know where this path leads. Words leap out at me. Schizophrenic. Crazy. Inventing things. Some of those words have been said to me. At me.

"Silas." My hands are shaking. "He started a few weeks ago."

Paul frowns. "I don't remember him. What does he look like?"

I'm in too deep to stop now. "Black hair, greenish eyes, darker skin. About five-ten, five-eleven. He looks Hispanic, maybe. Our group isn't that big, Paul."

"Noomi," Paul says, a trace of worry showing in his furrowed brow. "There's no one named Silas in your therapy group."

MAGNETISM

"Matter is very complex when looked at from a fundamental point of view—as we saw when we tried to understand dielectrics... Every electron has such a spin, which corresponds to a tiny circulating current. Of course, one electron doesn't produce much magnetic field, but in an ordinary piece of matter there are billions and billions of electrons ... Our equations lead... to the end result that parallel currents attract, or that currents in opposite directions repel." —Richard P. Feynman, *The Feynman Lectures on Physics, Volume II*

I push my spoon around in my bowl. Not eating. I barely slept. Halfway through the night I moved to Ada's room, trying not to wake her as I slipped between the covers, too exhausted from the onslaught of the shadows—preying on my anxiety and self-doubt—to stay in my room, alone and afraid.

The phone rings. I know who it is.

"I have to tell Dr. Chase about this," Paul said. As if it was his fault. "I'm sorry, Noomi. But I have to put it in your file."

I'm not inventing him, I wanted to say. But the words stuck in my throat and wouldn't come out.

"I'll write her a note for school," my mother says on the phone, her English perfect, her accent minute but distinct. I push my yogurt away and bring a slice of toast to my mouth, slathered with butter and rose jam in an effort to make it more appetizing. But today, the fragrant sweetness turns my stomach. I avoid my mother's eyes, though she's staring at me like she can see down to my bones. "Her teachers will understand." Pause. "Thank you. I'll talk to you in a few hours."

The silence as the call ends. The weight in the room like the air before a storm. The gold rims of our coffee cups. The tapping of my mother's fingernails against the table. The emptiness that settles in on me, the uncertainty. The words that will ring in my head for hours.

Head case. Mentally ill. Panic attacks. Imaginary friends.

Mom sits next to me and puts her hand on mine. I want to pull away, but I don't.

"Do you want to tell me what happened?"

I shrug, my eyes cloudy.

"Yes. No. It's hard, Mom. I want to tell you these things, but not if you don't believe me."

"I believe you." Her knuckles are hard against my own. A finger under my chin, lifting my eyes. I meet her gaze. "I believe you."

"There's a new kid in our adventure therapy." My voice catches. "His name is Silas. But Paul says there's no one in our group named Silas." Saltwater at the corner of my mouth.

Then I remember. I sit up straighter. "You saw him. Sitting on the curb next to me after the concert. When you picked me up."

She looks at me blankly. And then shakes her head. "I'm sorry, Noomi. I don't remember seeing you with someone there that night. But maybe I've forgotten. I was tired—it was a long day at the hospital."

I stand abruptly, pulling my hands from hers. "I can prove it. He gave me a drawing. I can show you."

I run upstairs, into my room, scrabbling on my desk for the crumpled drawing. I remember so clearly looking at it in the night, trying to keep the shadows at bay. Where is it? I turn over papers and pull out the drawers. Check on my bed and under it, and then in the trash can, wondering if it fell in somehow.

But it's not here. It's nowhere.

My heart pounds and I stop moving. The fear creeps back in.

You are a head case. You are crazy.

A jingle behind me. I whirl. Ada standing there, holding my keys.

"Looking for these?" A smirk on her face tells me she thinks she's being very helpful. I cast one last look around my room and walk out.

"I wasn't." I bite back my frustration about the drawing, careful not to take out my anger on my little sister. "But thank you anyway."

I follow Ada back down the stairs at about half the speed I ran up them, reluctant to face Mom and be forced to admit that the thing I was ready to claim as proof of Silas's existence is nowhere to be found. She's still in the kitchen, sipping her tea and staring at the wall, but she looks up when I walk in.

"Well?" The expectation on her face is more than I can bear. I look away, unable to meet her eyes.

"Forget I said anything." I pull on my jacket and grab my book bag. "I'll see you later."

"You have an appointment with Dr. Chase at 10:30," she shouts after me. "Do you want me to be there with you?"

"No, thank you!"

"This is important, Noomi!"

Dr. Chase can't help me! I want to scream. But instead I walk out, Ada following. I can hear Mom's light footsteps behind us. She stands in the door frame, watching us, but says nothing. Her long hair, the color of mahogany, glimmers in the morning light. The tension between us pulls like elastic, threatening to snap any minute. It stretches and warps, distorting the energy around us. I put the car in gear and drive away.

Exhale. Release. Breathe.

Thoughts dart like minnows. I shouldn't have to prove myself. I shouldn't have to prove I'm not crazy.

But then, would I believe Claire if she said she could fly? Would I believe Kali if she said she had an invisible twin?

Ada, in the back, is silent. When I glance in the rearview, she's staring out the window, watching the world go by. The picture of contentment. But she meets my eyes for a second before she looks away again, and I see the worry. The fear, the wondering.

I drop Ada off and drive a mile down the road to the high school.

First period is English.

"What is Hamlet telling us in this passage?"

Kalifa asks if I'm okay. I nod. I'm fine, I say. But there's a tension that won't dissolve. A bitter taste I can't wash down.

Second period. Art. I work on my sketches, wishing I had Silas's drawing back. Where did it go? Did I invent that, too? He's ten times better at drawing than I am. If he even exists. Halfway through the class, I throw my pencils down, disgusted with my lack of talent.

I drop my mother's note at the front desk, where they look at me suspiciously. I haven't been in and out of classes as much as I used to be, and I always have a note from my mom, but the front desk ladies are suspicious of everyone. They think anyone's failure to attend class is a moral offense, and it's their job to keep everyone in line.

In the car, the fear comes in waves as I worry about what Dr. Chase will say. What she will think. I am not schizophrenic. I know Silas is real. I know I'm not crazy. But the doubt lingers.

"I'm sorry, Noomi, but there's no record of a person named Silas in your adventure therapy group." These are the words she says in the first three minutes of our meeting.

There's no pity in her voice. No condescension. I wonder how she sterilizes her tone so no emotion comes through. I watch the second hand *tick-tick-tick* around the wall clock. I feel her searching my face, my body, inquisitive. There's a new photograph on the wall today. It's Mount Hood, cloaked in snow, leaping prominently from the hills. I wish I were up there, in the whiteness, or walking through Silas's desert full of robots.

I wish I were anywhere except here.

"You think I'm inventing him."

"I think we should consider the possibility that you're seeing and hearing things that don't exist to other people."

I want to argue with her. I want to tell her she's wrong, that Silas is real, that he's a human being who with just a few words, helped me fight off the shadows that have haunted me my whole life, which is more than any shrink has done. More than she's done. I want to tell her that I've seen him at school, at therapy, that I have one of his drawings.

But I can't do any of these things because I no longer believe myself.

"He's not a student?" I ask, timid. "I saw him last week at school. In the morning. He was with a group of younger boys on the lacrosse team. I saw him there."

And then he disappeared, I remind myself. Vanished.

But I let that part of the story go unsaid.

Dr. Chase stares down at her iPad. I can feel the vacant space like lines of magnetic energy, stretched between us, poisoned with uncertainty and disbelief.

"It's Voladores," I say.

"What is?" Dr. Chase asks.

"His last name. Silas Voladores."

Her fingernails tap against the iPad. The thickness in the air. I wish there were a barometer to measure the pressure in this room.

"I'm sorry. There's no one by that name at your school."

I am quiet.

Dr. Chase lets out a breath and leans over the iPad, looking at me intently.

"Noomi, I want Silas to be real. Is there any other name I could search? Is this a nickname he's using? A pseudonym?"

Suddenly I'm tired of it. Tired of seven years sitting through therapy meetings and counseling sessions with nothing to show. Tired of sitting in an office with this woman who has no idea how to help me. Tired of everyone thinking I'm crazy and inventing things and I don't know what I'm talking about. "It doesn't matter. Silas isn't important. Can we forget about him?"

"He's important if you met him and talked to him."

"No, he's not. If he ever comes back, I can just pretend he doesn't exist. Happy?"

"That's not—"

"I don't care what you want, Dr. Chase," I mutter, my voice growing louder as I go on, "or what you think will make me better. Nothing any of my therapists has said has ever helped me. That includes you. So far, Silas Voladores is the only person who has been able to help me fight the shadows. So please forgive me if I would prefer to continue allowing him to exist, even if that means I never tell anyone else about him and I never say his name again."

Finally, I've told the truth.

I meet her eyes, expecting her to back down, humbled, blown away by my devastating words. But this, apparently, is as much a fantasy as Silas. She stares me down. I'm convinced she doesn't need to blink except to appear more human. Her square glasses are shining in the low light from outside. We play a game of chicken for ten seconds, which doesn't sound that long but on an atomic scale it's long enough for billions of particles to be born and destroyed again, and I think about that fact as every second ticks by and neither of us backs down.

In the end, I'm the one who looks away.

"Tell me about the shadows."

"I've told you before."

"Tell me again."

My breath rattles through my teeth.

"I don't want to waste my time with someone who doesn't believe me."

"I can't help you unless you talk to me."

"You can't help me, period!"

Dr. Chase sighs dramatically. Finally, I've got a reaction out of her. She presses a button on her iPad and the screen goes dark. She sets it next to her and leans forward, her elbows on her knees.

"Okay. Listen to me, Noomi. I'm going to make a series of promises to you right now that I hope will help you trust me." Finally, I look at her. "First, I'm not going to put you on medication because it's clear from your history those haven't helped. Second, I'm not going to hospitalize you unless I believe you're in danger of hurting yourself or someone around you, which I am required by law to do as a medical provider. Third, I'm not going to take you away from your family or your friends unless the first two conditions apply.

"You're a straight A student, one of the brightest in your class. Stellar recommendations from all your teachers. You have a family who loves you, friends who care about you, and a very bright future. For me to take any of that away from you because you're—well, because you met someone who may or may not be in your therapy group—would be one of the worst things I could do to a patient. Okay?"

I'm frozen in place, unable to move. But there's that water on my cheeks again. And the memory of the flames licking my skin, warm and welcoming instead of deadly. It's time to face my fears, I told Dr. Chase the last time I was here. If I'm going to make good on that promise, I have to try something new.

"Okay."

"Please help me understand," she says. "Tell me about the shadows."

I take a deep breath, lean back, and look away. "Thinking about them when they're not there is like having a broken ankle and, instead of being given crutches, being told you can only walk on that foot," I say. "It's painful."

"I'm sorry," she says, "but if we're going to find out what's causing them, I need to know more about them."

"I call them shadows because I don't know what else to call them. When it happens, my vision goes black. Sometimes it's like someone has slung mud on my eyes. Pulled down a curtain in front of me. Sometimes it creeps in from the edges. Sometimes it's from the shadows of things around me." I pause. "I guess that's why I call them shadows. Because sometimes they detach."

"The shadows of, say, buildings?"

"Or trees. And they grow until they block my vision. But it's not like a cloudy day. It's total darkness. Like being miles inside a cave with no flashlight. And the blackness isn't even the worst part." I laugh. It rings hollow, echoing around the room. "The worst part is the emptiness."

"What does it feel like?"

"It's like a vacuum inside my body and it's sucking my soul out. But it's gradual. First, I feel tired, sleepy. Then exhausted, bone deep. The tiredest I've ever been. Then I don't have any emotions left. Then I can't even think, and all thoughts disappear. That's usually when I black out."

"What happens next?"

I shrug. "I wake up. Anywhere from a minute to fifteen minutes later. One time someone found me lying in the park because I had fallen over while walking Kuri. Kuri was barking at me, but I couldn't hear or see anything. I told the man I had passed out because I hadn't eaten anything that day." I laugh again, but this time it comes out more like a cough, and I feel like I might vomit. "It's always easier to believe that teenage girls are desperate to lose weight than that they're seeing crazy things, isn't it?"

For the first time in a long time, Dr. Chase's expression softens.

"Noomi," she says. "Listen to me. Really listen." I drag my eyes from the ground to look at her. "No one doubts that the things you're seeing are real. Real to you. And that's all that matters. No one thinks you're crazy. And, Noomi—" She pauses, and looks away for a second, before turning back to me. "I was one of those teenage girls who was desperate to lose weight. Part of the reason I went into psychology was because I was anorexic for four years in high school and college. I weighed ninety pounds when they checked me in. I was hospitalized for a month. I missed a semester of college.

"Our battles are *real.* I know what it's like to see things other people don't—a fat girl in the mirror, for instance—and to have those things swallow you whole. Just because you're the only person who sees these shadows, or who can talk to Silas Voladores, doesn't mean they're not real. But in order to treat them, we have to understand why you're seeing them and where they're coming from. Okay?"

I nod, blinking hard.

"Okay."

"Tell me about Silas."

CATALYST

"Whether 'tis nobler in the mind to suffer the slings and arrows of outrageous fortune, or to take arms against a sea of troubles, and by opposing end them?" — William Shakespeare, *Hamlet*, Act III Scene I

"I heard she jumped off a cliff one time."

"She's a schizo."

"She had to be hospitalized because she tried to kill herself."

"Lauren told me she was hospitalized *twice*."

Dr. Chase said no one thinks I'm crazy, but three soccer players and a girl from the dance team seem eager to prove her wrong. They're standing at the end of the hall, casting what they must imagine are subtle glances my way every few seconds. I look around, wondering how many people are listening. They're not even trying to be quiet. As they discuss my sanity with all the discretion of a stadium announcer, shame and anger smother me. At least two dozen people are milling around, getting books, chatting with friends. I bury my head in my locker.

"Lauren isn't allowed to go over to her house anymore."

Whether 'tis nobler in the mind to suffer the slings and arrows of outrageous fortune…

Their words burrow into me, rub against my skin like grains of sand. I throw my textbooks into my bag and slam my locker door. My next class is just up the hall. I have to walk by them to get there.

"You don't get to say shit like that," comes another voice. Kalifa is standing down the hall, eyes flashing under her headscarf. "You don't know anything about her."

"Listen to the terrorist," one of the boys says, laughing. I grit my teeth. "Seen any of your buddies from Al-Qaida lately?"

"It's no wonder you and straitjacket-girl are friends." The girl this time.

I drop my bag. Stalk down the hall. Heads turn. People stare.

"Noomi," Kalifa says, a warning—

"Hey, watch out, she's gonna—"

"You miss the tie-breaking goal against Albany and you think you have the right to make fun of *anybody*?"

Claire's voice rings through the air, and I freeze, my arm half-way up, my fingers already curled into a fist.

"The only thing anyone should be making fun of today is your embarrassing performance on the field last night." Claire stops, standing shoulder-to-shoulder with me. She smiles. "Zoe. How are you? I don't think you want your mom to know about the ounce of cush my brother sold you for that little hot tub party last weekend. Do you?"

Zoe's face turns from pale to red to a sickly green. Claire's smile is feral.

"Coach Thompson would love to hear about that, too, don't you think? Pretty easy way to lose your spot on the dance team—and any hope of a scholarship."

Claire's older brother has been operating a nice under-the-table business selling marijuana to high schoolers to earn cash for his books and meals while at college. It's dangerous, but he's made a ton of money. The side effect is that Claire has blackmail on everyone who's ever bought anything from him, since our school has a zero-tolerance policy on drugs and alcohol.

A group of freshmen start to applaud. Claire turns and bows as if on stage. Zoe crosses her arms and opens her mouth, but nothing comes out.

"Now clear out," Claire says. "And leave my friends the fuck alone."

The offenders turn and walk down the hall, muttering to themselves as they go.

"That's better," Claire sighs.

"Way to take out the trash," Kalifa says.

Claire wrinkles her face and waves her hand under her nose. "It was all stinky too."

"You looked like they popped the pin on your grenade," Kali says to me.

"I'm fresh out of words for people like that."

"Ready for calc?" Kali says. "What a relief to deal with cold, hard numbers."

"I'm ready for just about anything except other humans," I reply. I retrieve my bag from where I'd left it by my locker. As I turn to Claire and Kalifa, I see a familiar face out of the corner of my eye. It's Silas. Leaning casually against the lockers, no book bag in tow. He's watching us, looking like he's been there this whole time.

I meet his eyes.

You're not real, I tell him angrily. You're the reason they think I'm crazy.

He straightens, pushing off the lockers, and turns to walk away. I can hear his footfalls echo with every stride.

You're a figment of my imagination, I insist.

"Noomi?" Kalifa's voice cuts through my thoughts. "You coming? We're late."

I nod and force myself to turn away from Silas's retreating figure.

"Yeah. Let's go."

I can't resist. I turn to look at him one last time.

But, like before, he's vanished.

See? I berate myself. It's all in your head. He's just an illusion, like the shadows.

But that doesn't explain how I can douse myself in gasoline, strike a match, and walk away a minute later.

IMAGINARY THINGS

"I can't believe that!" said Alice.

"Can't you?" the Queen said in a pitying tone. "Try again: draw a long breath, and shut your eyes."

Alice laughed. "There's no use trying," she said: "one can't believe impossible things."

"I daresay you haven't had much practice," said the Queen. "When I was your age, I always did it for half-an-hour a day. Why, sometimes I've believed as many as six impossible things before breakfast."

—Lewis Carroll, *Through the Looking Glass*

Evening light flutters across the table, a cool breeze from the window blowing in as the sun sets. I look up from my sketch to watch Ada. She's drawing a dog and a cat playing together. Neither are well-drawn, but you can tell what they are. Which is better than a year ago, when I had to ask what her drawings were, and she would stamp her feet when I couldn't tell the difference between a horse and dog.

"Noomi, do you have the green pencils?"

I check among my hoarded colors. "Pea green, blue-green, or Ada-green?"

"What's Ada-green?"

"The color of your eyes."

"That one, please!"

"What are you using it for?"

"The unicorn horn."

Good thing I didn't ask what kind of dog she's drawing.

"What did you do in school today, Ada?"

I pick a bright yellow pencil and start adding pops of color to my paper.

"We practiced our cursive, and Mrs. Bailey read us a story."

"What story?"

"It was called *The Grandfather Tree.*"

"What was it about?"

"A young tree that grows into a giant tree and then an old tree. But he dies to make room for all his baby trees."

"That sounds really sad."

"Hmm," Ada says, thinking about this while she fills in a spot of blue on her unicorn's flank. "I didn't think it was sad at all."

"Why not?"

"Because the tree got to be a part of everything else in the forest."

"That does sound nice." I pick up a purple pencil and start filling in the shadows. Blue comes next, adding texture to brown and purple, and I fill it out with maroon, adding rich colors to the shadows I remember as bleak and monochrome, darker than our coldest, rainiest days, darker than the blackest cave.

"What are you drawing, Noomi?"

"Trees," I reply. "Trees on the mountain."

"Like the grandfather tree?"

"Maybe. But none of these trees were giant trees."

"Then they can't be the grandfather tree." There's a long silence while we draw, Ada giving her unicorn a bright horn and a tail that leaves stars in its wake, and my colorful shadows, so colorful they could never hurt me, so vivid they could never be empty. "What did you do in school today, Noomi?"

I think about this for a moment, always wondering how much I can tell my baby sister without hurting her, how much

I can confide without frightening her. But since recently I have been in the business of taking risks, I decide to take another.

"I almost hurt someone today."

Ada stops coloring and looks at me. "Why?"

I meet her eyes squarely. "Because he hurt me." Ada nods as if this makes perfect sense. She drops her eyes back to her paper and resumes shading her unicorn. "He called me crazy," I say. "I was angry. So, I wanted to hurt him."

"What did you do?" Ada asks.

"I almost hit him." I pause, reflecting on the moment—Kalifa's voice ringing through the hall. Claire smirking, taunting. Silas hidden in the crowd. "But I didn't."

"Why not?"

"Someone stopped me."

"Who?" She looks up again, squinting.

"Claire. She was smart. She was fighting with words, not fists. I was too angry to think with anything but my hands."

"I would be mad, too," she says, nonchalant. "I don't like it when people call me names. But Ms. Seifert says we have to be nice to those people even when they're mean to us." She looks up at me. "Do you think that's true?"

I choose my words carefully. "I didn't today. I think sometimes we have to stand up for ourselves. And that means fighting back. But we have to fight like Claire, not like me. With our brains, not our hands."

"That sounds smart." She smiles and resumes coloring. For a moment, we're silent, working on our drawings. Then Ada puts her pencil down with a flourish and sits up straighter. "There. I'm done."

"Show me." She holds the drawing so I can look at it. The dog is riding on the unicorn's back, and the dog is wearing a cape. "Is the dog a superhero?"

"No. He just wants to be able to fly with his friend. That's why he has a cape on."

"Where did you get the idea to draw a unicorn?"

"Mr. Romaro said I should try to draw imaginary things like in your picture."

I look at her sideways. "What imaginary picture?"

"Not an imaginary picture, Noomi." An exaggerated sigh as she reaches to her backpack on the floor. "Imaginary things *in* the picture." She pulls out a stiff, crumpled piece of paper. And sets Silas's futuristic desert landscape on the table.

"Ada," I say, my voice low, "did you take that off my desk the other morning? Why did you do that?"

She looks bashful through her bangs. "I wanted to take it for show and tell."

I smile against my will. Even when I'm angry, she charms me.

"That's sweet, Ada, but you know you need to ask before taking anything from someone, right?"

"I forgot." The way she looks away, fidgeting, twisting her hands around her pencils, tells me she didn't forget.

But I can't be angry at her. Not when I've realized what this means: I have Silas's drawing back.

And Ada can see it too.

"And besides, you know I didn't do that drawing, right?" I say, leaning across the table to orient the paper so we can look at it together. "Do you think I could possibly have drawn this?" I laugh and put my unfinished trees next to Silas's desert for contrast. Mine looks like the product of a third-grade art class. His is like a Picasso sketch. "I can barely draw trees, Sweet Pea. I could never have drawn robots that look this real." I pause, take a breath, and then ask my next question. "Do you remember the boy sitting next to me when you and Mom picked me up after the concert last week?"

"The one with the hood?" Ada asks. "And dark hair?" Relief washes over me. I lean back and rest my head on the chair. I'm floating, suspended in a new tranquility.

"Yes, that one. You saw him there?"

"Duh. He was right next to you."

For a second, I let myself drift in this revelation. Ada can see him too.

I point at the corner of his drawing. "His name is Silas. See where it says his name in small letters down at the bottom? Just like how Mr. Romaro tells you to write your name on your drawings so he knows it's yours. That's how you know it's not mine."

"Oh. I guess I should tell them in show and tell that you didn't draw it."

"I guess so."

I smile.

Ada can see him too. Suddenly, not so imaginary.

Silas is real.

Inflection Point

"The point along a curve at which a change in the direction of curvature occurs." —The Oxford English Dictionary, "Inflection Point"

I stare at him from across the campfire. The sky is dark blue, the color of deep ocean. Firelight flickers against his hood while Leah leads us through a guided meditation. Crickets chirp in the night. The unseasonal warmth dissipated today, giving way to cold air and colder winds. I shiver, though the cold can't do more than make my hair stand on end, and I listen to Leah and try to follow her breathing directions. But my eyes never close, and my thoughts are fixed on Silas.

You are real, I tell him over and over again in my mind.

"Allow your back and neck and head to align, to straighten. Allow your shoulders to drop and relax. Find a sense of dignity in your posture. Allow your eyes to close."

I watch Silas. At this distance, in the darkness, I can't tell where he's looking. But I imagine him staring back at me. I imagine him crumpling his paper and throwing it on the ground, into the ocean, into space. It's a strange mix of relief, anger, and confusion that churns inside me. The night sky fades to black. Above Silas's head, a few stars appear. Orion, the hunter. Cassiopeia, the queen. Gemini, the twins.

I imagine Zeus hanging my constellation in the stars. Noomi, the lunatic.

Are you real, Silas?

"With your inhale, allow your breath to fill the space in your lungs. With the exhale, empty the space. Inhale. Exhale. Feel the way your abdomen expands and contracts with your breath."

I breathe with Leah's instructions. The warmth of the fire contrasts with the cold air. In the southern sky, a storm is building. Leah continues, walking us through a mindfulness meditation while I stare across the fire at Silas. Clouds obscure the stars overhead, gathering, sweeping forward. I can feel, more than hear, thunder rumbling in the distance.

Leah opens her eyes, shakes her shoulders, and smiles.

"Thank you, everybody. That's all for today. We'd better get home before the storm breaks. I'll see you on Sunday for this week's hike."

Everyone around me moves, but I stay seated. Paul stands quickly and avoids my gaze. Leah meets my eyes and opens her mouth, as if she has something to say. But she changes her mind and turns away.

Silas is still sitting there. Staring across the fire. Mirroring my movements. There's something gravitational between us. Like a meteor curving into the path of a planet, a collision imminent.

Which of us is the planet? Which the meteor, quietly waiting for doom?

When everyone has cleared out, heading to the parking lot, I stand and walk around the embers to him. I'm determined not to let him out of my sight—not even to blink. You won't disappear on me today, Silas. He doesn't move. As I get closer, I see that he's not staring over the fire, as I was, but into it. His eyes are fixed on the light.

"Hey," he says.

"Hi, Silas."

"Did you figure it out?"

"Figure what out?"

"Traveling."

I shake my head.

"No. I didn't. But I did figure out that you're not actually a member of this therapy group."

He nods. "That's true."

"So why do you come?"

"Leah's voice is soothing. I like her meditations. And I met you."

Rain is beginning to fall. The sky has taken on a purple hue normally reserved for autumn rains. There's an odd wind blowing in, and the air grows moist and chill around us. *Drop, drop, drop*. It patters onto my waterproof shell, a necessity here in Oregon.

"How is it possible that you don't belong to this therapy group, Paul doesn't know who you are, and there's no one registered at my high school by your name?"

"I don't go to your school. I never said I did."

I shake my head. "What school do you go to, if not mine?"

"I don't go to any school. Not in this world."

I freeze. "You said that before. On top of the mountain. What do you mean?"

He turns to me with the same stoic urgency he had when he was scribbling his name on his drawing and crumpling it up. The rain falls harder now, turning the embers to smoke, creating a dance around us. It reminds me of a Radiohead song. *The rain drops, the rain drops, the rain drops*...Thunder rumbles. Silas turns so he's sitting opposite me, cross-legged as though he's still in meditation. We ignore the water now falling in larger *thunks* on my jacket, on the ground. A drop collects on his eyelash and he blinks it away. He leans toward me, his eyes gleaming by the reflected light of the fire, now hazy from the clouds and pattering rain.

"This is what I was trying to tell you, Noomi. Last week, when I gave you my sketch."

"Sketch?" I laugh. "Silas, that was way more than a—"

"That's not important," he interrupts. "The first time I met you, on top of that mountain, your eyes were as black as pitch." A chill runs up my spine. He knows. He raises a hand and gestures around us, at the stars overhead. "As dark as the sky right now."

He knows about the shadows.

"They're hunting you. I don't know why, but they're after you."

"The shadows," I say.

"Yes. The shadows."

"You know." The words pop out of my mouth like bubbles. "You know about them. You've seen them. Where?"

He shakes his head. "Not here. Not in this world."

"Stop saying that!" Anger rises, boiling over in a burst of rage. A flash of lightning in the distance, beating time with my anger. "You and your stupid *other worlds*. Your robots and suns and sand fish. None of it makes sense. The shadows aren't in some other world—they're *here*, with me. Anytime, anywhere. They're in *this* world, and I don't care about whatever places you've traveled, because those places don't mean a damn thing to me."

He doesn't move, his eyes fixed on me. I can see the bones set beneath his cheeks where he's clenching his teeth. Finally, he stands, towering over me, and offers me his hand. Reluctantly, I take it, and he pulls me to my feet.

"Do you trust me, Noomi?" He grips my hand more tightly and leans forward, staring hard at me.

"No." I shake my head. In the glow of the dying embers, his eyes wide and gleaming, he looks demented. For the first time, I feel afraid. I try to pull my hand back from his, but his grip is firm.

"Good." He smiles. "Because I'm going to take you somewhere you're not going to believe."

He closes his eyes and the world shifts. The sensation is like falling. Like falling backward into cool, refreshing water. Like falling and falling and plummeting deeper and deeper into the ocean but never drowning and there's no water on your face and everything is black, so black it's terrifying, and I wonder if the shadows have finally found me and are going to kill me. But I can't move so I can't panic and my body crushes in on itself like I'm going through the smallest, tiniest door you can imagine, and I look down and I can't see myself, there's nothing to see, there's none of me left, and why am I not dead? And then suddenly—

I'm standing again.

In the middle of the desert.

With figures wearing white robes and hoods walking past me, hundreds of feet away, like the ones from Silas's drawing. There's a wall of metallic creatures on my left, some of them ten stories tall, walking or floating in a straight line toward some point on the distant horizon.

The sun is hotter than I've ever felt it before. The rain is long gone, a distant memory. Not a cloud dots the pristine, blueish-green sky. Green? In the sky? A breeze—not cool but fiery and full of sand—blows into my eyes, my hair. I squint around. Vibrant plants pepper the landscape. Silas is standing next to me, watching me with the faint trace of a smile on his face.

"Welcome to the State of Los Angeles, 2765."

Uncountable Infinity

"In 1861, Cantor presented a striking argument that has come to be known as Cantor's Diagonal Argument. One of Cantor's purposes was to replace his earlier, controversial proof that the reals are non-denumerable. But there was another purpose: to extend this result to the general theorem that any set can be replaced by another of greater power." —Keith Simmons, "Universality and the Liar: An Essay on Truth and the Diagonal Argument"

I throw up an arm to shield my eyes from the onslaught of the desert. "What just happened? Where did you take me?"

"I told you."

"But…that's not possible. That's crazy. We were standing by the fire, and now we're…" I look down at the sand beneath my feet, the wind billowing my clothes. "Here."

"Exactly." Silas's face changes, his brow furrowing and his mouth twisting upward. It looks strange because I've never seen it before. He's smiling.

"How?"

"I brought us here." He stares upward, still grinning. "I'm a Pathfinder."

"A what?"

"You are too. You should know."

"A what?" I repeat.

"A Pathfinder."

"You keep saying that like I should know what it means."

"You should." He stamps his feet in the sand, settling in, his hair blowing in the wind. "I can't believe no one's told you, or you haven't figured it out on your own. We're Pathfinders, Noomi, and that means we can travel to other worlds."

I stare at him. Blink hard against the grains of sand bombarding my eyes, and against the impossibility of this idea.

"What do you mean, other worlds?"

Silas waves his hand at the line of hooded figures walking past, at the floating robots in the distance, points up at the sun, round and orange, glinting there. "This is another world. A parallel world. The universe is porous, Noomi. There are holes in the fabric of spacetime, and we can find them and travel through them. They're called *paths*. And we are Pathfinders."

"Holes in the…spacetime? Are we…time traveling?" My voice comes out thick with shock and confusion, my head reeling as though I've jumped off a merry-go-round. Time traveling. *You can go anywhere, anytime*, Silas said to me before.

I could visit my father.

"No, we're not time traveling." The fragile hope in my heart withers as quickly as it bloomed. "You can't go backward or forward in time in your own world."

"But…you just said—"

"We're in a different universe. One that split apart from yours in a hair's breadth of a nanosecond when someone made a decision that could have gone any one of a multitude of ways. There are uncountably infinite parallel universes in the world. I brought us to one of them." Silas pauses, staring at the horizon where a mountainous ship with a sail that reflects sunlight like water is floating low across the dunes. "I've fallen into some strange worlds before. When possible, I like to stick to the ones that most resemble mine. The others can be…tricky."

"Fallen?" I echo faintly.

"You can stumble into a Path if you're not careful. That's why I'm so surprised you've never traveled."

My head is foggy. I can't figure any of this out. Nothing makes sense. The physics of what Silas is saying are impossible. Dr. Chase was right. I'm seeing things. I'm losing my grip on reality.

This isn't real.

And yet, the heat of the sun. The sweat beading on my forehead, collecting beneath my now-unnecessary rain jacket. The grains of sand I blink out of my eyes. The wind, unfurling my black hair like a chimerical sail on the skyscraping ships in the distance.

What is real and what isn't?

Silas watches me carefully. He seems at ease in the sun. His long lashes are perfectly adapted to bat sand out of his eyes. His dark complexion and black hair make sense against the backdrop—I can imagine him in the line of walkers, white robes fluttering in the dunes. As if he belongs.

Maybe he does.

"Is this where you're from?"

He smiles and looks away. "No. But this is my favorite world to visit."

"Why?"

"It feels like home."

"Where is home for you?"

He doesn't move, but his face changes almost imperceptibly. His jaw sets and he squints a little. He raises a hand to shield his eyes from the sun.

"I'll take you there another time. This is a lot to take in. I've met a lot of Pathfinders, but I've never taken someone on their inaugural voyage before."

He's changing the subject, but I don't press him. There are things I don't want to talk about either. We're allowed our secrets.

"Do you want to take a look around?" he asks.

"What is there to see?"

He points. "There are some caves that way with shade and shelter."

A half-hour later, I've had enough of sand dunes to last the rest of my life. I'd stripped off my jacket and pulled it over my head like a hood, hoping for some relief from the sun, but I was under no circumstances about to strip down to my underwear. My shirt is soaked through, and my jeans are clinging to me like a second skin, sticky with sweat, twisting and rubbing in all the wrong places. It must be a hundred and twenty degrees. Sweat drips down my face as I sit in the shade of a small, dusty cave adorned by a few straggling succulents.

"Here," Silas says, handing me a strip of plant that looks vaguely like aloe, except it's a bright, shocking purple. "Suck on this. Sugar and water will rehydrate you."

I take the thick leaf and eagerly suck from the exposed inside. It tastes a little like pear, maybe, or melon. Not as sweet as either.

"If I had known you were bringing me to a shoot for Star Wars, I would have picked different clothes."

"Technically, we're in Los Angeles, not Tatooine," Silas says, smiling at my grumpiness.

"Tell me again how all this works?" I close my eyes and lean back against the wall of the cave. "You said earlier we're in the State of Los Angeles. But you also said we're not time traveling. So where are we if we're in Los Angeles but we're not in the future?"

"We're in a different world, very similar to yours, just different enough." He pauses, thinking. "I don't know what the future of your world looks like, seven hundred years later. And no one will know, until your world makes it there." Shakes his head. "In this world, the nation-state of Los Angeles began colonizing other planetary systems about two hundred years ago. This is one of those planets. It's in the process of being terraformed." He points at the line of massive robots on the horizon. "That's what the robots are doing. Carrying enormous quantities of building material, metal, ore, water, and agricultural products from the space port to a colony."

I feel as though my brain is being kneaded like Ada's Play-Doh. "So, we're in the future of another world that's like mine but different?"

"Exactly. This place," Silas gestures around and above him, to the sun distantly overhead and at the desert landscape, "is one of myriad other worlds that were created based on the multitude of decisions that are made every single day. As we think of it, time moves backward and forward. In reality, things are a lot more complicated than that, but one aspect is relatively simple. As time moves forward along a one-dimensional line, the number of worlds increases exponentially at every instant. As time moves backward along that same line, the number of worlds decreases exponentially, all the way back until you only have one single world left, which is the only world that existed prior to the Big Bang."

I think of Mr. Arcadio's gift to me: *Flatland: A Romance of Many Dimensions*, and remember the Square visiting the King of Lineland, whose poor people could only move in a single dimension along a straight line.

"How do you know all of this?"

Silas shrugs. "I've met a lot of other Pathfinders. We talk about the worlds we've visited. We share what we've learned."

"What makes us Pathfinders? Why are we different from everyone else?"

He watches me out of the corner of his eye, not looking at me directly. "It's different things for different people."

"What do you mean?"

He pauses; diverts his attention from me to some tiny creature crawling on his arm. Then stares at a vibrant, spiky blue plant that adorns the entrance to the cave. Finally, he speaks.

"No one really knows what exactly causes it." His voice is flat. "For a lot of people, there's some concentrated burst of power that allows them to travel. Getting struck by lightning, for instance. Or a near-death experience." He pauses again. Fidgets. Stares between his legs at the sand beneath us. "For some, it seems to be genetic. There's no other explanation. A highly recessive gene, maybe, or one that only activates under very rare circumstances."

"Is that how it is for you?" My voice is soft. There's a scar in his voice, a wound that never fully healed.

"Yes," he says. "I don't know why I'm a Pathfinder. No one ever told me I was. I stumbled into a world one day when I was young, and almost died. It was underwater, and I nearly drowned before I was able to find a new Path and get home." He barks a laugh. "That's the tricky thing about Pathfinding. You can never really tell what you're getting into."

"What do you mean?"

"You can't look into your destination universe before you choose a Path. Well, maybe some species can, but I can't, and I haven't met any humans who can. You can feel the edges of a world. Get a distant sense of it. Like looking at a painting from very far away. Otherwise, it's just guesswork."

"So humans aren't the only ones who can Pathfind?"

"Oh, no," he says, laughing.

I smile. I like when he's smiling and laughing. There's something stoic about him in those moments when he's cloudy, like a cliff face or a mountain, rocky and cold. But when he lightens up, when he smiles—it's radiant.

I want to be close to that.

"Some species on our very own Earth can Pathfind. I ran into an elephant traveling one time. Another human Pathfinder I met told me she saw a colony of bees Pathfinding. I'm not sure I believe her." He stares up at the sky. "Surprisingly, no other primates. There seems to be a threshold of intelligence, a certain *type* of intelligence you have to achieve in order to Pathfind, but no one I know has figured out what it is."

There's a pause. I breathe. I can hear his breath too. In and out. Mixing with the wind whistling outside this cave. The spiky plant in front of me, the foreign creature—it looks furry—on Silas's arm, the sand dunes slowly but surely shifting into new shapes.

I try to imagine telling this story to Dr. Chase the next time I see her. Sitting in her office staring at the sailboat painting as I have a thousand times. I'm a Pathfinder, I say to her in my imagination. What does that mean? she asks. It means I can travel to other worlds. I see her eyes widening. She types frantically on her iPad. A prescription is handed to my mother after our meeting. *It may be time*, Dr. Chase says, *to consider institutionalization.*

No. I can't tell her this.

I can't tell anyone.

"Silas," I say, "can we go home now?"

Fluid Dynamics

"The arrangement of the molecules is continually changing, and, as a consequence, any force applied to the liquid produces a deformation which increases in magnitude for so long as the force is maintained."—G. K. Batchelor, *An Introduction to Fluid Dynamics*

Silas doesn't take me home. Instead, he tells me I need to practice Pathfinding until I can find the threads of our world, peer through the fabric of spacetime, and confirm that it is, indeed, mine.

"It's easier to go home than to leave. You have a sort of internal compass that will direct you to the world of your birth. Like true north, your sense of direction will always lead you home."

"Why?"

He shrugs.

"Just another thing Pathfinders don't really know?"

"There are some theories," he says evasively.

"Tell me." I summon a tone of command. But the heat is getting to me, and water from the melon-cactus was hardly enough to revive me.

Silas narrows his eyes. "No," he says. "We're going home. I'll tell you another time." I sigh, but don't argue. "The easiest way to learn is to close your eyes." I do so. "That colorful darkness behind your eyelids—those are the threads of spacetime you can use to find a Path."

My eyes pop open.

"No, those are blood vessels in our eyelids illuminated by the light," I correct.

"That's what your teachers told you."

I cross my arms and glare at him.

"Haven't your teachers ever taught you something you later found out was wrong?" He stares at me. "Maybe for ordinary people, that's true. Maybe it's even partly true for us. But whatever it is, in that vivid darkness, you can find a Path."

"Find?" I ask. "Or make?"

"Find," he says emphatically. "Paths are very difficult to make. But finding them, that's easy. Your world is particularly porous. There should be loads of them."

"Why are they difficult to make?"

"It can be dangerous," he says. "The energy required to create a path is volatile. You can hurt yourself. Or those around you. Or you can get lost or trapped." Fear floods through me. I hadn't considered the impact this ability could have on those around me. Will the shadows find me? What if they find Claire or Kalifa, or my mother—or Ada?

How do I protect them when I can't protect myself?

"Are you ok?" Silas bends to look at me. His eyes are greener now, emerald like spring grass in the mountains, standing out in crystalline bursts against the dusky landscape. It's strange that his eyes should change color like this. So much of this is new, like a vivid dream, that moment of lucidity right before you wake up.

"Do your eyes always change color when you Pathfind?" My voice is a low trickle, like a spring from the ground.

He straightens, pulling away.

"I don't know," he says. "Do they?"

"Silas," I whisper, "am I dreaming?"

He shakes his head. "Focus, Noomi. You need to go home.

But you need to learn to Pathfind too. Close your eyes and stare at those blood vessels. Get a sense of them."

I close my eyes and try to relax, breathing in and out. Silas places his hands on my shoulders, and a chill runs through my body. His touch is calming. I focus on the lines dancing against my eyelids.

"They move," I say. "They shift."

"Yes," he says. "That's because we're hurtling not just through space as this planet moves through its universe, but through time as well. The fabric is constantly moving. Finding a Path is about relaxing and watching until you feel a glimmer of something. It will be a snag. Like catching your sweater on a nail and being pulled back. When you find a Path back to your world, it'll feel like walking into your house after a long day."

I watch as the shapes fly or float or burst into my vision. There are navy blues, purples, and reds. Splashes of green and ember-orange. There are so many colors in the darkness. So rich and full. So unlike the shadows. Then I feel it. A snag. A pull. Like a needle pulling thread. It smells like Mom's spiced coffee and tastes of musty earth and wet air. There's a purple hue that makes me think of the deepening sky where Silas and I were sitting around the fire.

"That's it," he says, his voice low and soft. "Focus on it. Stare into it. Peel back the layers of the other worlds and Paths around us. Push past the fog."

My eyes fly open as I realize I've been forgetting a big piece of the puzzle. "Silas, how does time work? What if I miss the window and we end up back home too early—or too late?"

"We're animals," he says, shaking his head. "Subject to the laws of physics and biology, even if those laws are more complex than what you've been taught in school. Time carries us—and our physical worlds—forward, and we can't escape those confines, although it may pass differently in one world than it does in another. For instance, time passes more quickly here relative to your world. That's why this civilization is so much more technologically advanced than yours. They've had more time to develop."

"How much time has passed in our world?"

"*Your* world," he corrects gently. "I'd guess twenty to thirty minutes."

A shiver races down my spine. "I'm late," I whisper. "I was supposed to be home. My mother has no idea where I am."

"Let's go, then. Focus."

"Can't you just do it?" I ask desperately. There's a pressure on my chest like a vise.

Silas shakes his head. "You have to learn. I don't want you to get stuck somewhere and not be able to find your way home."

Reluctantly, I nod. I don't want that either. I take a deep, calming breath, letting the pressure slough off me like water, then close my eyes and find the threads, searching again for that tenuous connection. I feel it—the pull. The snag. I let the first one slide by, afraid to dive in. As I stare into the darkness behind my eyelids, I can feel the currents as much as see them, like being underwater in the ocean, where the water is flowing in so many directions at once, the waves rolling over you toward shore and the undertow tugging you into the deep. The rushing and pulling of a million billion water molecules all moving according to an infinitely complex system of motion.

One current feels familiar. The threads tug at me. They catch me, pull me, reel me in.

"Slow down," Silas whispers. "Look first."

I stare into the jade bloom in my eyes and feel glimmers of crackling heat, smell fir trees and cool night air.

"Good. Now let it take you."

I sink into it and again it feels like falling, but this time instead of water it's silk, smooth and cool against my skin. And then I feel as though I am being compressed. It's the same feeling I had the first time, except now it isn't so terrifying because I know what it is. I feel myself being passed through the eye of the needle, my whole essence compressed into infinitesimal nothing. Then released again, expanding, exploding outward, and my feet catch on soft decomposing pine needles. The smell of wet earth and humus permeates the air, and the embers in front of us are dying.

"We're standing on the other side of the fire."

"Yes," he agrees. "Very good for your first time."

Rain is falling in earnest now, and the sky has taken on a greenish-purple hue that portends more to come. I pull out my phone, hoping my mother hasn't sent me thirty panicked text messages. I glance at the glowing screen and see a new message from her. *Running late, still at the hospital. Be home in twenty minutes. How was your session?* The times tamp tells me she sent it about five minutes ago.

Relief floods through my bones.

"I should go," I say. "It's late, and my mother will be expecting me."

Silas nods. He turns and walks away, deeper into the park.

"Wait!" I call after him, my heart fluttering in trepidation. How will I contact him? I don't want to lose him, now that I've found him, now that I know what I know. He turns, looking at me. "When will I see you again?"

"I don't know," he says.

"You haven't answered half my questions."

"I don't have all the answers."

"I need your help," I implore. "I need you to help me fight the shadows."

"You don't need my help, Noomi. Not in this world. Not in any world."

I do need your help, I think futilely as he walks into the darkness. I can't do this alone.

But he's gone.

Resonant Frequency

"Consider a string, such as a guitar string, that is stretched between two clamps. Suppose we send a contiuous sinusoidal wave of a certainfrequency along the string, say, toward the right. When the wave reaches the right end, it reflects and begins to travel back to the left. That left-going wave then overlaps the wave that is still traveling to the right. When the left-going wave reaches the left end, it reflects again and the newly reflected wave begins to travel to the right, overlapping the left-going and right-going waves. In short, we very soon have many overlapping traveling waves, which interfere with one another. For certain frequencies, the interference produces a standing wave pattern (or oscillation mode) with nodes and large antinodes... Such a standing wave is said to be produced at resonance, and the string is said to resonate at these certain frequencies, called resonant frequencies. If the string is oscillated at some frequency other than a resonant frequency, a standing wave is not set up. Then the interference of the right-going and left-going traveling waves results in only small (perhaps imperceptible) oscillations of the string."
—David Halliday, "Standing Waves and Resonance" *Fundamentals of Physics*

Spark. Ignition. Reverse. Pedal.

The rain is coming down hard. I turn on my wipers and shift into drive, push the pedal. There's an emptiness in my core. An unknown. Uncertainty. What just happened? Is it real? Am I a Pathfinder? Or is my mind playing tricks on me, conjuring something fantastical to trick me into believing I'm not crazy?

According to everything I've been taught, what Silas and I just did is impossible. The laws of physics tell me I've lost my grip on reality. Mathematics is incompatible with Pathfinding. And there's no way human cells could possibly be compressed into nothing and rebuilt on the other side.

And yet I can douse myself in gasoline and watch it burn off my skin without a trace.

Memories from the last hour rush over me. The falling, the compression. Landing in the desert, sweat dripping down my face. Silas's eyes, fading from green to iridescent to green again. The gentleness in his face when he smiles.

Is it real? Is any of it real?

The rain grows harder, coming down from the sky in great sheets. I try to forget about Pathfinding, to focus instead on getting home safely. But the uncertainty sits in my gut. Rotting. The rain adds to the melancholy, the dissonance growing to a swell. Who do I believe? What am I? What is real and what isn't?

There's a dark patch on the road where a streetlamp is out. I drive through it and the peculiar emptiness flashes through me, the blackness devoid of color. I gun the car past the patch before the emptiness can settle into my bones. The feeling fades as streetlamps paint the asphalt with sepia-colored light.

Before turning onto the highway, I pull to the curb and take a few deep breaths. Don't let them find you here. Focus, like you did on the threads behind your eyes. Focus on getting home.

Blinker. Gas. Turn.

The highway is dark and bleak. Greyscale. Color seeping out of the world. The universe is porous, Silas said. It feels like the whole spectrum of light is being drained out of those pores. The first fleeting fear washes over me, the one that always fades soon after, drained away like every other emotion. I crank up the music, hoping for a distraction, something to focus on, to energize me. But the rain pounds on the roof of the car and the shadows are here, crowding out my vision, creeping at my spine.

I pull to the side of the road. No use fighting it. Can't drive like this. Darkness looms like malignant trees with sticky fingers. The gloaming. Every streetlight is dark.

They're here, I think dully. I've lost. Against my will, my muscles relax. Settling into the seat. The leather welcoming. Blurring. I feel undefined. Erased.

I close my eyes.

The colors are still here but fading fast. Deep red, there. Blue and purple, there. A splash of green. The blackness so complete it obscures my vision of the threads, the fabric. I try to peel it back, but it's deep. Like everything has been drenched in ink. But then I feel the snag. The catch of a Path. I don't hesitate, don't feel the edges to find out what world I'm falling into. I sink back and let the current carry me. Like being swept underwater.

The last thing I hear is the sound of thunder rumbling, and then I am gone.

The compression.

The falling.

The darkness.

I connect. My feet on the ground. I keep my eyes closed, searching with my other senses for the shadows. But the blackness is gone. The emptiness, gone. Full color behind my eyelids again, the threads of spacetime unobscured. My heart swells. Relief washes over me.

I did it. I escaped.

I open my eyes and look around, grateful, as always, for the return of my vision. This world is hot, too, like Silas's desert, barren and sandy. But here there are more familiar things, even if only through photos: cacti, succulents, dusty scrub bushes that rise no higher than my waist. There are a few scattered houses, ramshackle and dusty, half-crumbling. Where am I?

I walk toward one of them, feeling called in that direction. Stepping over shrubs and through little dirt paths, I make my way to the hut.

Crack!

There's an explosion of noise like a gunshot. My heart kicks in my chest and I drop to the ground, hands over my head.

"*Lo tengo!*"

A boy, no older than thirteen, is running out from behind a bush toward something fallen on the ground. He runs away from the house, and my feet are drawn in his direction. A sick feeling wells in my belly as I realize what he's got—a dead javelina, a wild desert animal that looks like a boar. My father used to talk about them, and as a child I loved when he would read me a story called *Los Tres Pequeños Jabalíes*, a Spanish version of "The Three Little Pigs" and the "Big Bad Wolf."

"*Muy bien!*" A man's voice, this time. Rich and musical and resounding. It strikes a chord so deep my spine vibrates to the pitch. It sounds like honey and caramel, like *horchata* and nutmeg, like autumn leaves and wam hands. My stomach clenches and unclenches as recognition dawns.

Resonant frequency occurs when one vibrating system produces a similar oscillation at a greater amplitude in a separate system.

It's my dad.

A man is walking out of the house toward the boy with the rifle, who is now standing still, staring down at the javelina. Though he is unfamiliar with a dark beard and dusty clothes, and he's older and more sun-baked than I ever saw him, once I see his eyes, almond-shaped and creased with smile lines, I know it's him.

My father is standing in front of me. Older. Darker. Dustier. Alive.

Dad! I want to cry. I want to run to him. I want to wrap my arms around him and hold him in all the ways I haven't since he died. But my legs are paralyzed. He won't know me. He won't know who I am. In this world, I am nothing to him. I don't exist. And yet, here he is, standing in front of me.

The last time I saw you, you were in your Sunday suit, clean-shaven, lying in a casket, your skin as pale as your shirt.

Something strange happens. He stops moving, standing stock-still. He bends at the waist, slowly, and then sinks to one knee. I creep forward, inching toward them until I'm only a hundred feet away, hidden in the bushes, watching as he leans to the left and then collapses, unmoving on the ground.

"Dad!" I cry, but my voice dies in my throat and what was meant to be a shout comes out as a whimper. Is he dying? Am I going to watch my father die twice?

The boy finally looks up from the javelina, glancing over his shoulder. When he turns, he lets out a gasp and runs to my father's side. My father. Padre, Papa, Dad. The words echo and collide in my head. The boy stumbles, tripping on something, and then rights himself to keep moving. He falls on his knees at my father's side—is it his dad, too? The thought occurs to me like lightning zipping through my skin. He puts his hand on my dad's back and shakes, trying to rouse him.

"Nana!" the boy shouts.

A woman bursts from inside the house, pausing only for a moment before dashing out to where man and boy are on the ground. Her grey hair billows behind her. It takes me a moment, but I recognize her too. She has flat cheeks and deep-set eyes, wearing a white-dusted apron tied over her jeans, and somehow looks younger here than in my world. My abuela, my father's mother.

"*Esteban, despiértate, despiértate, mi amor.*" Wake up, she pleads, rolling him onto his back and cradling his face with her hands.

The boy looks on helplessly. I'm on my hands and knees now, crawling forward, oblivious to the dust and dirt, trying to get as close as I can without being noticed.

Finally, my father opens his eyes and shudders. The sigh of relief that leaves my chest is like a breath I've been holding for a year. My grandmother presses her face to his. The boy lets go of his hand and stands up, trying to look tough.

My father stiffens, trying to stand. A moment ago, he looked strong and healthy. Now he is tired and weak. He clings to my abuela, and she helps him sit up.

Dad. The word comes out of my mouth not even a whisper, just a shape of my lips, my mouth going through the motions with no sound.

"*Las sombras, de nuevo?*" she whispers. The shadows again?

He nods.

Fear ripples through my heart. Did he have them too?

Something changes. The wind shifts. I flatten against the ground as my grandmother looks around, feeling the change in the air, too.

I have to go. I want to stay here forever, watching my father, learning about his life, but this is not my world. The longer I stay, the more I risk giving myself away.

I close my eyes and search for the threads, taking care to search for a Path that will lead me to a good place to return. I let a few waft past me—one smells of gasoline and burned rubber, and another feels so empty and dark I'm sure it must still be inhabited by the shadows. I try to look for one that will take me back to the car. I find one that is dimly yellow-orange and feels warm, and I focus on it.

"*Esteban, estás enfermo,*" I hear my abuela say. "*Necesitas ir al doctor, mi amor.*" You're sick. You need to see a doctor.

"Papa," the boy says, and I close my eyes tighter. So, it is his son. This must be a world where he never left the desert, where he never came north to go to college, where he married a different woman and had a different child and lived a different life.

I want to imprint his face onto my memory forever. Before I let myself fall into the spaces between the threads, I open my eyes for one last look at my father.

A metallic chill shivers through my veins. He is staring right at me. His eyes fixed on mine. Like a hawk. Like a hunter. The fire I heard so often in his voice is burning through his brown eyes, giving them a reddish tint. But he smiles at me, kind and soft, and the blaze turns to embers, warm like a cozy kitchen on a snowy day, and I let myself fall back into the Path I found, and he and my abuela and his son and the bloody javelina and the dirty scrub of the desert are all gone, and I'm falling through endless, soft, warm darkness. Then I'm back in my world and it's dark but at the same time brilliantly warm and bright, and it takes me a few seconds of breathing blackened air and soot to realize why.

Everything is on fire.

INCENDIARY

"And so you see, my love,
how I move
around the island,
around the world,
safe in the midst of spring,
crazy with light in the cold,
walking tranquil in the fire"
—Pablo Neruda, "Epithalamium," *The Captain's Verses*

Sideways.

I am sideways. A wooden four-by-four presses up against my legs and I'm compressed between soft bales of hay on one side and several hundred pounds of pressure on the other. The fire is all around me. In front of me. Behind me. The hay is catching. This world is hot, even for me. Red-orange-yellow-white. Crackling. The world smells like ash. It smells like heat. My skin sweating. Maybe I'll finally get my wish. The flames are warm and welcoming, like my father's eyes.

Like my father's eyes.

How did I get here? I was supposed to be back in the car. Where I am I?

What is happening?

Instinct kicks in. I have to get out. My legs are trapped under the beam. I try to move them, but the wood is too heavy. I roll over, off the hay that is incinerating around me, and squeeze my calves, dragging my legs under the pressure of the beam to the edge, where it finally rolls off me and collapses in the dust.

I scramble to my feet and glance around. I'm in a barn, old and crumbling, unused for years. It's familiar. I feel like I've been here before. A chunk of the roof is missing, and I realize: this is the Moreland's old barn, down the road a few miles from my house. I used to play here. Smoke rises in thick, dusty plumes, so much that it chokes me and I cough. I can't breathe. Panic sets in, and I stumble forward, through the flames.

But everything is old and dry and dusty, the wood rotten through, the beams already weak. The barn was crumbling anyway. The fire burning on one side of the building is sweeping through to the other side and the rafters collapse in front of me and my exit is blocked. I am trapped.

I try to breathe again, but smoke goes in my nose, stinging my eyes and making me cough harder. I drop to the ground. Crawl forward. Under the fallen rafters. The beams are on fire but there's a tunnel and I'm not worried about the flames. The opening is tiny. I flatten my body and press my chest into the ground and squeeze under the beams. The heat grows to a crescendo. My jeans have caught fire. Sweat breaks on my face, instantly boiling away. Still, my skin is intact. How am I alive? How is my body not crisping, blackening, melting before my eyes? I push forward through the dirt and finally through the collapsed rafters. The giant open door looms in front of me, and a waft of cool air blows in, the open darkness of night so promising and empty I wonder if I am dying, stumbling across the river Styx into the world of the dead. I take a few steps out of the barn and everything is dark and the world behind me is as bright as the Sun and then there are sirens in the air and rain on my body and I am alive. I am alive. I am alive. I am alive.

I fall to the ground.

Inhale, sweet

Muddy, soft grass.

Rain across my face.

Lightning strikes close but also far. The storm is passing.

Flashing red and white lights in the distance, sirens wailing. Two fire trucks barrel through the overgrown road and pull up in front of me. Men in navy and reflective green suits leap off the trucks and run forward, dragging hoses and cranking wheels, eyes wide and white, their hats reflecting strangely in the rotating lights. It's hard to see but I can feel their footsteps approaching, and I press my elbows to the ground and try to climb to my feet, but it's hard. I only make it part-way. I realize sitting there on all fours that I'm naked, my clothes have burned away, and the first thing they do when they reach me is throw a blanket around my shoulders and pull me to my feet, half-walking, half-carrying me to the enormous gleaming metal truck, and I realize I'm crying hard enough for there to be water on my face, or is that the rain? I can't tell—

DECOHERENCE

"The true reason for the prevalence of chaos is that large quantum systems are hard to isolate from their surroundings. Even the 'patter of photons' from the Sun...destroys the delicate interference underlying the quantum regularity. This effect, of large quantum systems being dramatically sensitive to uncontrolled external influence, is called decoherence. In the classical limit, the quantum suppression of chaos is itself suppressed by decoherence, allowing chaos to re-emerge as a familiar feature of the large scale world... Decoherence is a real physical process that is going on everywhere all the time. It takes place whenever a quantum system is no longer isolated from its surrounding macroscopic environment and its wavefunction becomes entangled with the complicated state of this environment" —Jim Al-Khalili, *Quantum: A Guide for the Perplexed*

Cracked lines. Shattered glass. Light distorted through water, waves bent and twisted so my eyes do not understand. Grating like shearing metal and screeching tires. Fingernails across steel. And the sterile, gaunt scent of alcohol and latex.

With wide, disbelieving eyes, the EMTs insist on taking me to the hospital. They strap me into a strange collar, and I'm supported inside the plastic framework that won't let me move or bend or twist. A pinch inside my elbow. Needles. The ambulance shakes and rolls as we zoom to the hospital. A bag hangs above my head.

What's your name? Can you open your eyes? Move your leg. Move your arm. Do you feel this?

I answer all their questions. The ambulance bay doors open. A countdown from three and I'm lifted into the air, weightless, onto a different bed. Now, now, everything disintegrates. Voices separate from bodies. A dozen people buzz around me. Sounds murmur together. Images partition and blur. My body rolls and moves and floats through the world without my help.

Decoherence. When all the possible quantum positions of a subatomic particle are combined onto a probabilistic map, and none has yet been found to be true or false. The cat is dead. The cat is alive. The atom is on one side of the wall, and the other. Both are true and both are false.

I am real. I am not real.

Silas is real. Silas is not real.

The shadows are real. The shadows are not real.

The shadows are gone. Where did they go?

A voice, high-pitched and urgent. "Noomi!" My mind latches onto it like an anchor. "You're alive, you're alive, *Alhamdulillah*."

Every syllable pulses over me, every accent as tactile as a dot of Braille. It takes me a moment to realize the words are spoken in Arabic. Soft, familiar hands wrap around mine, pulling me back from the edge. I feel unified. Stitched together. The doctor's white coat splits into two, then four. I see her name tag, focus on it. The world stops spinning as I read her name over and over while she walks with us. Saida Perez, M.D. Saida Perez, M.D. Saida Perez, M.D. Saida Perez...

"Mom."

"Noomi." Her hands are on the bar at my side. I am being whisked. I've read this word in books and it's happening to me now. Whisked away. Whisked down halls. Whisked into a new dimension. "Are you okay?"

"I feel blurry. A little sore."

"Dr. Perez, your daughter is going to be fine." The sound rolls over me, distorting and morphing into something impenetrable. A fog rolling in, bringing dank, chill air. "Her vitals are good. Everything looks good. We're about to do FAST. Please step back."

Objects float by, like I'm a visitor in an underwater museum. Heads and faces bob past. Trays of food and medicine. Doctors in coats and nurses in scrubs. Visitors. I smell rubber and disinfectant and can taste fear in the air. The bed is rolled into a room. I'm wearing a hospital gown; light cloth that rubs slightly against my chest. My gown is pushed up to my rib cage. Cold liquid across my abdomen.

"I'm not pregnant," I say.

"She's not thinking clearly." My mother's voice. "Was she drinking?"

"The EMT reported no toxins and no indication of TBI." But the voice is worried.

"Henry, do the CT."

"It might not be necessary, Saida."

Something cold and hard connects with my skin. I recoil. It presses against my side, rolls across my belly, up to my ribs, down to my hips. Someone is looking at a screen. Voices crosshatch and fade.

"Clean. No signs of bleeding."

No response. Hands clench in mine. Twist. Release. I am isolated again. I force myself to focus. Shapes and colors combine to make a nose, a chin, hair, eyes.

"Noomi," a voice says. I squint. "My name is Dr. Zimmerman. I'm a colleague of your mother's. Do you remember me?"

Nod.

"Can you tell me your full name?"

"Noomi Nailah Perez."

"What's today's date?"

"March 25, 2016."

"Where do you go to school?"

"Rocklin High."

Glances. Tension. Silence. Did I get it wrong?

"Very good, Noomi." More silence. The pale doctor with dark hair and chestnut eyes stares at my mother across the hospital bed. "Saida, there's no evidence your daughter was concussed. Any confusion is perfectly attributable to trauma. She's not burned in the slightest. No internal bleeding. Vitals normal. But the EMT reported she emerged from a burning barn right before the structure collapsed. Her clothes were incinerated. Do you have any idea what this means?"

"She got lucky," my mother says, breathless. She's staring at me like I'm a miracle. "I don't believe in God, but if I did, I'd be on my knees thanking him right now."

The doctor shakes his head.

"There has to be more to the story."

A new pair of eyes looms over me. Moss-green. Summer-grass green. They make me think of ferns and waterfalls.

Silas.

"Noomi," he says carefully, his voice deep with worry. "What happened?" He drops into a chair next to me and leans in, staring at me in that unmoving, treelike way. He looks like he hasn't moved for a thousand years.

"What are you doing here?" I ask.

Everyone looks at me. The nurse glances at my mother, who's staring straight at me.

"Don't talk to me," Silas says sharply. "They can hear you, but not me."

I glare at him. Why would he ask me a question if he doesn't want me to answer?

"Are you okay?" the doctor asks, moving closer to me, leaning over me.

"Sorry," I say to the doctor. "I…thought I saw someone."

I divert my gaze to Silas. *Why can't they hear you?* I want to shout. I visualize hundreds of arrows flying at him. Every single one misses. He smiles wryly as though he knows what I'm picturing in my head. *You're imaginary*, I tell him. *You don't exist.* He doesn't respond. Sits there, staring at me. Then leans back, reaches into his pocket, and pulls out a pen and folded piece of paper.

"Might as well work on this," he says, "since I'm going to be here a while." And then he sets to drawing. I crane my neck to see what it is, sitting up straighter in the hospital bed. But I can't see. Why are you going to be here a while? I want to ask.

"Noomi?" my mother asks, casting a hesitant glance at the chair Silas is occupying. I sit back immediately. Silas continues drawing, unperturbed. "What are you looking at?"

"Nothing."

"Saida," Dr. Zimmerman says quietly, watching me. "Can we talk outside?" She follows him, smoothing her skirt as she stands, casting one last glance my way.

A nurse buzzes around, checking on me, so I can't talk to Silas. Once again, I sit up a little, trying to peer over the edge of his paper to see what he's drawing without being too obvious. Dr. Zimmerman and my mother are talking outside. I can see them outside the glass, heads together. My mother quiet and reserved in comparison to Henry's expansive gestures and astonished expression. I can't hear their conversation. But I can imagine what they might be saying.

Your daughter should have been incinerated.

She got lucky.

No one gets lucky in a fire like that. There wasn't a mark on her.

She was wearing jeans. Denim can be a flame retardant.

Saida, she was naked when she came out of that barn. Something different happened. Your daughter does have a history—

Don't bring your biases into this. She's not dangerous. She's not violent.

Decoherence. All the infinite possibilities for a single particle interacting with every other single particle in a system getting mixed up and confused, and the particle is in every single possible place in that instant and all the possibilities are both true and false at the same time.

The cat is dead.

The cat is alive.

Your daughter is dead.

Your daughter is alive.

All are true. All are false.

The nurse sits down. In the same chair as Silas.

Silas is in the chair.

The nurse is in the chair.

Both are true. Both are false.

I stare at the two of them, overlapping images, for the half second that they occupy the same space. In a burst of motion, Silas leaps out of the chair, standing over both of us. And laughs.

"Occupational hazard," he says.

I narrow my eyes. Frown.

"Get it? Occupational hazard? She was occupying the same chair as me." He stops smiling, looks away. Takes a deep breath. "Noomi. I'm sorry. I know there's a lot that's confusing right now." I glare at him as ferociously as I can. "I shouldn't have left you. You're too new to Pathfinding. And the things that are after you are…I don't know what they are. I don't know why they're after you. But we can learn together. We can find out what they're after and why. And we can fight them together. Okay?"

Why? I want to shout at him. It's the question that's been echoing in my mind since the first time I jumped off our roof, foolishly thinking the leap would be enough to kill myself, only to find that my broken leg healed within five minutes of landing. Why? Why are these things haunting me? Why are you here, trying to help me? And why, for the love of God, can't I get rid of them?

I am no closer to the answers than when I doused myself in gasoline and struck a match.

No. That's not true.

My dad had them too. He and I have that in common.

I know that much, at least. I am one step closer. One small step, but that's enough.

Enough to keep fighting.

DISSOCIATION

"Dissociation (n): the act or process of dissociating: the state of being dissociated: such as a: the process by which a chemical combination breaks up into simpler constituents especially: one that results from the action of energy (such as heat) on a gas or of a solvent on a dissolved substance, b: the separation of whole segments of the personality (as in multiple personality disorder) or of discrete mental processes (as in the schizophrenias) from the mainstream of consciousness or of behavior." —Merriam-Webster, "Dissociation"

"She seems to be in perfect health," Dr. Zimmerman said to my mother. "But based on the police report, the circumstances around the accident, and Dr. Chase's recommendation, we've decided to keep her under observation for a twenty-four-hour period."

The nurse who's been babysitting me all night just left, and my mother walked out to get coffee and a bagel a few minutes ago. Finally, Silas and I have a moment alone.

He holds his drawing up to me. It's me. Wrapped in a scarf with the hood of my jacket pulled over my face. Green eyes shine beneath the hood. The rest of the illustration is in black pencil—only my eyes are in color. He holds the drawing next to his cheek for me to see.

"It's you. On the mountain. The first time I saw you."

It's eight in the morning. I have another eleven hours in my observation period.

"I'd been drawn to you for a long time. I could feel you across worlds. But it was the first time I found you in this world."

"You owe me an explanation," I say, shaking with fury. "Why can't anyone see you? Why do I look like a crazy person when I'm talking to you, but you can talk to me and no one can hear? How is it even *possible* that you can sit in the same chair as another human?"

"Remember how I said we have ties to our home world?" Silas says patiently. "If I was from your world, it wouldn't be possible. We start to dissociate in other worlds. Only in our home world are we truly ourselves. Solid. Formed." Dissociation. The chemical definition comes to mind unbidden. The separation of molecules into smaller molecules, atoms, or ions. Table salt dissociates into a sodium ion and a chlorine ion. Hydrochloric acid dissociates into a hydrogen ion.

"Our biological makeup is so much more complicated than salts or acids. We can't just dissociate."

"It's not like that." He shakes his head. "We're not dissociating into the air. We're dissociating into the Paths between worlds." He pauses, glances at the floor. "At least, that's what someone told me once. I'm not as good at this stuff as you are. Science isn't my strong suit." He sounds almost contrite, as if he's sorry he can't explain properly. "Because we can travel through those Paths, the particles that comprise our bodies are constantly seeking them when we're in other worlds. Trying to go home."

"Why?"

"We're pulled toward the place of our birth. Every time we Pathfind, we're creating copies of ourselves in other universes. We borrow energy from the world we're visiting to create a copy of ourselves there. But that energy has to be paid back. It doesn't take long before the multiverse starts trying to restore balance. We fray. We dissociate. We dissolve."

"How...how long?"

He shrugs.

"I'm not sure. It seems to vary. Some think it has to do with how porous that particular world is. Greater porosity means faster dissociation. Others think it has more to do with the proximity of one universe to another." I squint at him. How can universes be close to each other? "There are advantages, though. It means that whenever we're in other worlds, we can choose to be seen or not. We choose how we present ourselves to beings in that world. The better you are at Pathfinding, the more you can manipulate the laws of foreign worlds to choose your physical form."

"What about to other Pathfinders?"

"You could see me whether I wanted to be seen or not. You're aware of the disruptions in the energy fields in ways ordinary beings aren't. I can't hide from you."

I shake my head, trying to wrap my mind around all of this.

"That still doesn't explain why a barn went up in flames around me and I didn't die," I say, my voice hedging between anger and confusion.

There's a knock at the door. I glance up, startled, realizing that anyone could have seen me talking to the air, nodding and staring at someone not there. But the curtains are drawn. I exhale, and the door swings open. My mother is standing there with Ada, Claire, and Kalifa. Claire and Kali rush to my side in a blur of motion, while Ada sits in my mother's arms, her head pressed against her shoulder.

"Oh my God, Noomi—"

"You could have died—"

"Are you okay?"

"How do you feel?"

"Your mom called—"

"Something about a fire—"

"We wanted to come last night, but they wouldn't let us. They made us wait until now," Claire finishes breathlessly, squeezing my hand so tight I'm not sure I'll have fingers left when she lets go.

"Visitation hours," my mother pipes up from the doorway, where Ada is clinging to her, her legs dangling, too big to sit comfortably on my mother's small frame.

"It's a miracle," Kalifa says, awed. "Allah was watching you."

"Maybe," I say, my voice neutral. I hardly know if I believe myself. What if Silas is a delusion, a fiction, and the only explanation really is some sort of supernatural protection? Silas, with all his wild ideas, seems about as likely as a bearded man in the sky who occasionally chooses to protect certain people for no apparent reason.

Neither seems probable. But one is sitting next to me right now.

I glance to the side, looking for Silas. But his chair is empty. My heart sinks.

Was he ever there?

Ada slips off my mother's hip and comes to stand as close as the IV will allow. She looks at me seriously, biting her lip, and my heart cracks for my sweet sister, who can't possibly understand why all this is happening to me.

"Noomi," she says. "Did you do it this time?"

All sound crystallizes. Claire and Kalifa stop moving, staring at Ada. It's as if the room has suddenly frozen and the only thing still warm is my sister, nervously shifting from side to side, watching me, hoping I'll give an answer that makes sense.

"I got caught in the barn," I reply. "But I didn't start the fire."

She sighs. A tenuous hand reaches out and settles on my shoulder.

"Good," she says. "Well," she rephrases, "not good. But I'm glad you didn't do it."

I glance at Kali and Claire, both of whom know the vague outlines of my attempts at self-harm. We've been friends since grade school—it would be impossible not to know. But neither knows how intentional I've been in my quest for relief from the shadows. Claire is wide-eyed and worried. Kalifa seems less surprised. Maybe she guessed at the meaning between the lines when I told her my stories, when I explained why I was going to therapy, changing medications, joining adventure groups.

"I'm sorry you got hurt," Ada says.

"I'm not hurt, Peach. You don't have to worry about me."

"But you said there was a fire."

I nod. "There was, but I'm okay."

Claire sits on the side of the bed, reaches out and takes my hand. She smiles, blonde hair swaying like willow branches as she leans forward.

"Hey," she says, conspiratorially. "Look on the bright side: you got all three of us out of our calc exam this morning."

"Oh my God," Kalifa exclaims, slapping Claire on the arm. "Seriously? What is wrong with you? You're thinking about exams right now?"

"Really?" I reply, shocked. "Mr. Hansen excused you from the exam?"

"This is no laughing matter, Kali! He's been beefing this test all week as the hardest he'll give all semester." Claire wiggles her eyebrows at me. "He said to tell you that you don't have to take it at all—that's his get well present to you."

"Oh," I say, almost disappointed. "I was so sure I was going to ace this one."

"Noomi could have died and you're thinking about calculus." Kalifa shakes her head.

"Sorry for trying to focus on the positive!"

"At least you two will get to take it later," I say, sighing with mock melodrama. "Now we'll never know how I might have done on the Great Calculus Exam of 2016."

Kalifa grins. "And you won't get a chance to knock me from the top of the class until finals."

The Peacock

I Saw a Peacock, with a fiery tail,
I saw a Blazing Comet, drop down hail,
I saw a Cloud, with Ivy circled round,
I saw a sturdy Oak, creep on the ground,
I saw a Pismire, swallow up a Whale,
I saw a raging Sea, brim full of Ale,
I saw a Venice Glass, Sixteen foot deep,
I saw a well, full of men's tears that weep,
I saw their eyes, all in a flame of fire,
I saw a House, as big as the Moon and higher,
I saw the Sun, even in the midst of night,
I saw the man, that saw this wondrous sight.
—17th century English "trick verse" folk poem,
"I Saw A Peacock With A Fiery Tail"

They let me go home that night. The doctors found no evidence of trauma, mental or physical, and after the observation period, there was no reason to keep me at the hospital. The police wanted to talk to me about my experience at the barn. My mom said that was routine whenever there was property involved—the police wanted my statement to include in their report—but the thought of trying to explain how I came to be in a burning barn in the middle of a lightning storm sent a cold thrill of fear through me. But Dr. Chase insisted this could wait, claiming that reliving the experience so soon after the incident would only worsen my condition, the officers backed off. Dr. Zimmerman signed me out, and I walked hand in hand with Ada the whole way.

At home, Mr. Arcadio is waiting for us, standing in the dim porch light outside our house, holding a wriggling Kuri in his arms. He sets the dog down and Kuri rushes forward, leaping into Ada's outstretched arms and licking her frenetically.

"Noomi," Mr. Arcadio says, wrapping me into a fatherly hug. "I was so glad to hear you're safe. How do you feel?"

"A little out of sorts," I say. "But that's less because of the fire and more because of the hospital bed."

He pulls back, holding me at arms' length. "It sounds like it was a close call."

"I'm lucky I got out when I did."

"It's a good thing you knew what to do," he says.

I stare at him blankly. It's a good thing I knew…to get out of the barn?

"I guess instinct kicked in."

He nods. "You found a path to safety."

I freeze. *You found a path…*Does he know what that means? Silas's words ring in my ears. *We're Pathfinders, Noomi.*

"Thanks for watching Kuri," my mom says. Mr. Arcadio seems not to have noticed my reaction. I shake off the strangeness. Just a coincidence, I tell myself. Path is a common word. It doesn't mean anything.

"It was no problem." He smiles. "I'm always happy to help, especially with a cute little monster like Kuri."

"I'll call you tomorrow."

"Or send me a text. I'm not so old, you know. My grandson started texting me recently. He even taught me to use emojis." He turns to leave, but then hesitates. "Oh, Noomi…" He reaches back into the house, picking something up from the table in the foyer. "I got this from the library for you. I thought it might divert you while you're recovering." He hands me a book.

I read aloud. "*A Brief History of Time* by Stephen Hawking."

"You've taken such a liking to chemistry in the last few years. I thought this might provide a segue into quantum mechanics."

I glance up at him. He is smiling, and I start to feel strange. Like I'm in a bubble. Why is he giving me a book on quantum physics? Why now, in this moment?

"I hope you enjoy it as much as I have."

He turns, heading down the steps, down the street. He lives just a few blocks away. I watch him go, the strangeness deepening, feeling like I'm floating as I walk into the house, follow Ada up the stairs. Like I'm seeing heat waves rising from the floors. Mr. Arcadio' s odd choice of words. The house is a foreign body. I am heavier, weighed down. My footsteps leave imprints on the hardwood floors. My breaths echo; everything is unfamiliar. I look around corners before I start walking, unsure what I'm looking for. The shadows?

Or Silas?

Where is he, anyway?

His absence confuses me. Before I left the hospital, he told me he would meet me again as soon as he could. That he was afraid to leave me alone because the shadows could come back at any moment.

"How are you going to stop them?"

"They don't seem to like me," he replied reluctantly. "They want you alone."

"Is that why they left when you found me on the mountaintop?"

He didn't have a good answer, and I still don't trust him. He's withholding information from me. He hasn't told me everything he knows. And even then, I don't know for sure that this isn't all some crazy hallucination.

"Mom says I have to go back to school on Monday," Ada says mournfully as she loads toothpaste on her brush. "I don't know why I can't stay home with you."

"Because you have to go to school to be smart like Mom and Dad," I reply, setting my hand on her head. "Look. You're almost up to the bottom of the mirror."

"I know," she says, melancholy, not looking up.

"What's wrong, sweet pea?"

"Nothing." She stuffs her toothbrush in her mouth and starts brushing. I follow suit.

Two minutes pass in silence, the only sound the rustling of our brushes while we stare at each other in the mirror. She turns on the water, spits, rinses, and then looks at me.

"Why aren't you hurt, Noomi? Do you have superpowers like the X-Men?"

I manage a laugh. Ada's favorite cartoon is the X-Men. I'm not surprised she thinks I'm like them. Maybe I am.

"I got out of the barn before it got too hot." I tell her the same lie everyone's been using to explain my miraculous escape from the fire, although this can't explain how my clothes burned clean off and my skin was unblemished. "Superpowers didn't help me escape."

"What about the time with the gas?"

Emptiness settles on my shoulders. "What time?"

"The time you poured car gas on yourself and started a fire." My jaw clenches so tight my bones hurt. "I could feel the heat from the bushes. It smelled like it does at the gas station. And you weren't even hurt."

"You saw?"

"I didn't mean to. But Mom said lunch was ready and told me to find you."

The heaviness of it. A hole carved into me. Black and blue like the deepest bruise, chiseled out of my stomach with a rough stone. My baby sister, watching me douse myself in flame and strike a match. Of course I knew she was there—she was the one who banished the shadows when they found me right after—but I thought that was later. I didn't know she'd been there when I struck the match. The idea of her watching, hiding in the bushes, while I tried to char myself to the point of never returning, is horrifying.

How could I do this to her? How will she grow strong and healthy and vibrant when she's seen so much of this darkness? But I could ask the same thing of myself. How can I grow strong and healthy and vibrant after I watched our dad die?

I can't. I haven't. I am wilting, withering, the shadows eating me from the inside out.

But I can't let that happen to Ada.

Never.

"Why didn't you say anything?" I kneel in front of her, wishing she hadn't been holding onto this memory for the last few weeks, wishing I'd had a chance to explain when it happened, there, in the moment.

She shakes her head, unable to speak.

Ada knows too. The number of people who know my secret is growing. Ada, Dr. Zimmerman, Silas. Even my mother will recognize the truth eventually. As the secret expands, it becomes more real. The more people witness this incomprehensible ability, the more people know about the shadows, the less I doubt myself.

"I'm not a superhero," I tell her. "But I might have one superpower. I can't hurt myself. When the barn caught fire, I was safe. The fire washed over me, and I should have died. I don't know why I didn't. But I'm trying to find out."

She perks up. "I know!" she says. "You should be a firefighter! Then you can rescue people in danger and you'll be safe!"

"You're right. That's what I'll do. When I finish high school, I'll learn to be a firefighter. How does that sound?"

"Good," she says solidly, like a judge banging a gavel, as if the matter were settled. She smiles. "You should sleep with me tonight. I know last time I didn't keep the shadows away, but

I promise this time I will." The tenacity in her little face is like helium, inflating me with hope.

I go to change into pajamas. The strangeness washes over me again. I flip the lights in my room, feeling odd in street clothes, out of my hospital gown. I pull off the jeans and tee my mom brought for me, take off my bra, and throw on a sleep shirt. The feeling of being watched starts as a prickle between my shoulders and grows, like the moon eclipsing the sun. I glance around. There's no one. But the feeling grows. Spindly fingers walk up and down my spine. I shiver. Flip off the light and walk quickly into Ada's room.

She's staring at the door, eyes as round as sand dollars.

"Ada?" I say. "Are you okay?"

She shivers, too, and then looks up, clear-eyed, as if shaking off a trance.

"I thought I saw someone there," she whispers. "But it's no one."

"Who?" I ask. "Who did you see?"

"I thought it was a man. Tall, with blond hair."

It doesn't sound like Silas, but I ask, "The boy who did the drawing?"

"I don't think so." Ada shrugs and turns away, hopping into bed and pulling the covers up over her knees. "I don't know if he was really there. Ommi says the house makes noises sometimes, and I should't be afraid."

I crawl into bed next to her and flip off the light. Come and find me, I say to the shadows, challenging. I can escape you now. But the memory of the barn—the flames licking at my hair and body and rolling over me like a wave, the beams collapsing around me—reminds me that even if I am indestructible, the world around me isn't.

"Mom doesn't always have all the answers," I say quietly, like I'm sharing a secret. "Sometimes adults are so stuck in what they know that they forget they don't know everything."

"Like the time she didn't believe us about the peacock," she whispers.

I giggle at the memory. When Ada was four and I was thirteen, we were playing house and I was letting her boss me around, telling me to clean my room and pick up my toys, as she pretended to be the mom and I her impudent toddler. She stopped pretending to sweep our "house" and stood transfixed, staring off into the distance where, not more than a hundred feet away, was an extraordinary bird with green, blue, and purple plumage. We ran inside, aghast, to tell our mother. She refused to believe us or even to come outside for a good ten minutes, until Ada dragged her outside by the hand to show her the bird. A peacock had escaped from an eccentric collector down the road, we learned, after she finally called animal services to report the presence of a large male peacock in our backyard.

"What was its name again?"

"Bubbles," she responds.

"Who names their peacock Bubbles?" I laugh.

"Hey!" Ada chastises. And then, shyly, "I like that name."

"Dream about Bubbles for me," I say, tucking the covers in around her. "And remember him every time you think Mom has all the answers."

I close my eyes. A face appears as I do, staring at me in the dark. Silas's dark skin and green eyes, framed by winged lashes. I open my eyes again, unsure if I'm imagining him, or if he's here. But there's no one. The haunting presence in the house is just me, I tell myself, my frayed nerves. Ada too. We're both uneasy after all the stress from the fire, the hospital, the police, the doctors. I lie back. Put my head on the pillow. The threads of spacetime shift and sway like curtains behind my eyes, becoming clearer every time I look. I try not to get sucked into the vortex of the moving threads. I relax, sink into the pillows, and try to stay rooted.

Is this real? I ask myself for the thousandth time. As I drift off, I pretend it's not, that none of this is happening, even as I realize the impossibility of my wish.

It is. It's real. No matter how hard I wish it weren't.

"How much do you love me?" Ada's voice floats up to me in my sleepy haze.

"As much as all the stars in all the galaxies in all the multiverse," I reply.

"Is that enough to stop trying to hurt yourself?"

My eyes fly open. I roll onto my side, propping myself on my elbow. Feeling the motion in the bed, she opens her eyes too, reluctantly. She looks at me as though she'd rather be having this conversation with her eyes closed.

"Ada." I look her in the eye. "I promise. I won't try to hurt myself again."

"Pinky swear?"

I hold my pinky up to her. She crosses her own in mine and smiles. The gravity of the moment settles around me.

"Pinky swear." I hold tight to her little finger for another second. And then she closes her eyes again, but grabs my hand and pulls it closer. She stills, and I lie down, wrapping my fingers around hers.

"Noomi," she asks, her voice slow and creaky. "What's a multiverse?"

"I'll tell you in the morning, Sweet Pea."

BIOLUMINESCENCE

"Bioluminescence is light produced by a chemical reaction within a living organism. Bioluminescence is a type of chemiluminescence, which is simply the term for a chemical reaction where light is produced. (Bioluminescence is chemiluminescence that takes place inside a living organism.)" —National Geographic Encyclopedia, "Bioluminescence"

I run my fingertips across green leaves. Inhale the warm scent of moisture and humus. Insects chirp and flutter. Wings buzz in my ears. The trees are enormous—the size of houses, of clouds, of skies. Vines crawling with purple and orange flowers criss-cross in ladders up and down the trees. Dense shrubbery all around makes it hard to pick a path. I press my palm to the bark of one of the trees. Hard and rough, it scrapes against my fingers. The air smells of decay and growth at the same time. The humidity oppressive and uplifting. So thick, it collects on the fine hairs on my arm. So thick, I can feel it in my lungs with every breath.

I am walking.

Birds call and holler high in the trees. Pairs of eyes loom out at me from the leaves above. I watch them, unafraid. They do not look at me. I turn to see an enormous creature, some sort of giant rodent, making its way through the underbrush. It lumbers toward me, snatching with long, curved claws at boughs laden with dark green fruits. I've seen creatures like this before, but smaller: sloths, with hooked toes, striped faces, and long tongues. The noise it makes increases with every step, as branches tear and snap and I hear it chewing, stepping, breathing.

It walks right through me, like a gust of wind blowing in, through my body. Wind through the branches of a tree, shifting without moving. The hair on my skin stands on end.

Is this a dream?

I remember the nurse sitting in the same chair as Silas for a split second, occupying the same space. Was she the ghost? Or was he?

Only in our home world are we truly solid, he said.

Am I Pathfinding?

If this is a dream, I'm astonishingly lucid. It feels too vivid, too present, to be real. Like watching sharks glide by in an aquarium: a hair's breadth away, impenetrable.

When Ada was smaller, she used to sleepwalk. She would get up and go to the bathroom, or to the kitchen downstairs, or hide in a closet. We found her asleep in a coat closet one morning, passed out in her pajamas, curled up next to an old pair of shoes. Another time my mother heard her in the kitchen, opening a drawer and taking out silverware methodically. It was one of the reasons I started sleeping in her room—to keep an eye on her.

Have I sleepwalked into a new world?

I close my eyes and sink deep into my heels.

Inhale—smell the woody, wet air.

Exhale—let the muscles in my body sink deeper into my legs, my feet. My spine condenses, like I'm settling into something smaller.

Inhale—the air is different now. Moist, still, but now dank. Granitic. Cold. Wet like moss and concrete after rain.

Exhale—straighten, rolling onto the balls of my feet. Open my eyes.

It's as dark as the spaces between the stars. Apart from the papery fluttering of my eyelids, nothing has changed. I can see nothing. I'm blind.

Still, I am not afraid.

I stretch out my hands and press my fingertips to a cold, stony wall. My hands walk along the wall, fingertips seeing, my feet carrying me forward. I put one foot in front of the other, tentative, like a creeping spider.

After ten or so minutes of walking like this, a cerulean hue appears somewhere in the distance. Light. There must be light ahead. I keep moving, stepping carefully, my fingers crawling across the wall, my steps more confident with every stride. Soon the color is bright enough to illuminate my surroundings, and I stop, staring at the walls of the cave around me. It's not tall—no higher than fifteen feet—and compact. I stretch my other hand out, touching both walls at the same time. They're wet, dripping. It smells of chalk, limestone, mold. I'm in a tunnel, with darkness growing into utter blackness back the way I came, and forward into an ever-brighter blue-green, beckoning to me.

As I walk, the tunnel widens and the light grows. It opens into a broad cavern where the source of the light is revealed: a deep, crystalline pool that stretches almost as far as the eye can see. It glows, aquamarine, illuminating an enormous cavern.

Bioluminescence. I breathe, watching the water. A chemical reaction by which living organisms create chemicals that react with oxygen to release their own light. The surface of the pool is perfectly still, untouched by wind or currents. The cavern is huge, and the pool, not uniform in shape, must be several football fields in length. It stretches off to the left, curves and undulates around a corner. To the right, it angles straight out, bounded at the far end by a smooth wall that juts up out of the pool.

I am standing on the only visible shore in the cavern. Where am I? In my own universe, on my own planet, in some hidden underground cavern? Or on a foreign planet where this is the whole universe to the glowing creatures in this pond?

Or is this a conjuring trick, an invention dredged from the caverns of my mind?

I shake my head. It doesn't matter. It no longer matters if I'm dreaming or awake.

The water is calling to me. I walk toward the quiet shore as if summoned.

Bend. Dip my hands into the water. Ripples run outward from where my fingers have disturbed the calm. Cup my hands and pull the water to me. It glows blue. The color of icebergs, of deep snow on a mountaintop.

I close my eyes, relishing the sweet chill of the water in my palms. But as my eyelids flutter closed, the world shifts again. The water evaporates from my palms.

Wait, I want to shout. I wasn't done yet.

The cool underground air is replaced with the smell of dust and raw scrubbed dirt. The heat is almost tangible on my skin; the light from the sun bright and hot.

This world feels familiar.

I open my eyes, and in front of me is a grave.

Noomi Nailah Perez. November 3, 1998 – August 1, 2009

August 1, 2009 was a year after my father died of a heart attack. It was the first time I tried to kill myself.

I'm in a different world. A world where I succeeded.

Someone is standing beside me. A middle-aged man, leaning on a shovel. He's staring at the grave with the same fixed, absent expression I feel. His face is hardened and tough, with creases around his eyes and mouth and tanned, leathery skin. His hair is stiff and dusty as he runs a hand through it. It's a hot summer day and sweat runs down the sides of his face. His eyes look familiar. Deep brown and almond-shaped.

"You were buried," he says, in a voice as hard and dusty as his skin. "I dug your grave. You're not a Pathfinder in this world. Your abilities couldn't save you."

"I jumped off the roof," I reply. "Three stories high and I jumped." I pause, remembering the moment in my world when I did this. I didn't think I was actually going to die—I was ten, and children always believe themselves immortal. "In my world, I was trying to get away from the shadows."

"You broke your neck," he says, nodding. "But really, you died because your heart was broken."

"What happened to Mama?" I whisper. Something tugs at me. Like when the snow melts off the mountains in the summer, and the dams fill up, waiting to be released into the rivers below. Something is filling up inside me.

"She fell apart. Lost her job at the hospital. She lived in an inpatient facility for several months. When she got out, she started drinking. I think she'll pull herself together. But she has years to go."

"And Ada?"

"Lives with your abuela now."

There's a long pause while we both stare at the small, dark headstone. It's hot. The Oregon grass has turned to willowy, golden stalks. The wild wheat is ripe and ready. The fields will be full of farmers this time of year, cutting and baling hay, harvesting the wheat, picking blueberries, raspberries, and blackberries, plowing and preparing for the winter grass seed.

"How do you know these things?" I ask. The man looks at me for the first time. I've met him before, I know it. His eyes look so *familiar*. But I can't place him.

"I've spent a long time traveling between the worlds that were created at the moment when your father died and you became a Pathfinder. I've learned a lot in that time."

"Why?"

"I'm looking for answers."

"To what?"

"How to help you."

I shake my head at the hollowness inside me. The absence of grief, of fear, of any feeling at all. Similar to the vacant shell I become when the shadows carve me out. I want to reach out, cry out, to find those feelings. This is *wrong*, something says within me, but the voice is buried so deep I can barely hear it, let alone reach it.

"People keep trying to help me," I say. "Silas. My therapist, Dr. Chase. Even Mr. Arcadio gave me a book he said would help, and he said something strange before I…" I trail off. The gravedigger's eyes widen almost imperceptibly as I say the last name. But his expression is unchanged. "Am I asleep?"

"Yes," he says. He focuses on me, and now he sounds more like a professor than a gravedigger, accenting his syllables and speaking more formally. "But you're in another world too. There are many things you don't understand, and it will be a long time before you do. But you will learn. You have to." He leans in and takes my hand, his skin rough against mine, and pulls my hands, palm up, between us. He stares at me for a long moment before looking down. I gasp when I follow his eyes.

My hands are gleaming blue.

"Pathfinders are not the only things capable of moving between worlds," he says. "Whatever you encountered in your last world left traces of themselves on you. So, too, with the shadows. Wherever you go, whenever you Pathfind, your eyes are black and full of them."

"How do you know?" I ask, my breath short. The dam in my chest is creaking behind the weight of everything it's holding.

"Your friend Silas is also a friend of mine. But that's not important. The shadows are growing stronger, and they have a new ally in their quest. Their goal is to destroy you. If they succeed, they'll have a portal through which to devour your entire world."

I open and close my mouth, gaping at him. Growing stronger? A new ally? He shakes his head as I try to interrupt, questions buzzing through my mind like bees.

"You'll wake up soon, Noomi. Time is passing, and this is the safest place for me to tell you what I know." He pauses, meets my gaze, and then continues. "You are a Path, Noomi, and wherever you go in spacetime, the Path moves with you. You alone are the gatekeeper, the sole barrier that prevents the shadows from entering your world and sucking it back to oblivion. But as long as you live, you can fight them. And, in time, you may be able to close the Path and close your world off to them entirely."

"But how?" I ask, the questions coming out like a flood. "Why is it so hard to close the Path? Why can't you—or some other, more powerful Pathfinder—do it for me?"

He looks at me gravely. "For another Pathfinder to close the Path inside you would kill you. Are you prepared for that?"

"It would kill me?" I look away, blinking rapidly, surprised to find tears in my eyes. Ada's face drifts up to me. Her green eyes aglow with curiosity. Then I see my mother, warm and passionate, picking us up in her scrubs from the OR after school, telling us about her latest surgery or her newest challenge at work. Kalifa, coming to my defense at school the other day. Claire, on stage, performing in last year's rendition of *Les Miserables*. Kuri lapping at my cheeks. Silas's iridescent eyes.

"I was ready to die for so many years. Or so I thought. But I'd tried so many times and failed, I think I knew I wouldn't succeed. I always knew it wasn't really the end."

When I look up at the gravedigger, he's smiling softly, watching me, as if he can see everything running through my head. "No," he says. "I thought not."

"How, then?" I ask, rubbing my blue hands against my cheeks. "How do I close the Path?" Feeling the rushing waters breaking the dam, I let loose the question that's been weighing on me for years. "How do I fight them?"

"Two things," he says. "First: train. Silas will help you. Practice Pathfinding. Practice honing your energy so you can find a Path to another world at the drop of a hat. Practice seeing the gaps—where a Path might be, where one could be made. When you're ready, you'll know. You'll feel it."

He grips my hands, pulling them up to eye level between us. "But in between now and then, the shadows will haunt you. To fight them, you must be like these tiny beings: luminescent. You must find your own light, so bright it will shine in the deep places within you."

He drops my hands, and immediately the world tilts and shifts, swirling into nauseating colors that blend together into a blinding light, and I fall backward as if pushed off a cliff, except there is no ground, and I'm falling,

falling,

falling—

SCHRODINGER'S CAT

"A cat is penned up in a steel chamber, along with the following device (which must be secured against direct interference by the cat): in a Geiger counter, there is a tiny bit of radioactive substance, so small, that perhaps in the course of the hour one of the atoms decays, but also, with equal probability, perhaps none; if it happens, the counter tube discharges and through a relay releases a hammer that shatters a small flask of hydrocyanic acid. If one has left this entire system to itself for an hour, one would say that the cat still lives if meanwhile no atom has decayed. The first atomic decay would have poisoned it. The psi-function of the entire system would express this by having in it the living and dead cat (pardon the expression) mixed or smeared out in equal parts.

"It is typical of these cases that an indeterminacy originally restricted to the atomic domain becomes transformed into macroscopic indeterminacy, which can then be resolved by direct observation. That prevents us from so naively accepting as valid a 'blurred model' for representing reality. In itself, it would not embody anything unclear or contradictory. There is a difference between a shaky or out-of-focus photograph and a snapshot of clouds and fog banks." —"The Present Situation in Quantum Mechanics: A Translation of Schrödinger's 'Cat Paradox Paper,'" Erwin Schrödinger. Translator: John D. Trimmer.

Techno thumps in my ears as I type notes onto my computer from the reading for my Latin class. I take a sip of tea, draining the final, lukewarm drops from the mug. I'm enjoying yet another quiet afternoon at my local coffee shop while I'm temporarily out of school on doctors' orders. I glance down at the book, double-checking my quote—and then leap about a foot into the air when a backpack slams onto the table.

"Ugh!" Kalifa exclaims loudly, her voice slightly muted beneath the pounding beat of the music in my ears. "I'm so mad, Noomi, I can't even tell you."

"What's wrong?" I take off my headphones and set them next to the computer, though the music continues playing, the beat audible through the oversized headphones.

"Mr. Terrell took two points off my author project because I didn't submit it *in the right font.*"

"That's not fair." I reply, indignant on her behalf.

"I know!" she shouts. "I would have had a perfect score if not for those two stupid points. But because I printed it in Garamond instead of Times New Roman…"

"Did he have any style guides in his syllabus for the project?"

"Well …" Kalifa hesitates. "It does say at the bottom of the project requirements that everything has to be in twelve-point, double-spaced, Times New Roman font."

"Oh. Well. Kali …" I cock my head at her. "That sounds pretty cut-and-dried."

"But I'm so tired of Times New Roman!" she exclaims, passionate again. "I swear, the second I get to college, I'm going to banish Times New Roman from every single one of my assignments," she fumes.

"Kali," I say gently. "It's just a font. It can't hurt you."

"Apparently it can! Those two points might knock me from the top of Mr. Terrell's class, which could threaten my valedictorian status." She takes a deep breath and looks down at my table, covered from end to end with open books, notebooks, and pieces of scrap paper. "Why are you reading Stephen Hawking?" she asks, surprised.

"I'm not." Not right now, anyway.

"That doesn't explain why it's sitting open next to your Latin textbook."

"I've taken an interest in quantum physics."

Kali cocks an eyebrow at me. "Some casual reading while you're out from school?"

I shrug. What can I say? I'm curious about how I can sleepwalk into a universe where I killed myself years ago. "Mr. Arcadio gave it to me," I explain. "It's interesting."

She stares at me for a moment longer, before picking up her backpack again. "Are you ready to go? We've got ten minutes to get to the other side of town."

Ah, yes. My appointment. Kali volunteered to drive me to Dr. Chase's today, since Mom is working at the hospital and I'm currently not allowed to drive. Not after the barn fire. Not after my car was found, untouched, the driver's seatbelt still clicked in, a mile down the road from the Moreland's barn. Not while everyone gets nervous just looking at me, like I might combust at any moment.

I close my textbooks and put everything back in my bag, following Kalifa out the door to her car. She starts the engine, and the Rolling Stones "Paint It Black" starts blasting from the speakers. Mick Jagger is Kalifa's current pop-culture obsession. She's been listening to *Aftermath* all week.

"Thanks for giving me a ride."

Kalifa smiles, smoothing the folds on today's silvery headscarf. "No problem." She glances at me. "Thanks for listening to me vent about the author project. I know you have more important things on your mind. When are you coming back to school?"

I laugh. "It's okay. I like being distracted by normalcy. Dr. Zimmerman says I can come back on Wednesday, as long as my therapist agrees."

"Good," she says. "We miss you."

I reach out and take her hand, giving it a squeeze. "I miss you too." Her fingers are long and fine, with a perfect French manicure on every nail.

"Do you..." Kalifa looks away, staring out the windshield. "Do the doctors have any idea what happened?"

I shake my head. I want to tell her and Claire everything. The shadows. Watching my dad die. Trying to kill myself. Silas. Pathfinding. The explosion. Everything I've been bottling up.

"I have something I want to tell you," I say. "A lot of things, actually."

"Want to spend the night this weekend?" she asks. "Girls only. I won't invite Basi. You and Claire can come over, we can watch movies, make popcorn, and jump in the hot tub."

"That sounds great." I make myself smile while my stomach does a flip. Now I'm committed. Will they think I'm crazy? Will they believe me? Will they still want to be friends when they've seen the emptiness inside me?

A dark thought occurs. I can prove it. If I cut myself in front of them and it heals, they'll have to believe me.

We drive the rest of the way in silence, letting Mick Jagger and Keith Richards fill the space between us. "Thank you," I whisper, barely audible, as Kalifa parks in front of the small, drab building. I jump out of the car and close the door. She waves and drives off, the beat pounding from her speakers as she pulls out.

I turn to walk inside, wishing I were still in the car with Kali instead of going to meet Dr. Chase. I remember the last time we met, and how much better I felt after. How much more I trusted her. I try to summon those feelings again—that she had earned my respect.

"How are you feeling?" Dr Chase asks, after our initial greeting. I'm sitting on the couch. Facing her. Trying to meet her eyes, finding it impossible. They are always so blank, expressionless. Unreadable. I look at her earrings instead: two triangles dangling from a small gold hook. A warm spring breeze blows in through the open window.

"I feel okay."

"Tired? Stressed? In any pain?"

"Stressed, definitely. Not tired. No pain."

"The doctors gave you a clean bill of health."

"Yep."

"I was glad to hear the Morelands decided not to press charges."

"Me too."

"Can you tell me what happened?"

"I've told the police everything I remember." My voice is carefully neutral. I gave my statement yesterday. It was a short and uninteresting affair. Nothing like I'd expected: hours of interrogation, grilling me about how I got there, whether I set the fire, my history. Instead, the whole process took about fifteen minutes.

"I'm sure you have. Maybe we could talk not about the particulars of the experience, but about your reaction to it."

"Now? Or at the time?"

"Both."

Of course she wants to know if I have anything special to share. I wish I could summon more emotion, put more feeling into this conversation. Anger, fear, sadness—even relief or gratitude to have escaped from such a devastating fire.

But all I feel is curiosity. So, instead of answering her question, I start asking my own.

"Yeah, I have had a lot of thoughts," I tell her. "Do you know anything about physics?"

"Like classical mechanics?" she asks, surprised.

"No. Quantum physics. The interplay between subatomic particles, particles vs. waves, quantum indeterminacy, different theories on the mechanics of time, et cetera."

"A little," she says, her voice as guarded as mine. "I read a book on quantum physics every few years, trying to stay current. But I'm no expert. Why?"

I take a deep breath. "I'm thinking about the possibility that there are many universes, each defined by different choices as time progresses along a straight line." She pulls back, a look of surprise on her face. "Do you think it's possible that there's a universe where I didn't escape from the fire?"

Her mouth opens and closes for a few seconds like a fish. "I don't know much about quantum mechanics, Noomi, but I suppose it's possible."

"What do you know about the many-worlds theory?" I lean in, elbows on my knees.

"Not much." Her voice a delicate tension between casual and terse. "It sounds like you know more than I do."

"There are some theories about the particle-wave effect and quantum unpredictability that postulate there must be an infinite number of universes," I say, plowing forward. "Subatomic particles have the possibility to be in multiple places at once—but only based on predictive models—and some physicists theorize that every time a particle is faced with a 'decision,' so to speak, of where to go or how to behave, the universe splits into alternate worlds where, in one world, the particle went one direction, and in another, the particle went a different direction. Which would mean," I finish, "that on a macroscopic level, it's possible I could be alive in this universe and dead in another."

"Yes," Dr. Chase says, "that's very interesting." She looks up from typing notes on her iPad and stares past me, looking at my ear just as I was looking at hers, not meeting my eyes but not dodging them, either.

I start to regret my decision to open up to her.

"It's just a theory," I say, to fill the silence.

"I have to wonder," she says at last. "Why have you been thinking about this?"

I shrug. "Because it's interesting."

"You seem very...dispassionate. Analytical. You've just come out of an incredibly traumatic experience. You were hospitalized for a full day." She leans in. "You might be using this fascination with a theoretical question to repress the trauma you experienced and any emotions surrounding it."

I stare at her. "I'm not ready to talk about the fire."

"Okay," she says, relenting. "Let's work with this. Why are you so interested in the idea of multiple universes?"

Because I've been to them. Because the things that haunt me are from another world.

"Because according to all the laws of physics, I shouldn't be alive right now," I say.

"The doctors have admitted they're not sure how to reconcile the police report with your bill of health."

"So I'm wondering how it's possible that I'm alive, sitting in front of you. It's strange to think that I'm alive because of a fluke. My friend Kalifa said, 'Praise Allah.' But I don't believe in God. The truth is, I shouldn't have survived. I have to consider the possibility that in another universe, on another path, I didn't."

"Is this connected to your attempts at self-harm?"

"What do you mean?"

"Do you think that was the *cause* of the fire?" she asks slowly.

"What does *that* mean?"

"The police report said there were traces of gasoline in the barn. That the fire started in one location and grew incredibly hot before exploding. All signs of arson."

A chill runs through me.

"If you think I set that fire to kill myself," I ask, drawing out every word, "why am I alive?" She stares at me silently. "The officer who wrote the report watched me emerge from the inferno. My clothes were completely burned away. If I was trying to kill myself, I did a damn good job. Except I'm sitting in front of you."

Dr. Chase doesn't respond to my dramatic closing argument. She hasn't so much as moved. I lean in, waiting. Still, she doesn't react. The chill on my skin grows. A creeping dread walks its fingers up and down my arms. The shadows feel present, the emptiness and coldness sucking at me, but my vision is fine. I can see crystal clear.

But Dr. Chase's eyes, normally such a brilliant blue, are black. And the color is seeping outward. Blossoming. First into the whites of her eyes. Then into her teeth. Then her fingernails. Black like ravens, like tar pits, like the hole in the sky where the new moon should be.

I stand up. Recoil. Hand over my mouth.

It's not in *me* this time. It's in *her*.

In the real world.

The shadows on the chairs are growing larger. The orange pops on the sailboat painting I love to stare at are fading to grey. The blue is already darker. Navy. Now deepest violet. Now black.

I stumble backward over my chair.

"Help," I whisper, to no one, to nothing. I am helpless. Trapped. Can I Pathfind out of here? Will that save Dr. Chase, her stupidly colorful office, or the people around her? Or will the shadows follow me to some other world and destroy it, too? What can I do?

Silas, I think, a silent scream for help, the only name I know to call. *I need you.*

A riffle of air washes over me. A reverberation in my chest. Without warning, he's beside me. "Close your eyes, Noomi," he says gently, his hand on my arm.

I obey. The world shifts. I fall backward, collapsing onto a mattress of nothing, the *compressed* feeling I'm getting used to. I inhale, breathing in the sweet scent of wet leaves and forest floor.

I open my eyes. We're standing in a tall, deep forest of bamboo.

The shadows are gone. I breathe in a sweet sigh of relief and fatigue. I bend over, pressing my hands to my knees, exhausted.

"What happened back there?" I ask. "How did you know to come?"

"I don't know," Silas says. He frowns. "I felt it when you said my name. Like a drumbeat. I looked for you and saw the shadows were everywhere. I came as quickly as I could." I reach out for his hand, needing a source of strength. He pulls me up, looking at me gravely. "I didn't realize how bad they were. The shadows. I'd never seen them in your world before. Only in you."

I shake my head. I haven't either. I don't have the strength to say it.

"Where are we?"

"There's someone I want you to meet," Silas says. "Someone who knows how to fight them."

QUETZALCOATLUS

"Quetzalcoatlus northropi /kɛtsəlkoʊˈætləs/ is a pterosaur known from the Late Cretaceous of North America (Maastrichtian stage) and one of the largest-known flying animals of all time. It is a member of the family Azhdarchidae, a family of advanced toothless pterosaurs with unusually long, stiffened necks. Its name comes from the Mesoamerican feathered serpent god, Quetzalcoatl." —Wikipedia, "Quetzalcoatlus"

It seems like forever that we walk through this forest with bamboo stalks so tall and leaning I'm surprised they don't topple. The wind rattles through them like wood chimes, and the fluttering of the long, thin leaves sounds like whistling. Birds chirp and chatter overhead, so I know we're in a world not so different from mine. I follow Silas as he tromps through the woods, feet crunching on the leaves.

"Where are we going?" I venture after a while.

He doesn't respond.

I check my watch, which is ticking along normally. Almost fifteen minutes have passed. Is my watch keeping time in this world, or my own? The light through the trees is growing brighter, an aura that arcs and dances through the greenery.

Eventually, we come to a thicket of bamboo trunks that have been bent into a sort of cave or tunnel. Silas ducks under it and I follow, walking into the woody cavern, using slivers of slanted light to guide my feet. It's not long before the bamboo cave opens into a round bowl of woven, dead stalks, where the tall trees have been cleared away and the sunlight shines down freely.

"In this world," Silas whispers, leaning into me, so close I can feel his breath, "the dinosaurs aren't extinct. The asteroid hit, but some of the flying dinosaurs managed to survive. They took a different path of evolution, and..." He trails off.

The words thrum in my heart as I look around the clearing. Two pale green rocks, smooth and oblong, the size of bowling balls, sit in the center of the woven bamboo stalks. It smells strange and musky here, almost gamey, and when I look at my feet, grey fluff, like hundreds of dust bunnies, has collected between the woven bamboo. A tumbling wind blows in my face, and Silas puts one hand to his forehead to shade his eyes, looking up. The sun is blotted out as something enormous comes to drift over us, and gusts of wind are blown down onto us like a landing helicopter, blowing my hair around and into my face.

An enormous set of wings is descending on us.

I yell and grab Silas, pulling him down by the shirt, but he slaps my hands away and stands, watching. I straighten as I realize his lack of fear and watch, astounded, as the creature descends.

"If I tell you it's time to go, we have to leave immediately," Silas shouts over the wind.

Her wingspan must be the length of a city bus, and her body, thin and elongated but barrel-chested, is surely the size of a horse. The talons, grey and scaly and horrifically sharp, curl and close beneath her as her legs pull up and she lands, flapping gently, on top of the stones, which I now realize are not stones but eggs. As she lands, I glimpse shocking amber streaks on the undersides of her wings, as bright and pure as gold leaf. She wriggles a little and settles in on top of the eggs, folding her wings beside her. There's no more than a few feet between her and us—even so, it seems her nest is far too big for her. The walls of the bowl curve up and out, flatter than they are high, but she takes up a relatively small portion of the space, leaving plenty of room for us.

"What is she?" I whisper.

"I call her Lefka," he says. "Her full name is Lefkaquatl. She's known to Pathfinders as the feathered goddess." He bows to her.

I stare at him, and at the bird—*dinosaur?*—giant, white, and feathered, with an enormous hooked beak that could reach into my chest and pull my heart out with one deft swipe. Her chest is large, her tail is at least six feet long and almost delicate, stretching out behind her and turning upwards with the curve of the nest. She is elegant, with the calm expression and predatory eyes of a hawk.

She opens her beak and I recoil instinctively, pulling my arms over my face. But instead of pecking me to death, she lets out a series of musical chirps, as sweet as a nightingale.

"Silas," she says. "You come."

My head is buzzing with strangeness. I understand her. She understands us.

"This is my friend, Noomi." Silas gestures to me. "I told you about her."

"The one with black eyes." The words are musical, more like listening to a song picked out on the piano than a language—and yet somehow recognizable syllables emerge from the throaty notes she sings.

"How can we understand her?" I ask.

"Pathfinders can always understand each other," Silas says simply.

I stare at him, a million more questions burning in my chest from this single response.

"Why have you come to me?" she asks.

"The storm clouds," Silas says. "The evil shadows. They've found a way into Noomi's world. I think they're coming through her. She needs your help. You're the only Pathfinder I've ever known who's defeated them."

"The storms are not evil, Silas," she harmonizes, shuffling on her eggs, nestling herself deeper on top of them. "They are balance. As worlds are created, so they are destroyed. The shadows have swallowed countless worlds." Her deadly head swivels from Silas to me. I fight the urge to step back. "If they have found a path through you, they will swallow your world."

"But," I protest, "my family. My sister. My friends. I can't let the shadows take them."

"Then you must keep them out."

"How?"

She breathes in an enormous inhale, feathers ruffling, then releases it, singing, "When the shadows fell over my nest, many egg cycles ago, I closed the skies that allowed them in. But fledgling Silas says they are coming through you. That you are their sky. Then you must close yourself."

"I don't understand," I whisper.

Silas turns to me, urgency on his face.

"Think, Noomi. When did they start attacking you? Did anything strange happen? Have you ever been electrocuted, or struck by lightning, or had a near-death—"

"My dad," I whisper. "He had them too. I saw him while Pathfinding."

"Tell us," Lefka sings. "Tell us of your nesting parent."

"He died. When I was nine. He had a heart attack. He was in Ada's room, playing with her. She was only a year old. I heard him hit the floor. I ran to her room, and he was on the ground. He heaved for breath a few times and reached for me. Ada started crying. He touched my hand and tried to say something. But he couldn't speak. And then he died."

I look into the piercing eyes of the great bird, black and flecked with gold.

"The story does not begin there," she says.

"When I was Pathfinding to escape the shadows...in the car, before the fire. I saw my dad." I can hardly get the words out. Not once since the fire has the memory left my mind. But I still haven't processed it. It's been floating around in a haze, corroded by the memories of the crash, of the hospital. "He ... he had a different child. A son. His son shot a javelina, and my dad came out to celebrate, but the shadows came. He passed out, and I heard my abuela asking him if it was the darkness again."

"The loss of a parent is too great for a hatchling to bear without wounds," the giant white bird sings, her voice melodic and soothing. "And in his death your father inflicted something terrible on you. You must heal the hole within you, and the storms will not be able to move through you."

"But how?" I ask, my voice raising in protest. "I don't understand what I have to do."

"Nor do I, fledgling," she cries, her voice rising in a high-pitched operatic trill before descending to her usual alto. "I can push my hatchlings out of the nest. But they must fly themselves."

"How did you do it?" I whisper. "Fight them."

"I am old and wise and strong," she says. "I have lived many egg cycles, and I have seen many worlds. I brushed my wing against the hole in the skies that let them in, and they were gone. You are a fledgling. It will be harder. This is your first fight, and it will not be easy."

"Why aren't they here now? In your world? If I'm here, why don't they follow me?"

She raises her head and trills, her beak raised to the sky, in what sounds like it might be a laugh. "They do not dare challenge me now. Like me, they prefer easier prey." She opens her mouth in a giant cry and cranes her neck into the air, her wings unfolding in a mesmerizing show. A chill runs down my spine, and suddenly I'm afraid. Silas takes a step back.

"Leave, humans. I enjoy you, but I am hungry. I do not want you to be my next meal."

Silas lays the flat of his palm on my forearm and closes his eyes. I follow suit, and in an instant we're tumbling back through the pores of the world, and I feel as though Lefka's dusky feathers are raining down around me, falling on me, cushioning me, until I'm flat on the ground again with a thump.

I glance around—we're on the sidewalk outside Dr. Chase's office. This world feels like home. The little slatted sign that says *Dr. Emma Chase and Dr. Jeremy Pritzkin, Clinical Psychologists*, is within an arm's length.

Silas is watching me, his hand still on my forearm.

"Are you okay?" he asks.

"Yeah." My voice comes out so soft it can barely be heard. "Thank you for helping me." I glance at the sign, and then through the door. "What will have happened…inside?" I ask.

"Without your energy to draw from, the shadows will have gone. Your doctor should be fine. Confused, maybe, but no worse."

"Maybe now she'll understand what I'm going through," I say ruefully.

"Noomi," he says. His hand is still on my arm. My skin tingles. "Why didn't you tell me about your dad?"

I shake my head, looking at the ground. It's all happening so fast. I gather my thoughts and put my words together.

"When could I have? When we were at the hospital, there were just a few minutes when I could talk to you. Then—you disappeared. I haven't seen you in days."

He nods. "We haven't had much time together, I know. But I want to earn your trust. I want…" He hesitates. "I want you to trust me, because I want to help you fight the shadows."

"Why?"

He meets my eyes, a fractured smile on his lips. "Because you deserve someone to fight with you. Someone who knows what you're up against."

The words of the gravedigger from my dreams come back to me.

"Silas," I say. "I met a man while Pathfinding. It was accidental—I did it in my sleep. He said I have to find my own light if I'm going to fight the shadows. What does that mean?"

"I'm not sure. It sounds like a riddle. Like what Lefka said—'the storms will not be able to move through you.'"

I sigh, frustrated. "Everyone speaks in riddles. None of it makes sense."

He takes my hand. My heart skips a beat. His hands are warm and soft, like desert shade.

"We'll learn. Together."

REVOLUTION

"Revolution; noun 1a (1): the action by a celestial body of going round in an orbit or elliptical course, also : apparent movement of such a body round the earth (2): the time taken by a celestial body to make a complete round in its orbit"
—Merriam-Webster, "Revolution"

Today is Ada's eighth birthday, and this year it conveniently falls on a Saturday. Mom and I took advantage of the opportunity and allowed Ada to invite ten of her friends to a birthday party based on one of her favorite subjects: astronomy. All eight planets, plus Pluto and the asteroid belt, are hanging from the ceiling in crude rendering on giant balloons around the first floor of our house. The Sun, in piñata form, is in the living room, where all the furniture has been cleared to prevent damage during the piñata's eventual destruction. My mother and I are trying to maintain order, while Mr. Arcadio, who my mother enlisted to help with the party, seems hell-bent on promoting chaos. Kalifa also generously volunteered to help and is attempting to keep the more adventurous of the children away from my mother's collection of antique Syrian teapots.

"Here's Jupiter. How many moons does Jupiter have?"

"Sixty-seven!" Three kids call out the right answer, and I proudly note that Ada is one of them. Someone else ventures, "Sixteen!" and one boy says, "One hundred and thirty-eight!"

"Sixty-seven is correct. On to Saturn. Who can find Saturn first?"

"Oh my," I hear Kali sigh, as eleven sets of feet stampede from the kitchen to the stairwell, where Saturn floats, a cardboard cutout of her glorious rings glued precariously to her middle.

Mr. Arcadio narrates their adventure around the solar system like a grandfatherly version of Ms. Frizzle. At the end, when he leads them back to the sun, he blindfolds Ada and hands her the stick to smash the piñata. Her aim is true, and after a few good whacks the papier-mâché Sun collapses under her stick, and the candy tumbles to the ground amid a chorus of cheers. Ada stands there in the shower of candy, letting it wash over her with a smiling joyfully as if caught in a summer thunderstorm. Mashing a Reese's cup contentedly between her teeth, she ventures over to Mr. Arcadio, who is sitting on the couch, looking thoroughly tuckered out, which I think serves him right for getting the kids so riled up over a bunch of planets.

"Mr. Arcadio," she starts, as I begin cutting the moon-themed cake. From my vantage at the kitchen island, I can see them both in profile and can just make out their voices over the sounds of children arguing about various pieces of candy.

"Please, Ada, I've been telling your sister for years. Call me Mal."

"Okay, Mal. I have a question."

"Shoot."

"What do birthdays mean?"

"It means the Earth has gone around the Sun in one full revolution since your last birthday."

"But why's that special?" She takes a Jolly Rancher from her pocket and unwraps it. "Why do I get to have a party today and not yesterday?"

"It's special because it means we've arrived in the exact same place in space that we were a year ago."

"But Noomi says the whole Solar System is hurtling through the universe too, which means we're not in the same place at all."

Mr. Arcadio's laugh, warm like caramel and honey, fills the room. "You're getting too smart for me, Ada. Do you want to know something interesting?"

Her head bobs. He leans in and whispers. But when Ada replies, her voice is as loud as before.

"Was my purpose to help Noomi?"

I freeze, my knife halfway through a slice.

Mr. Arcadio sits back. I have to strain to hear him. "I don't know. Only you will know for sure."

"That must be why I have so much light inside me," she says. "To scare Noomi's shadows away."

"Yes, Ada. But it's your job to figure out where the light is coming from."

"Oh, I already know that."

"Really?" Mr. Arcadio pulls back, looking at her in half-mocking, half-genuine surprise.

"I have a lantern inside me," she announces. "I just need to figure out how to shine it at Noomi's shadows."

Mr. Arcadio sits back. A wide smile spreads across his face.

"Noomi?" Kalifa is suddenly at my side. She glances at me, worried. I haven't moved in almost a minute, focused on eavesdropping. "Are you okay?"

"I'm fine." My hand trembles as I finish cutting the cake.

"What happened?"

"Nothing." My smile is strained as I lift the slice and transfer it to a little plate. I continue watching Mr. Arcadio even as Ada wanders off, distracted by candy and her friends, feeling removed from my surroundings, distant from the clashing voices and youthful excitement. He knows something. There have been too many hints, too many coincidences. First the book he lent me. Then the odd comment after I got out of the hospital. And when Ada mentions the shadows, he doesn't balk. Doesn't act surprised.

He knows about them. Knows they're more than what they seem.

But *how* much does he know? Why hasn't he told me before?

And what on Earth is Ada's lantern?

SCORPIO

"Scorpio—Intense, penetrating."
—Chani Nicholas, *You Were Born for This*

"Okay, how about this one: Would you rather lick a shoe or kiss a frog?"

"Kiss the frog! Do you have any idea how many bacteria are on the bottom of a shoe?" Kalifa shivers violently and makes a gagging motion. Claire and Kali are lying on the bed together, their faces resting in their palms. Kalifa's hair is down and out of her *hijab*. I can count on two hands the number of times I've seen her without her *hijab*, and it's always a thing to behold. Shining brilliant and smooth, her tawny hair gleams under the pale holiday lights she's strung across her room. "Okay, my turn. Noomi, would you rather see what's inside a black hole or see what's inside a quark?"

"Quark," I reply instantly. "I bet once we know what's inside quarks we can figure out what's inside black holes."

Kalifa shrugs. "That's what they thought about atoms too. And then electrons. And protons. Your turn, Noomi."

Claire picked the music tonight, so we're listening to James Blake's *Overgrown*. His melancholy croon soaks into our bones as we sit on Kalifa's bed in our pajamas, letting our hair dry after an evening of soaking in her hot tub.

I turn to Claire. "Would you rather …"

… die by drowning or by jumping off a cliff? I swallow the words on my tongue. Don't think like that, I tell myself.

"… ride a unicorn or a dragon?"

"Dragon," Claire says immediately. "Unicorns are totally overrated. They're the cheerleaders of the magical world; they don't do anything but glitter and look pretty. But you can set people on fire with a dragon." She grins.

I wonder if there's a universe where dragons and unicorns are real. If Lefka exists, surely dragons do too.

A small, repetitive thought creeps up at me. The doubt; the dread. None of this is real. I am inventing all of it. Silas. Lefka. Pathfinding. The shadows. All of it a fiction. The product of a tortured mind.

I turn away from my friends, suddenly too ashamed to go on. Self-conscious, I grab Claire's iPad and start fiddling with the music. Searching for a change. Something to break these thought patterns that do nothing but harm.

"Noomi," Claire says from behind me. "Would you rather tell us what's really going on with you, or bottle it up forever and ever?"

There's a moment of stillness. My finger hovering over the button that says *play*. Everything goes quiet. Kalifa slaps Claire on the leg and hushes her. But the silence in the air tells me we cannot go back from this.

I swivel to face them.

"I can't choose neither, can I?"

Claire shakes her head. "Rules of the game."

Rules of the game, I repeat in my head.

"Okay," I say, standing up. "I'll tell you. But I need you to come outside with me. I can't talk about it in here."

"Sure," Kalifa says. "Let's go."

Ten minutes later, we're all padding around Kalifa's subdivision. Claire's flip-flops patter against the asphalt. I try to listen for the sound my chucks make against the pavement, but my footfalls are too quiet. In a few minutes we've come to the little creek that runs through Kali's neighborhood. Claire leans on the bridge with her elbows on the wooden railing and I press my back against it and cross my arms.

"Look," I start. "This isn't easy to talk about. I'd choose not to if I could."

"That's okay," Kali interjects immediately. "You don't have to talk about it if you don't want to."

"—But by choosing neither, you're choosing the second option," Claire points out. "You're choosing to keep it bottled up."

"Does that mean I haven't broken the rules?" I ask.

"No, it just means you cheated your way into a loss," Claire retorts.

"Claire! She can do whatever she wants."

"I know I can. And I want to tell you. But—" I suck in a breath "—it's harder than you know."

The only sound for the next several seconds is the water through the stones in the creek. The silence is heavy. An unusually clear night has given way to some of the brightest stars I can remember seeing in town.

"Remember when we were kids, and you could see the stars on every clear night?" These aren't the words I meant to say. "Before the haze from the city started drifting in."

"Things were clearer then," Claire agrees. "Look," she points. "Leo. That's my sign."

"Claire," Kali says, with a side-eye. "You're not still on that horoscope stuff?"

"Of course, I am! 'Leo: Attention-seeking. Loves the limelight. Performance-oriented, outgoing, and social.' Could that describe me more perfectly? I don't think so.'" Kalifa and I roll our eyes. This flash of normalcy feels like sweet relief after the tension. "Oh, come on, you guys, you both so perfectly embody your sun sign, it's not even funny."

"Don't," Kali says, a warning in her voice. "I'm not at all like a Virgo."

"You just think you aren't," Claire exclaims.

"There's Boötes," I say, pointing, trying to distract from their budding argument. "Like on your scarf." Before we came outside, Kali wrapped her hair in a blue silk scarf with white dots, depicting several constellations from ancient mythology.

"Also known as the herdsman," Kali says.

"How do you know that?" Claire asks.

"I like constellations enough to wear them on my *hijab*. Why would you think I wouldn't know the stories?"

"But you don't believe in horoscopes."

"Just because I don't think the stars have the power to predict our future doesn't mean I don't enjoy looking at them."

"Horoscopes don't predict the future," Claire says tartly. "They tell us how to interpret the present."

"I'm a Scorpio," I say, cutting off their lively debate once again.

"Mysterious and reserved but charismatic," Claire says immediately, as if quoting from a textbook. "Interested in the darker, unexplored side of life."

"Named for the scorpion that stung Orion." Kalifa points to the sky where the constellation can be faintly seen among the other stars. "Which is why Orion is always on the opposite side of the sky, running away."

"Scorpio signs are usually very smart," Claire says, "and you're definitely at *least* as smart as I am."

I jab her in the ribs. "I'm sorry, *who* sets the curve on every chem exam?"

"I'm sorry," Claire mimics, "*who* sets the curve on every calc exam?"

"You two are so lame," Kalifa says. "No one will remember who got what grade when we get to college."

I laugh. "Says the girl who two days ago was worried about losing her valedictorian status over a choice of font!"

She crosses her arms and looks away.

"Scorpio is a water sign," Claire continues. "They tend to be deep thinkers and serious-minded." I nod, oddly satisfied to be described so accurately. "Intensely focused on their passion projects, always working on transformation, healing, and rejuvenation."

My skin prickles. "That's so accurate it's a little scary."

"See!" Claire turns to Kalifa, triumphant.

"You cherry-picked the descriptions of a Scorpio to fit Noomi because you know her so well," Kalifa retorts.

Suddenly, the confession tumbles out of my mouth. "I wanted to tell you the truth tonight. But I don't know how to start. The truth is, I don't know the truth. But what you said," I nod at Claire, "about how Scorpio signs are interested in the darker side of life—well, that's more true than you know."

"You're not making much sense," Claire says.

"Shhhh! Let her talk," Kalifa hisses. "Besides, you read *horoscopes*. I would have thought you'd have a high tolerance for nonsense by now."

I laugh. "You both know about my panic attacks. You know what the doctors say, anyway. But they're so much more than that. It's like…" I fumble and look away, trying to describe something I've tried to describe a thousand times and failed every time. "Maybe it's like drowning. You're in a storm, and your ship goes down, and you're fighting to stay afloat but it's impossible. You're sinking, and you can't move or swim because your muscles have gone dead from fatigue, and it's dark, and you can't breathe or see or feel or hear, and all around you is just this *nothingness*, the immense weight of nothingness, and the ocean swallows you whole."

"Noomi," Claire says, "your eyes…"

Kalifa's hand grazes my cheekbone. "They're black."

"It happens," I say, trying to blink it away, and finding only water there instead, "when they come."

Silence as empty as the spaces between the stars.

"They?" Claire asks at last.

"The shadows. That's what I call them."

"But if they're not panic attacks, what are they?" Claire hesitates. "How can they make your eyes…turn colors?"

I shrug. My heart pounds in my chest. "Demons from another universe?"

Claire laughs, breaking the tension. Kalifa slaps her on the arm. But I laugh too.

"It sounds crazy, doesn't it? You probably think I'm crazy."

"On the contrary," Kalifa says, "I don't think you're crazy at all. I think that we should take inspiration from our idols of science. When Marie Curie was confronted with a problem she didn't understand, did she give up and call it 'ghosts' or 'magic'? No, she did not. She persisted with her experiments to find a reasonable, scientific explanation. When Isaac Newton was trying to understand the laws of gravity, and conventional mathematics couldn't explain acceleration, did he decide it was witchcraft? No, he *invented an entirely new field of mathematics*. Are we supposed to sit here and accept that these are *demons* or *inventions* when we know perfectly well there's a scientific explanation somewhere?" Kalifa looks me square in the eye. "Whether these attacks—demons, as you call them—are coming from inside you, from your mind, or from somewhere else—wherever that may be—there's an explanation. With hypotheses, research, and experiments, we can find the answer. And we can stop them."

"I don't know if I want to be the subject of scientific inquiry," I reply warily. "That hasn't always gone well in the past."

"I'm just talking about doing some reading," Kalifa soothes.

Claire's eyes are wide as she reaches out to take my hand. "We don't think you're crazy, Noomi. We know you well enough to know you're perfectly sane. And whatever you're dealing with—these shadows, or whatever they are—you shouldn't have to face them alone."

Kalifa nods. "Whether they're demons or panic attacks or something in between, we can fight them together."

"And besides," Claire says, uncharacteristically shy, "we don't want to lose you."

Kali squeezes my hand. "Whatever we can do to help."

Never again, I think fiercely, will I underestimate my friends.

YGGDRASIL

"Stark on the open field the moonlight fell,
But the oak tree's shadow was deep and black
and secret as a well."
— Edna St. Vincent Millay,
She Had Forgotten How the August Night

The van shakes and rattles as we clunk over a series of potholes. I glance behind me at two girls laughing and showing each other pictures on their iPhones, snapping selfies as we bump along the road. A third girl, sitting next to me, is new to our group and, like me, doesn't seem to fit in. She looks at me and rolls her eyes at the behavior of the others. Her hair is straight, sharp, and hay-colored, and her long, flat bangs do an excellent job of hiding her brilliant blue eyes.

I try to remember her name.

Bree. That's it. She introduced herself a few weeks ago.

I turn back to the window as we roll past a meadow, full of young grasses and trees in the flush of spring growth. Paul's humming softly as he drives, which does nothing to replace the emptiness in our ears now the radio's dead. We pass a cliffside, winding along a river, dotted with meadows and trees on all sides. It jostles a memory. A few years ago, with my first wilderness therapy group, while we were hiking down into a river valley, I threw myself into a hundred-foot crevasse and found myself in the gorge moments later, unharmed, without a scratch.

There was no pain. Only disappointment.

I remember the vertigo, standing over the cliff, waiting. I stared down and hoped. The shadows flicked across my vision, a harbinger of more to come, and I jumped, desperate to stop them this time. My stomach fell out of my body and the shadows disappeared. The world came alive in vivid color. I watched with double vision as I fell through the canyon, drawing what should have been a second into minutes, hours, days.

When I hit the rocks, I felt my body bend. Bones crinkled. Muscles stretched and released and came back together. I timed it, counting the seconds aloud as I watched my limbs heal. It took two minutes and five seconds for the bleeding to stop.

I sat in the gorge and waited for someone to find me. No one did. Eventually, I got up and walked to the river, where I was able to rejoin the group.

That was my fifth attempt. I was gone for an hour and a half. I told them I'd gotten lost. It wasn't until the rafting incident that one of the counselors began to suspect my absences were purposeful.

Paul pulls the van into a small parking lot at the trailhead. I slide the door open, and we all get out to unload our packs. This is an overnight trip, so we're loaded with sleeping bags, tents, water, and food for an evening around the campfire. There was some debate about whether or not I would be allowed to come, just a few weeks after the incident at the barn. But when the police determined that the fire was most likely started by a wayward lightning strike—therefore unlikely to be a poorly-thought-out arson or suicide attempt on my part—and Dr. Chase and Dr. Zimmerman both gave me a clean bill of health, my mother decided it would be better to pretend I'm normal than to continue treating me like a prisoner.

"Hey, Noomi," a voice says next to me. It's Bree.

"What's up?" I ask.

She shrugs. "Just saying hi. What are you in for?"

"'In for...?'" It sounds like she's talking about a jailhouse.

"Yeah. Why are you in adventure therapy?"

"Same reasons you are, I guess," I reply. "My shrink made me."

She giggles, cupping her face behind her hands. She looks like a cartoon character, her eyes are so wide and blue.

"My shrink made me, too," she says. "But I mean *why* did your shrink make you?"

"I jumped off one too many cliffs." I shoulder my heavy backpack and turn to walk with her.

"How did you survive?"

"Secret parachute."

She giggles again and doesn't pry. I'm grateful. "Want to know why I'm in?" Without waiting for an answer, she leans in and whispers, "I tried to stab a boy in my class." Despite her hushed tone, there's pride in her voice.

"Oh?" I raise an eyebrow. "Tell me more."

As we walk, I notice she has a fresh tattoo of a butterfly on her forearm. It looks like a watercolor, with blue, green, and yellow wings. I wonder how she convinced her parents to go for that. Or maybe it wasn't a fight. Maybe they have dozens of tattoos and were excited to bring their daughter to the parlor with them.

"He was a year older than me. We had theater class together. He kept using his phone to take pictures up my skirt and down my shirt. I must have told the teacher a half-dozen times, but he didn't care." She rolls her eyes. "So, the next time he did it, I was ready. I had an exacto blade." She says this as if it were natural. As natural as an apple falling from a tree. As the sun rising in the morning. Maybe it is. "The judge told me I would have to go to counseling and anger management to avoid juvenile detention. Of course, nothing happened to him."

I stare at her. "Did you hurt him?"

"No." Her tone is mournful. "He caught my arm before I could get him. I didn't even break the skin. And when I told them to search his phone for the photos of me, he had already deleted them all."

"I'm sorry," I say. For all the trouble she's been through, I almost wish she'd at least tasted revenge. "I'm glad he didn't get hurt. But the teachers should have done something about him."

She scoffs, lowering her voice to a whisper as we join the group circle. "They would never do anything about someone like him."

"All right," Leah says, clapping to draw our attention. "Let's get moving. We want to get there in time to make camp before it gets dark."

She turns to lead the way and the group falls into step behind her. At the end of the line, I follow Bree, who charges uphill with the intensity of an ant carrying food home to the queen. Paul steps softly behind me, bringing up the rear, still humming songs I don't recognize.

All around us the hills and valleys are alive with signs of spring. Green-gold leaves abound, unfolding a thousand little wings in the trees and grasses. Only the oaks are hesitant, their crooked fingers spindly as they creak up to the sky and wrench to the ground, hung with lichen and weighted down.

I see you there, oaks, I whisper to them. I'm afraid to bloom too. I reach my fingers up to touch a branch looming over us as we walk.

My next thought comes unbidden.

I wish Silas were here.

"Oaks are lovely, aren't they?" Paul says, his voice carrying from behind me. "They have a long history in mythology."

"Oh?"

"You don't know?" he says, and I turn to glare at him for a moment.

"I'm a STEM girl, Paul, not a literature-and-mythology type." I return my attention to the rocky path at my feet. "My friend Kalifa probably does, though," I say, wishing she were here too.

"You're hardly illiterate," he counters. "I've seen you with your nose in enough books over the last two years to know that's not true."

"Maybe I'm just asking for a story about an oak tree."

Bree glances back at the two of us, arching a brow. I cock my head slightly, staring at her. I don't know her well enough to guess what she's trying to say. After a second, she turns away, resuming her charge up the hill.

"I can oblige," Paul says. "Have you heard of Thor's Oak, Yggdrasil?" He says the word like *ig-drah-sill*, and I roll it over on my tongue a few times before I reply with a slow *no*. "In Norse mythology, Yggdrasil was the bridge between humans and the world of the gods. The legend says it was an ash tree, but there's a famous incident in early Christian history that bridges the gap between the mythology and the history of the Norse oak."

"What was it?" I ask.

"There was a giant old oak near the town of Hesse, Germany. It was worshipped by pagans in the nearby town who considered it the bridge between the spirit world, the world of the gods, and their own. It was known as Donar's Oak. Old German for Thor's Oak." He stops to take a breath, his words coming out heavier as the ascent becomes steeper. I can hear his footsteps quiet behind me, and I stop too. He gestures to a white oak, broad and welcoming with its arching, low-hung branches in this forest of tall, straight Douglas firs. We stare at the tree together and I try not to be too conscious of Paul breathing lightly next to me, how tall and warm and comforting he seems. I wonder what it would be like to be next to him, pressed into his side, his arm wrapped around my shoulder.

And then he takes a step forward, and his arm brushes mine, both of us a little sweaty from hiking. I can feel the perspiration on his skin. He glances at me, and in his eyes I see a flash of the opalescence I've come to associate with Silas and Pathfinding and then—

Black spots pepper my eyes.

I sway—

My hand goes out for balance—

I come up empty. Paul is past me and there's nothing to reach for.

The black spots grow. Panic rises in my chest. I take a deep breath, try to blink them away. Inhale. Exhale. The shadows flush out of my vision. I straighten and look ahead.

Paul is staring at me. When I meet his eyes, they are black as pitch. Black as Dr. Chase's were in her office.

Am I seeing clearly? Are the shadows his? Or mine, reflected in his eyes?

He continues his story, his voice normal, as if nothing happened, while my nerves begin to fray. His eyes are fixed on me. "The Christians came into Germany to convert the pagans and found that they worshipped this giant old oak tree. A missionary named St. Boniface decided to chop it down to make sure the pagans couldn't continue their idol worship."

I can't break eye contact. Neither of us move. And then Paul blinks, and for an instant before the lids close over his eyes, the iridescence flashes again.

Ink splatters across my vision. I am drenched in it. It pours over me like a wave. I stumble, unsteady, throwing my arms out for balance.

"They used wood from the tree to build a church to the Christian god, and Donar's Oak was destroyed." What is he doing? Why is he doing this? His voice now sounds like it's coming from far away. Weight settles on my shoulders, my hips, my knees. I try to draw another breath, but it doesn't come. I totter. The ink spreads, dappling, bleeding through the blood vessels in my eyes. One hand to my temple, one hand wide, seeking something to hold onto, something steady, something—

"The bridge between worlds was destroyed." His words echo through the halls of my mind.

What is he doing to me? I falter and gasp, but air won't come.

"And they burned the rest of the tree."

Blindly, I push forward, trying to stumble past, but as I do I collide with him completely, and I feel his long limbs against mine, his body so thin, skeletal almost, and I feel like I'm clutching something that will collapse the instant I put my full weight on it. But momentum is carrying me forward and there it is, the falling sensation, the experience of floating in space or falling off a cliff or Pathfinding into another world.

Paul seems to collapse beneath my weight, and we tumble into what I now know is a Path to another world. Then something strange happens: a hand reaches out to grab mine and the falling ends. I am stabilized, reset, solid in my own world.

"Noomi?" Warm fingers wrap around my own. "Come on," the voice says. It's Bree. I can't see her, but I can hear her.

She tugs gently, pulling me away. My foot moves. I take the first step, and my body separates from Paul's. Light floods back in like a curtain pulled back. Bree's straw-colored hair reflects the sunlight dancing from above. I clutch her hand like a lifeline as we step into a rocky clearing. I suck in a long, cool breath and my head clears. A flowering meadow lies ahead as the trail flattens for a moment. The oaks are behind us.

Questions flutter and multiply. I can hear Paul's steady footsteps pick up again behind me. His breathing light and easy. It seems nothing happened.

"Are you okay?" Bree asks.

"Fine," I reply, breathing hard. "Just out of shape."

"You should join the soccer team," she says. "That'll get you fit in no time."

Once again, I'm grateful she doesn't pry. Behind us, Paul starts whistling what sounds like an Irish folk song.

Just another lovely spring day, it seems.

But I know better. Paul's eyes were iridescent, like Silas's when he takes me to another world. He was taking me somewhere.

Paul is a Pathfinder.

And this is the second time the shadows have come when he's been near. The first, in the coffee shop, sitting awkwardly across the table from me. Now—so visceral, so tangible—trying to drag me through the pores of the universe, bringing them to me—

Or was he bringing me to them?

ELECTROMAGNETISM

"Electromagnetism is responsible for far more than just electricity and magnetism. It is the force that binds negatively charged electrons to positively charged atomic nuclei, ensuring that stable atoms can be formed and that chemistry—including the chemistry of life—can happen." —New Scientist, "Electromagnetism"

I silence the growing cry in my body that tells me to call for Silas like I did at Dr. Chase's. Not yet. I tell myself again and again that I can handle Paul on my own. I don't need Silas for everything. The fire grows as a few of the other kids help Leah and another counselor build it up. Paul is nowhere to be seen.

As I pitch my tent in the fading light, Bree approaches.

"Need a hand?" she asks.

I glare at my messy tent, poles everywhere, stakes not yet in the ground.

"Sure," I reply. "I've never pitched a tent that doesn't stand on its own." Truthfully, my hands have been shaking too hard to fit the poles together.

"Here," she says. "You have to extend the poles to their full length."

I watch in admiration as she darts around the tent, pounding the stakes in with a fist-sized rock, fitting my hiking poles into the folded corners. The butterfly on her arm catches a ray of pale pink sunlight. It seems to take wing, flying off her skin and into the night. "Put that pole in at the bottom," she instructs, pointing to a sliver of fabric at the foot of my tent. I shake off my fascination with her tattoo to oblige. Moments later, the tent is upright.

"That was impressive." I cross my arms. "Do you camp a lot?"

She shrugs. "Yeah. My dad used to take me and my brother camping when we were younger. But mostly I got good at this stuff when I was in wilderness therapy last summer." She stares at the ground. "We were out in the back country for weeks."

"How old is your brother?"

"We're twins."

"I don't know how old you are," I point out.

"I'm sixteen. A sophomore." A year younger than me.

"You're not at Rocklin High, are you?" She shakes her head. "That's why I haven't seen you."

"I'm at West Albany." She glances down at my tent. "You clearly never go camping."

"That's not true," I protest. "I've been camping a few times. Always with these adventure therapy groups."

"Well, they didn't teach you very well." She smiles.

"They're always too busy meditating to teach me about camping," I reply. She laughs harder.

"So do you have a crush on Paul or what?" she says abruptly.

I stop laughing. My stomach clenches. The awkwardness of being called out about my halfhearted, illicit crush on our counselor mixes uncomfortably with the dark memory of this afternoon.

"What are you talking about?"

"I've watched you at our meetings. You're always flirting with him. You seemed enchanted on the hike up." She pauses. Watches my reaction as I fumble for words. "It's okay," she says, her voice measured. "I had a crush on one of my teachers last year. It's not weird or anything."

Well, it kind of is. "I don't have a crush on him," I say, willing it to be true. "I just think he's interesting. He's really smart, and he doesn't care about rules. I like people like that." I pause, thinking about the way he made me feel this afternoon. Pools of darkness, dragging me in. "But, now that I think about it, I can see why you thought that."

She narrows her eyes. "If you say so."

I see Leah, a hundred feet away, waving her arms at us, the lone stragglers who haven't joined the rest of the group around the fireside. "Let's go," I say, desperate for a change of subject.

"Want to go join your boyfriend?"

I roll my eyes, annoyed. "He's not my boyfriend."

We walk to the campfire in fragile silence. Paul isn't there yet. He must still be setting up his tent. A quick glance around reveals nothing—the fading light is shrinking the world, and I can't see much beyond the campfire. I sit next to Bree.

"Before we start preparing dinner, we'll go through a brief meditation," Leah says. A hush descends. Where moments ago nine teenagers and four counselors were buzzing with noise and movement, now everyone is quiet. Leah is good at these meditations. Her voice is low and calming—even I can't deny it's pleasant to listen to. She incorporates aspects of Zen Buddhism into relaxation techniques in ways that have apparently been quite successful for other students. I've overheard more than one of my fellow group members telling their parents how much her meditations have helped them. There's a dark voice in the back of my mind. I try to argue against it, but it's persuasive—and angry.

She loves when everyone has to shut up and listen to her.

She's just trying to help, the rational voice counters.

She loves being the center of attention.

She's a therapist. Her job is to help kids.

Yes, she's helpful. So fucking helpful. To everyone except you.

I swear under my breath. Don't think like that. Bree opens her eyes and looks at me, questioning.

"It's nothing," I mutter. I promise myself I'll listen this time. I'll trust her. I straighten my spine and nestle into the patch of grass beneath me.

Someone sits down next to me, and I look up to see Paul settling down, sitting cross-legged, his hands resting gently on top of his knees. My stomach clenches.

"Everyone, please close your eyes," Leah says, leading by example.

Paul looks at me, an odd smile on his face. His blue eyes suddenly frightening. Too blue. Icy and unwelcoming. My body revolts. This is wrong. This is what happened earlier. I fight the urge to stand up and walk away, to my tent, down the mountain, into the woods, never to return.

"Start, please, by focusing on your breath," Leah says, and Paul closes his eyes. He inhales, so loudly I can hear it over the crackle of the fire. "Breathe in. Feel the expansion of your ribs. Breathe out. The softening of your abdominal muscles as you exhale."

I stare at Paul, trying to understand. His face is relaxed, his body loose, his wiry legs carefully folded beneath him. The picture of tranquility. Do I interrupt the meditation and leave? Am I so afraid of him that I'll run away, hide in my tent, make a scene?

No. I won't run. I won't let him scare me.

"Relax the muscles in your cheeks, in your forehead," Leah says, and now I close my eyes and turn away from Paul, obeying Leah's gentle instructions. "Soften your eyelids, your jaw. Relax your neck and shoulders. Release any tension there. Give your body permission to rest." She carries out the syllables, the words. Pulls them like dough as far as they will stretch.

I follow her voice, trying to do as she says. I pretend it's not Paul next to me, but Silas. I imagine the warmth of his skin and hair, the comforting sensation of his body near to mine. I imagine the dark green of his eyes, how perfectly it would blend with the wild, mossy colors here in the fading light of day.

"On the next exhale, release any tension in your abdomen, your belly. Let your muscles soften."

I feel a prickle at the nape of my neck. Contrary to Leah's instructions, my body tenses. I look to my left. Paul is staring at me, his hand an inch away from my knee. I force down the fear and stare at him.

Don't, I tell him silently.

He gives me that odd little smile again, and I swallow hard.

"Relax your thighs, your legs. Feel the weight of your body as it rests against the ground."

I know what you did, I say silently. Paul's expression never changes. You betrayed me.

"Think about the earth beneath you. Relax into it. Feel the connection to the earth beneath your hips. Inhale. Exhale."

His eyes never leave mine.

And then he touches my leg. The oil-slick colors flash again in his irises. And the world goes dark.

Abrupt nothingness. Abyssal absence of light. All-consuming.

I blink, and my breath catches.

What is he doing? It's like there's nothing left in the world. Not a shred of color, not a line or dot or shape to take up space.

In place of sight, there's a heightened body consciousness I've never experienced before. Usually when the shadows come, they drain all sensation from me—sight, sound, feeling, emotion. But now, I'm aware of every inch of prickling skin.

Every muscle is tense and ready to spring. My eyelids open and close. My heart races; I feel my ribs expand. My breath quickens; I feel air rush in. Paul's hand tightens on my knee; I feel the pressure from each individual fingerprint, pushing against my jeans, threads scraping delicately against my skin.

I close my eyes as if to shield myself from the blackness and the world changes. Here, lids clenched tightly against the darkness, I can see things.

Strange things.

Colored lines of every imaginable hue pulse before me. They fold and dance, the whole world lit up in lines of neon that undulate and twist. They're pretty, I think, as I watch them in flux. Dimly, I can see that they outline things in the physical world—trees, rocks, the other humans around our circle, glowing lines of energy from the fire. I think of lines of magnetism, electromagnetic force fields that bend particles, large and small, into mathematically predictable patterns of ebb and flow. I'm looking at the threads of spacetime. These are the fibers that bind the worlds together. I could see them before, when I closed my eyes and focused intently, when I was practicing finding a Path. But this is different. This is how they're supposed to be seen. This is what the world must look like when we're not blinded by frail human vision.

Paul's hand tenses on my knee, and the world starts to shift. Now there's a heaviness bleeding in. The vacancy, the exhaustion, the apathy. Pressing against me. The lines at the edges of my vision start to dissipate, collapsing in on each other. The colors dull and fade to grey. And ahead, in the lines of color, I can see a Path. It looks like a funnel—a hole in the threads that leads down, and there at the center, all color dissipates entirely. There's nothing left but darkness.

It's a Path to the shadows.

Paul clenches his hand around my knee, and everything in me screams to push him away. I push his hand off me, but he grabs my fingers and laces his hand with mine, tightly, so tightly I can't break free no matter how I struggle, twisting my wrist back and forth, wriggling my fingers, trying to shake him off, and I realize that the vortex, the hole in the fibers of the world is moving closer to us. We're headed straight toward it, and I'm not sure if we're moving or if it is, but in a few moments we're both going to fall in, and I start to panic, breathing hard, shaking my hand to loosen his grip, but his fingers are a vise around my own. Listlessness, fatigue, emptiness settle on my shoulders.

Thin green lines collect in front of me. At first, they look like nothing more than dewdrops. Then they accumulate, braiding into strands, like a fraying rope. They beckon. Call to me. I reach my right hand to the threads, stretching. They dangle tantalizingly in front of me. I stretch further, but Paul yanks me back. He doesn't want me to touch them, I realize.

I relax for a moment, releasing all the tension in my body, pretending to let the fatigue and emptiness force surrender to the vortex, and then—

I leap forward, and my left hand comes free of Paul's, my right is stretched out in front of me even as the lines, now a bright sun-leaf-green, turn to slate-green, turn to steely grey, now just a breath out of reach. Desperate, I stretch my body as far as it will go. I reach for the lines. Curl my fingers. Catch two of them between my fingertips. Pull, a voice somewhere says.

I pull.

My bones stretch.

The familiar feeling of falling hits me like a train as sensation rushes back into my skin, my bones, my muscles. Brilliant lines of color flash back into existence as I plummet through the unending ocean of a Path—

—I am flattened—

—emptied—

—the threads that bind the worlds together so colorful they might be electric—

Bright purple and vivid orange bubbles erupt around me.

"Noomi!"

CHROMA

"Chroma measures the strength, wavelength purity, or saturation of colour."—Michael Allaby, ed., "Chroma," *A Dictionary of Earth Sciences*

I hear my name not in my ears but against my skin.

My head turns slowly toward the sound—no, not sound, but waves, pulsing waves of some thick viscous substance I can't begin to describe. I am floating, weightless, enmeshed in the wildest colors I've ever seen, more than I could ever imagine, more than can possibly exist.

The voice I hear—against my skin, in my eardrums, does it matter?—isn't Silas. I don't know why I expected him to be here. A hope more than an expectation. But it's not him. I squint, recognizing the man's face even as his shape and outline blends into the brilliant background.

It's the gravedigger.

He's dimly recognizable, his face made up of colors I can only describe as some extraordinary hue of green and orange, the brightest crayons in the box taken to their functional limits. I hold my arms in front of me, staring in fascination at the cerulean and violet mixing with colors so foreign I don't have words for them, so new and astonishing that if I weren't seeing them with my own eyes, I could never even dream they existed. I can feel the liquid around me in the same way I imagine a fish in the ocean would feel the water: the pressure, the force as it pushes around you and on you, but the suspension, too, the ability to move through it and in it and to feel it move with you.

"You," I say. The words pulsate through the liquid substrate. "What are you doing here?"

"I called you here," he says. "I threw you a lifeline, so to speak, when I realized what Paul was doing."

"The…green threads?" I ask. "That was you?"

"Yes."

"Where are we?"

"A world very far from yours." The words torque in shots of chlorophyll green, sunflower yellow and shocking pink, rippling outward from his mouth as he speaks. I can listen to it, I realize, as the waves from his words wash over me. Like how fish can feel a shark approach. I can't help but smile, delighted by the incomparable variety of liquefied color around me.

"It's like nothing I've ever seen before."

"The farther one world is from another in the multiverse," he says, "the more distinct their physical laws will be. We call this region Chroma."

We? But I only have time for one question at a time.

"That doesn't make any sense. Shouldn't all worlds be governed by the same set of laws?"

The man shakes his head, creating ripples through the iridescence around him.

"The only fundamental framework every universe shares is at the most elementary level of particles," he says. "Quarks. Leptons. Bosons."

"But the interactions of the particles build outward to create the laws of physics."

"Ah," he says. "Yes, Noomi, you're right. But also wrong."

"How can I be both right and wrong at the same time?"

"How can the cat be both dead and alive at the same time?" He smiles. "The interactions of the fundamental particles build outward to create the laws of physics. But you understand the wavefunction and the instability that creates at a quantum level, yes?"

Quantum wavefunction? I remember reading about that in one of the books Mr. Arcadio gave me. A particle's possible location in space and time, as well as its momentum, can be mapped using a probabilistic wave-based function. I think that's what it said. But what does that have to do with this colorful world?

Instead of answering, I look around, trying to distract myself from the impossibility of his question by admiring the impossibility of my surroundings, the fantastical colors I could never have imagined. There are shades of blue deeper than the darkest ocean and whiter than the laziest cloud. Hues of red and orange so pale they seem to fade to nothing, and others more fiery than the sun. And there are colors that defy nomenclature that would require a whole new language to describe. I think about the Inuit cultures and how many hundreds of words they have for *ice*, and the jungle-based civilizations who have over three hundred words for *green*. I need those words right now.

Reluctantly, I turn back to the older man.

"I'm only in high school," I reply. "I'm good at physics, but I'm not *that* good."

"There's only one thing you need to know for this purpose," he says, the words washing over me like waves. He sounds like a professor; he sounds, once again, familiar. "The interactions of quantum particles are impossible to predict. All the laws of physics can do is estimate, based on a complex set of variables, how a particle will behave. On a large scale, as millions and billions of particles interact with each other, this creates instability, leading particles to behave in ways that follow certain sets of laws, but only according to probability curves. This is called quantum decoherence. Given this unpredictability, is it so impossible to believe that particles could interact slightly differently in different worlds, which could, throughout the expansion of time and space, build upon themselves to create vastly different outcomes and phenomena?"

I pause, trying to follow his line of thought.

"It's not impossible."

He nods. "As worlds split apart on the time-space continuum, their governing laws and systems become more and more distinct. This world, far afield from yours, is governed by an entirely different set of laws, one where photons, rather than electrons, are assembled together with quarks to create physical bodies."

"Why are there so many colors?" I ask. "Colors I don't have words for?"

"Here, your eyes are not bound by the cones within your pupils. You are made up of the material we are floating in. You don't technically *have* pupils, or cones. Your sentience here is an accident; and it's not wise to remain here for long, lest you, like the laws that bind you, begin to dissociate."

Fear tugs at my chest, a reminder that I'm not indestructible everywhere. What did Silas say? We fray. We dissociate. We dissolve.

"You said you threw me a lifeline. Why would you save me just to bring me somewhere that can destroy me?" The gravedigger laughs. The ripples from his motion ring across my skin and in my mind. Like a buzzing fly that won't go away, I can't shake the thought that his gestures and expressions are familiar.

"This place won't destroy you. On the contrary, it's a sanctuary—if a temporary one. The shadows can't find you here. At least—not yet." He pauses.

Yet? A million questions are running through my mind. When *will* they be able to find me here? Why are they coming for our world? How did you call me here? What is Paul doing to me?

He turns to look at me and it feels like I'm pinned, frozen in place, unable to move so long as our eyes are locked. "That man was leading you into a different world. Where the things you call shadows come from." His eyes are full of iridescent swirls and bubbles of a thousand colors that are as eerie as they are enticing. "You've been there."

I nod, remembering my dream of bamboo forests that morphed to columns that were then swallowed by the shadows. It's hard to recall the darkness, the heaviness, the weight, while I'm surrounded by so much color.

"Only in a dream."

"Remember this place, Noomi. The shadows can't find you here. If ever you need a quick escape, this is where to come. Here the vibrancy never fades. And it never will, unless the beings that are trying to consume your world consume millions more. They must eat their way through half the space-time continuum before they find their way here."

Beings? "Are the shadows alive?"

He doesn't answer. Instead, he turns away and stares off into what looks like a never-ending ocean of paint. Channels of it glide by us in iridescent streams. Bubbles of deep red and purple swarm over us. Pools of it form above and below, bleeding into their surroundings, blending together to create new, discrete colors.

Finally, tired of waiting for an answer that won't come, I ask a different question. "How is this a place of refuge if I can't stay here?"

"You can't stay in any world forever, Noomi. You will always be called to your home world. Over a long enough timeline in any world other than your own, you'll dissociate back into the fabric of the universe. The energy that binds you must ultimately be given back to the world it was taken from."

That doesn't answer my question, I think, annoyance morphing into anger. The colors that make him up, red, yellow, and green, bleed into my own violet-aquamarine, combining into wildly foreign colors, shiny and iridescent, colors I cannot name.

"Silas will be waiting for you when you return to your home world."

I remember his words when I met him in the dream: Silas is also a friend of mine.

"Call Saida and ask her to pick you up. Do not speak to that man again. He is trying to deliver you to them."

"But why?" I ask, coming to the source of my desperation. "Paul was my friend. Why is he helping them? Why now?"

He shakes his head, his expression troubled. When he finally speaks, his words surprise me.

"I don't know, Noomi. I've never known a Pathfinder to work with them."

I am quiet for a long moment, digesting this, before another question ripples up inside me.

"Who are you?" I ask.

"One day, maybe, I'll answer that question," he says. He comes closer, reaching a liquefied hand out to cup my chin. "On one timeline, in one world, I dug your grave. In another, I watch over you. Someday you'll recognize me. But until then, it's best that we remain...acquaintances."

I nod, and he releases my chin. I can understand a need for privacy. Or secrecy.

"We need to go." He looks down at his hands, and I follow his glance. His hands are fraying, his fingertips beginning to lose their structure, to dissolve into the swirling colors around us. "Our time is almost up." He closes his eyes, and I know he's searching for a Path home—wherever home is for him. I follow suit, letting my eyelids close, batting against my strange, gelatinous skin. In the darkness, the lines of the worlds appear, and I find one that calls to me, that sings of clear mountain air, mossy forests, and wood smoke. I fall back into it, wishing I didn't have to leave.

But something nags at me, even as my feet hit the ground, as I land solidly in the darkness, surrounded by trees and cold evening air and the smell of a distant campfire.

"There you are." Silas's voice rings out in the darkness.

The nagging becomes more persistent. I realize what's bothering me as his silhouette emerges from the trees. The gravedigger called my mother Saida. He knows her name. But even then, most people don't call her that. They call her Dr. Perez. Who calls her Saida?

The strangeness becomes more apparent as I think about it.

He knows my mother's name.

Gaslight

Gaslighting, an elaborate and insidious technique of deception and psychological manipulation, usually practiced by a single deceiver, or "gaslighter," on a single victim over an extended period. Its effect is to gradually undermine the victim's confidence in his own ability to distinguish truth from falsehood, right from wrong, or reality from appearance, thereby rendering him pathologically dependent on the gaslighter in his thinking or feelings." —Encyclopedia Britannica, "Gaslighting"

"Silas," I stutter, suddenly exhausted. I tremble, my knees starting to give way. He did warn me. Pathfinding is exhausting, he said. In a breath, he's at my side, supporting me, arms wrapped around my shoulders.

"Thank you," I sigh, relaxing into his hold. Warmth. Safety. "Who is he?"

"Who is who?"

"The gravedigger."

"What are you talking about?" He lifts my chin to look at me. "Noomi, are you all right?"

"I'm fine." I straighten, lock my knees, regain my balance. "The man who told you to come here, to find me. Who is he? He said he's watching over me."

He stares at me. "The person who told me to come here is a woman. Well…" He pauses. "At least, I think she is. At any rate, she's not from this world. She's not from any world you'd know."

My mind is fuzzy. I frown, staring into his forest-green eyes, thinking of all the shades of green I know and all the new, unimaginable greens I just saw.

"Noomi!" A voice booms through the forest. My heart crashes to a halt. I lock eyes with Silas. His are wide and worried. The voice rings out a second time, "Noomi, where'd you go?"

"It's Paul," I whisper. "He's close. I should have found a Path further away from the group."

Silas shakes his head. "There aren't many Paths from the color world. She had to make a new one to rescue you. You found the best one you could have. We need to get moving."

Silas takes my hand and leads me through the trees. "I have good night vision," he says.

Exhausted though I am, we stumble down the mountain, tripping over branches in the darkness. Silas finds a trail; it must be the same one that led us up here.

"We shouldn't be on the trail," I hiss. "They'll follow us."

"Noomi!" Paul's voice echoes through the forest again, closer than before. "Where the hell did you go?"

"We have to move," Silas says. "They'll have flashlights, they can go twice as fast as we can. We haven't got a chance unless we're on the trail."

But a light is dancing through the trees behind us, visible now, not more than two hundred feet away.

"Run!" I say, panicking, and now it's my turn to pull Silas, dragging him down the hill, tripping over rocks and roots as I go. But this is the wrong decision, there's too much noise, pebbles and dirt and branches are scrabbling everywhere and it's *loud*, so loud someone's bound to hear us, and then—

My foot lands on a slick rock and my whole body goes out from under me. I fall to the ground and Silas falls in a heap on top of me and I feel like I'm being crushed, but of course nothing breaks, there's no blood, no pain. Just the sound of footsteps jogging behind us and then a bright light in our faces and we're staring up like deer in the headlights, shading our eyes with our hands because the light is so bright it's practically a searchlight—maybe it is—

"Noomi," Paul says, the whites of his eyes gleaming and his cheekbones hollow. He looks monstrous in the shadowy light, though I'm not sure if that's because he actually looks scary or because I know what he's up to now. But the shadows are starting to crowd his flashlight, crawling out from inside me, glooming the light from the bulb and obscuring his face as they drip all around him. When he speaks, his voice is condescending, pretending. "What happened? Did you have a panic attack?" He looks at Silas, and his expression shifts. "What are you doing here?

I gasp. Revulsion crawls up my stomach and into my throat. "You can *see* him?"

And the shadows dissipate.

Paul opens his mouth to speak, and then closes it again, glaring at me. Silas pushes himself off me, stands. He holds a hand to me and pulls me from the rocks. Paul makes no motion to lower his flashlight, and I hold my arm up to shield my eyes from the light.

"You told me Silas didn't exist!" My voice is hoarse. I'm livid, trembling. "You told Dr. Chase I was inventing things. You made me believe I was inventing things! And now it turns out you can see him too?"

"Of course, I can see him," Paul says. His blue eyes glow in the backwash from his flashlight. "But none of the other humans can. I'm a Pathfinder too."

"Probably from some slimy world that's already been devoured by the shadows," Silas says. "That's why you're helping them. So, they'll keep you alive."

"And because no one else can see him, Noomi," Paul continues, ignoring Silas, "who do you think they're going to believe when I tell them you've had a breakdown and need to be committed? The delusional student or the gifted counselor?"

My jaw falls open. I stare at him, agape. Already the shadows are back. I can feel their weight on my shoulders, pressing me down, bending my spine toward the ground. Darkness dripping into hollow patches of moonlight, blooming in the bright white of the flashlight.

"Then they'll flood in through you, devour all the energy in your cruel, ignorant world, and there will be nothing either of you can do to stop it." He's staring at me, through me. His back straightens and his shoulders seem to swell. He's growing in height like a sapling in the spring. The shadow he casts stretches and looms like the trees around us. Only his blue eyes are visible, flashing like lightning in the darkness.

Silas crosses the space between him and Paul and throws a right hook. Paul's arms fly up to defend himself, but Silas's blow never falls. Instead he kicks out, his left foot crashing into Paul's knee, who cries out as his leg collapses. The shadows vanish. Light floods back into our world. Off-balance and lankier than he is strong, Paul can't recover in time to shield himself from the punch Silas throws, his fist connecting with Paul's nose.

He falls back, clutching his face, gasping. In the beam of his fallen flashlight, I can see blood dripping between his fingers.

Oh god, oh god, oh god—

"Run," Silas says. He whirls, grabs my hand, and pulls me in a sprint down the mountain.

My heart hammers as I scrabble for footing over the rocks and dirt. They're going to find us, they're going to lock me up, Paul is going to tell them all I've lost it. My fingers reach into my pocket, seeking my phone, even though I know I shouldn't check it now, should wait, but I can't. I pause for breath as my chest heaves and I glance at my phone, find that I have two dots, are we close enough now that I can call Mom? Can I escape this nightmare?

"Why don't we just Pathfind out?" My mind is whirling. There's no sign of Paul or anyone else, but I'm desperate to get away.

"Paul is closing all the Paths around us," he replies. There's an edge to him, a pulsing tension. Rage lurking below the surface I can feel and don't want to touch. But in my panic, I'm losing control, terrified energy bleeding out into everything I do and say. "Close your eyes and look for the threads. The only open paths lead us closer to the shadows. He's better than I gave him credit for. Many Pathfinders can't open and close Paths."

"Can you?"

He pauses before answering. "Yes," he says, his jaw tight. "But not as quickly. It takes time and focus. Right now, it would be dangerous. I won't risk it, not with Paul and the shadows all around us." He glances at the phone in my hand. "Do you have service?"

I nod, fingers flying across the screen, pulling up my mom's contact information and dialing her number. She picks up on the third ring.

"Noomi?" she says, her voice fluttering. "What's going on? Why are you—"

"I need you to pick me up." The words rush out like water in a stream. "Now."

"Are you okay?" she asks.

"No," I whisper. "I'm not."

WEIGHTLESS

"Weightlessness, *condition experienced while in free-fall, in which the effect of gravity is canceled by the inertial (e.g., centrifugal) force.*" —Encyclopedia Britannica, "Weightlessness"

Two hours later, Silas and I are sitting in the darkness a few hundred feet from the wooden sign that marks the trailhead and parking lot. The van we came in gleams under the tarnished moonlight. We sit in silence, exhausted from the terror of betrayal and the charge down the mountain. Silas's head rests on my shoulder, and he nods forward every few minutes, dozing off. I'm too wired to sleep, too exhausted to move or think.

I hear an engine in the distance. Silas sits up and shakes his head. A moment later, the white headlights roll into the parking lot. I leap to my feet and Silas slowly stands up behind me.

"Will you be okay?" I ask.

"I'll be fine," he assures me, his voice thick with fatigue. "I'll find a Path home and get some rest, check in on you in a few hours."

"Okay." My voice is strained. I don't want him to leave. But the car is driving up and in a few moments I'll have to justify making Mom drive two hours into the mountains and somehow retain a shred of credibility. So I give Silas a hug before the headlights fall on us, and then wave him back into the darkness as the car rounds the bend. The headlights are blinding. I hold my hand up to shade my eyes.

"Noomi," Mom cries, leaping out of the car, running up to me when she sees me standing by the side of the road. Ada is in the back seat, her fingers pressed against the glass, looking out at us with concern. "What's wrong? Are you okay?"

"Thank you for coming to get me. We have to go. It's Paul."

"Paul? I thought you liked him. What happened?"

"He..." I've had two hours to find an explanation that will make sense to my mom, but I I'm coming up empty. Tell the truth and she won't believe me. Tell a lie and I'll trap myself in it when he tells everyone I hit him. "He was being terrible, Mama," I whisper, my voice breaking.

"I thought he was one of the good ones," she says, smoothing my hair as she presses me to her chest. "Did he hurt you?"

"Not physically." She pulls back, staring at me.

"Sexually?" Her voice is pained, tense. I shake my head, unsure how to explain. There was nothing sexual about it, but the memory of his hand on my knee sends a shudder through my spine.

"Can we talk in the car?" I glance around, nervous. Leah or Paul could come dashing down the hillside at any moment.

"I need you to tell me what happened, Noomi, in case we have to go to the police. The other counselors will be looking for you."

"No," I say, setting my mouth in a thin line. "It wasn't sexual. Not really." My voice condenses, shrinking down into something so tiny I can barely hear it. I say a prayer in my mind: please believe me, Mom. Please believe me.

"It was...the shadows. He was...bringing them to me."

Her expression changes. Her eyes narrow, her mouth sets in a firm line. She frowns. My heart falls to the bottom of my shoes.

"Noomi," she says, her voice shaking. "You can't blame your panic attacks on your counselor."

"They're not panic attacks!" I explode, tears spilling out of my eyes and down my cheeks. "You've never believed me that these things are real, and they're hurting me! You won't listen to me when I tell you what's really going on!"

"Let's go," she says, turning to pull me to the car.

"No," I reply, jerking my arm back and away from her. I pull the Swiss army knife out of my pocket and flick it open. "I can prove it," I say, pressing the blade to the skin of my wrist as Mom watches in horror. I slice the blade against my skin but it's dull and the skin doesn't even break, and she shouts with fear and leaps toward me, grabbing my hand and yanking it away from my other wrist. I try to fight, but she pries the knife from my fingers and jerks away, out of reach.

"Noomi," she says, her voice shaking. "I have to take you to the hospital. I can't let you hurt yourself." And then, glancing at the car: "How could you do this in front of Ada?"

"Ada understands far more than you give her credit for," I snap. "I'm not afraid of what she thinks of me."

"Get in the car," she says, her voice lower and with a dangerous edge.

Angrily I open the door and throw myself in.

"Are you okay?" Ada asks from the back, her voice small.

"No, little Peach, I'm not. I'll tell you everything later."

Mom gets in, slams the door, and shifts into drive.

We pull away in terse silence. And then I can feel them again. The shadows. Just like earlier with Paul. The blackness pressing against my vision. They're everywhere. I close my eyes and rub my temples. The gravedigger gave me a way out. "If you ever need an escape, this is where to come." But I can't Pathfind here, sitting in the car with my mom and sister. The shock of me vanishing will frighten them off the road.

I have to fight them. Here.

I remember how I fought them with Paul, as Silas and I charged down the mountain. I did it then. How?

"I'm taking you to the hospital, Noomi," Mom is saying. Her voice sounds distant and distorted. Foggy clouds, devoid of light, settling around me. Oily tentacles snaking through the air.

I think back to the confrontation with Paul, but the air is already thick with them, and my mind is slow and groggy. What happened when he brought them to me? How did I fight them? He said something that made me angry. I remember that. I try to get angry again: at my mother for not believing me; at Paul for betraying me.

But the anger won't come. All I can find is listlessness. Apathy. Exhaustion.

"Noomi," Ada says. "Look at me." I open my eyes and turn, leaning over the center arm rest to look back at her, trying to get my bearings in a world that is swimming with disembodied shadows. I stare at her. She's a beacon of light. A tree of pale green tendrils of light shoot off from her body and dart through the car like vines. "Your eyes are black again." She's watching me, unmoving.

"What are you doing?" I ask, in a daze.

"It's my lantern." The light radiating from Ada seems to be waging war against the shadows, but the shadows are winning. "But it's not strong enough," she says, her voice growing higher—a gentle whine.

"What are you two talking about?" Mom says. It sounds like she's speaking from another room. From another world.

The fingers of my mind reach out tentatively, blindly, feeling in the darkness for a Path. But nothing catches; nothing snags. There are no Paths. There's no way out. The thought occurs to me dully, like an idea that comes to you as you're rousing from a deep sleep. Silas's words drift up to me as if from a dream: Paul is closing them all around us.

I try to remember the neon orange and violet colors from Chroma, or the pale blue bioluminescence of my hands after the dream. But the memories won't come. Everything is fading. Everything is dying.

"Look at her eyes, Mama," Ada says.

I can't move. I feel heavy and hollow. Mom stares at me. All I can see are the whites of her eyes. Then they too are swallowed by the darkness.

"They're so dark." Mom's voice is slow too. Slow and dull and empty.

"Look out!" Ada screams shrilly, her shriek piercing the air like a blade.

Fear thrums through me, and the shadows pull back like a bag pulled off my head, like a curtain being lifted, and I can see again but there's nothing to see, everything is black, the car is drenched in it, my mother's eyes are impenetrably dark, and something is terribly wrong.

Gravity—it's gone.

The car. We're soaring, weightless. Off the road.

Now bumping. Crumbling. With a sharp jerk forward, the airbags explode and we come to an abrupt stop.

Seconds pass.

Ada, in the back, starts crying. I inhale. The cold air against the back of my throat tells me: I'm alive. Ada's alive.

Instinct kicks in.

The car is relatively level. We must have gone off the side of the road and hit something. A tree? Guardrail? I can't see outside. It's dark, but natural dark. The shadows are gone.

Mom is quiet. Unmoving. Slumped against the back of the seat, her head lolling slightly to the side. I reach out for her hand. The airbags are in the way but I push them aside and find her hand. Put two fingers to her wrist.

There's no pulse.

There's no pulse.

"Mom," I whisper.

I scramble into action. Push my car door open. The overhead light comes on, but the door only opens a few inches before connecting with a tree, or a rock, or something. The metal grates against stone. I try again, pushing harder, panting. It doesn't open. I go the other way—squeezing through the middle of the seat into the back, jerking the lever on the door opposite Ada, who by now is sobbing. I don't try to calm her. To my relief, the door opens. I jump out and pull the driver's side door. It swings open. As I squeeze into the seat next to Mom, I can just make out the enormous tree we crashed into, the trunk at least four feet around. There's shrub and brush all around us and heavy shadows overhanging. I stare at her smooth face, barely touched by the wrinkles of age, pressing one palm to her cheek and two fingers to the vein at her neck. I hold it there, trying to calm my breathing, trying not to distort any sensation in my fingers with my panic.

While I wait, holding my whole body still and staring at nothing, I notice the clock on the dashboard.

9:37, it reads.

There.

A pulse beneath my fingers.

She's alive.

I press my fingers to her cheeks and then slap her lightly several times. No response. I look her over, searching for a sign of injury. Her chest is compressed between the airbag and the seat. I put my hands on her ribs, feeling for broken bones, a punctured lung.

"You're the doctor, not me." My voice breaks. I fumble in my pocket, pulling out my cell phone, thanking anything in this world that might be holy that I have two bars of service, enough to call someone, enough to dial 9-1-1 as quickly as my slippery, shaking fingers will let me. I press the phone to my ear with my shoulder while my hands resume searching, checking her torso, her spine, her shoulders.

"What's your emergency?"

"Help," I whisper. "My mom drove off the side of the road. She's not conscious."

"What's your location?"

I rack my brain.

"Highway 20."

"Do you know where?"

My mind flutters, blank and empty. Wind rippling through the open spaces like a tattered flag.

"West. West of the mountains."

"What mile marker?"

"We're…we're not far from the Table Rock trailhead. Ten, fifteen minutes west. That's all I know. Please come soon."

"I'm dispatching an ambulance and the nearest patrol cars right now. If you have any flares or emergency lights, put them on. The officers need to know where to find you. Now listen to me." I jam my fingers on the triangular button for the emergency flashers and try to focus on the woman's words. "Are you personally hurt in any way?"

"No," I reply. "I can't—" I can't be hurt, I stop myself from saying. "I'm fine."

"If at any point you start to feel dizzy, or your head or neck starts to hurt—"

"I'm fine. I promise you, I'm fine."

There's a brief pause on the other end. Then, "Did you check your mother for a pulse?"

"Yes. It's there."

"Is she breathing?" Oh, god. How could I have forgotten to check for breathing? I hold my hand over her mouth and nose. A faint breath rustles my fingertips.

"Yes, she's breathing."

"Can you see any serious injuries? Blood, bones?"

"No. Nothing."

"Okay. Listen to me," she says again. I press the phone harder to my ear. "It's possible your mother suffered spinal cord or nervous system damage, which could be why she isn't responsive. There could also be internal damage. But as long as her airways are open and she has a pulse, you need to focus on your surroundings. Look around you. Is there any open flame in the car engine?"

I stand up and scramble forward, glancing at the hood. "Not that I can see. It's crumpled but that's all."

"Good. Is anyone else in the car besides you and your mother?"

"Yes. My sister, Ada."

"Is she okay?"

"I think so."

"I need you to check over your sister. Go to her and make sure she's not bleeding, there are no broken bones, that she's responsive."

I leave Mom, leaping into the back seat where Ada is sitting as if paralyzed, the light that was radiating out from her now completely gone, tears streaking down her face, her hair a mess and her eyes glassy and wide.

"Ada, are you okay? Are you hurt anywhere?" She nods a little, and my heart flutters in panic. "Where? Can you tell me?" She presses her palms to her chest where her seatbelt is, and I unbuckle the seat belt to get a better look. I pull her shirt off and squint in the dim light to see what's wrong. A yellowish blue bruise is already forming on her chest where the seatbelt held her in place, but I can't see anything else. I press my fingers to her skin where her palm was a moment ago. "Here?"

She nods, her breathing calmer now, her sobs quieting. "Is Mom okay?"

I can't meet her eyes.

This is my fault.

"I don't know, Ada."

I couldn't fight off the shadows. I'm a danger to everyone around me. This wouldn't have happened if I had been stronger. If I hadn't panicked and called Mom.

If I were never here in the first place.

"Ma'am, is your sister okay?" The voice on the phone calls me back to reality.

"She's bruised, but I think she's fine."

"There's an officer in your area who should be there within a few minutes. Put on your emergency lights. Do you know where to find those?"

"Yes," I whisper.

"Good. Put on the emergency lights and take your sister and go stand by the side of the road. Not *on* the road, do you understand? By the side of the road. Do you have a flashlight or flares?"

"I don't know." My voice like a ghost.

"Check the back of your car for flares or a flashlight."

"This is my fault." I don't mean to say it, but the words slip out.

"It's not your fault, hon. There's an officer who'll be with you in just a moment, and the ambulance is on the way. I need you to stay calm, all right?"

This is my fault.

I should have died.

Ada reaches up with a thumb and wipes the tears off my cheeks.

"It's okay, Noomi," she says. "I'm okay."

It's not okay.

It will never be okay.

Black Body Spectra

"A blackbody is an ideal surface, which satisfies three conditions. First, it is a perfect emitter. Thus, for a specified temperature and wavelength, a blackbody emits more radiant energy than any other surface at the same temperature. Second, a blackbody is the best absorber of energy. Therefore, it absorbs all energies incident on it from all directions and at all wavelengths. Third, a blackbody is a diffuse emitter. In other words, the radiant energy emitted from a blackbody is only a function of temperature and wavelength but is independent of direction…Historically, Joseph Stefan in 1879 suggested that the total emissive power of a blackbody is proportional to the fourth power of the absolute temperature." —Mahmoud Massoud, *Engineering Thermofluids*

The lights in this room are too bright. They must do it on purpose, to make people uncomfortable. That's why the chairs hurt too—and why all I have on the table in front of me is a small cup of coffee. I don't even drink coffee.

"What were you doing in the woods away from your group?"

"I was afraid."

"What were you scared of?" I don't like the way he says *scared*. As if I were a child hiding in a closet rather than a teenager who will be able to vote and die in foreign wars in a year. As if he doesn't believe my fear is reasonable. As if he doesn't believe me.

"My counselor. Paul."

"Paul Abrahams?"

"Yes." My voice so quiet, like a butterfly's wings.

"Why were you afraid of Paul, Miss Perez?"

"He was…hurting me."

If I didn't know better, I'd swear the officer's face was made of oak. His expression never changes. Thin lines like wood grains run down his skin, the edges of wrinkles that will form over the next decade. His eyes, heavily lidded, lift to mine as he waits for an answer. It's only his eyes that move. His chin remains firmly angled toward the paper.

"Where was he hurting you?"

"I—it wasn't physical."

"Sexual?"

I hold his gaze, uncomfortable but determined. He *must* believe me.

"Sort of," I say. "He didn't—you know. But he was… harassing me."

"He didn't *what*, Miss Perez?"

I release a deep breath. "He didn't…we didn't do anything sexual. It wasn't like that."

Officer Larsen tilts back on his chair for a moment, surveying me, his lip slightly curled. I narrow my eyes and say nothing.

An hour ago, when they asked me to tell my side of the story, the officers acted like I wasn't in trouble. Officer Larsen read me my rights and told me that I had the right to refuse to speak to them any time, although it would help their investigation if I would tell them what happened.

Anything to help my mother, I thought as I walked into this cold, unwelcoming space. Anything to redeem myself.

Anything to keep Paul away, I thought, hoping desperately that by talking to them and telling them what happened, they would lock him up and keep him far, far away from me.

Oh, how wrong I was.

"Did Paul Abrahams attempt to have sex with you?" I shake my head, feeling like a child: timid, unsure, and out of control.

"I need a verbal answer for the record, Miss Perez."

"No," I say. "He didn't."

"Did he attempt to take off your clothes?"

"No."

"Did he take his clothes off in front of you?"

"No."

"Did he touch you inappropriately?"

I hesitate. I don't want to continue. Paul was my friend, and I'm about to ruin his life. My jaw clamps up and I stare soundlessly across the table at the officer. But then, didn't he try to take me to the shadow world? Didn't he lie to me about Silas?

"Please answer the question, Miss Perez."

"Yes. He did."

Earlier, with Ada in my lap and Abuela clutching my hand, whispering prayers to her god, I contemplated what was coming. Over and over, I wondered what the police would say, how I would explain to them what happened. I walked through every theoretical direction this conversation might go. Every myriad possible world, splitting open before my eyes as the officer questioned me. I knew I couldn't tell them the truth. I can't tell them about demons no one else believes are real, or that Paul touching me wasn't about sex but about dragging me through the pores in our world into a destroyed corner of the universe so the shadows can suck the energy out of our world. The very thought of trying to explain all that is laughable. The police would think I'm insane. They'll drug me into a stupor, lock me up, and throw away the key.

Until recently, I might have believed I was insane too. I might have believed I was the one losing myself. But Claire and Kalifa saw the darkness in my eyes. The shadows blinded my mother on the road. It's not just me anymore.

Mom hasn't woken up yet. The doctors are keeping her unconscious until they're sure they won't have to operate. Abuela won't leave her side, and Ada, though mostly unharmed, hasn't spoken a word since the EMTs arrived at the car.

I think of Chroma, the color world, the viscous, brilliant colors bleeding into everything, the gravedigger's liquid hand touching my cheek, the strange familiarity of his expression, and his words: here the vibrancy never fades.

But I don't feel colorful. I feel as black as the shadows. An old science fair project from freshman year emerges from my memory. Kalifa and I researched black body phenomena, also known as thermal radiation, for the project.

Black bodies absorb all radiation that falls upon them, and therefore are non-reflective, we wrote. *The energy must be emitted, however, or the temperature of the body would grow to infinity. The energy is radiated out across all wavelengths in a way that corresponds to the overall temperature of the body. Black holes are examples of black body phenomena, as are stars.*

"Can you describe what Paul did to you, Noomi?"

Black bodies are so named because at room temperature, the thermal energy they radiate is not visible to the human eye.

"He...we were supposed to be doing a group meditation. I was angry at him. He'd done something earlier that made me mad."

"What was that?"

"He said..." Again, I search for a lie that will make sense. What *had* Paul done? I still don't understand how he brought the shadows down around me like black curtains. It was so quick—faster than they'd ever come before. One minute I was walking in the green of the forest; the next, the ink was everywhere.

"He said mean things about one of my friends. I think it was a joke, but I was mad anyway." A lie, but harmless enough.

Larsen shrugs. "Okay. Go on."

I take a deep breath. "I was mad at Paul. He came over and sat next to me in the circle. Too close. Awkwardly close. I tried to move away, but it was dark, and no one noticed when he moved closer. Then Leah—our group leader—started the meditation. We're not supposed to move around when we're meditating. So, I sat there. And Paul...put his hand on my knee."

I pause, remembering what happened after that. Wondering how to translate it for the man in front of me.

As the temperature of the black body rises, the thermal energy it emits approaches the low end of the visible spectrum. First, it glows a low, dim red.

"What happened next?" the officer asks.

"He—" I take a deep breath, closing my eyes. "He slid his hand up my leg, and I brushed him off. It made me feel...bad. I didn't want him to touch me. He did it again, and I brushed him off again. When he did it again, a third time, that's when I left." That's as true as it's going to get.

"That's it?" Larsen asks, disbelief in his voice. "That's all he did? Put his hand on your leg?"

"Yes," I say. I fix the officer with a cold stare. "It was enough."

"Enough to make you run away?"

At the approximate temperature of the Sun, the black body appears on the yellow-green visible light spectrum.

"Yes."

He holds my gaze for a long second before looking at his papers. "What happened then, Miss Perez?"

"I stood up. I left the campfire. But Paul stayed. Maybe he thought it would look weird to follow me." I'm talking fast now, the lies tumbling out of my mouth, spilling across the ground like marbles. "So, I left, but I didn't know where to go. To my tent? Paul would find me there. I was panicked. So I ran."

"Where did you go?"

"I kept running." I pause. "I don't think they noticed I was gone, and when I didn't hear anyone following me, I stopped. Then…I heard Paul calling my name."

"Did you see him again?"

I am quiet for a moment. "Yes."

"Miss Perez, Mr. Abrahams has told us that you hit and kicked him. He has a black eye and bruised ribs. Did you physically assault Mr. Abrahams?"

As the black body surpasses approximately 8,000 degrees Kelvin, the light emitted takes on a vibrant blue hue.

"No," I whisper. "Paul is lying. I didn't hit him." But I can't say the second part: Silas did.

As I fight the urge to say his name, something flashes through my mind. Not quite a memory. I press my fingers to my temples as it rolls over me. Cavernous spaces that press in on me. Dark green and grey colors weaving around me, above me. Breathing something not quite like air. Gasping for breath.

But then it's gone. As quickly as it came. I glance up at the officer, but he's staring at his file and hasn't noticed anything. I feel around in my mind for what it could be. A buried memory? A forgotten dream?

But nothing comes.

"For the record, you claim that you did not physically assault Paul Abrahams in any way?" Larsen asks.

"That's right."

"The last time you saw Mr. Abrahams, did he appear to be hurt or injured?"

"No." Another lie.

"You have no knowledge of how Mr. Abrahams would have come to have a black eye and bruised ribs?"

I shake my head. "No."

Larsen pauses. He glances at my file, riffling through the pages. "All right then, Miss Perez. What happened when Mr. Abrahams caught up to you?"

"We—I—just kept running." At the word *we*, the officer glances up at me.

"We? Was there someone else with you?"

My heart pounds. "I didn't mean to say that. It was just me and Paul."

"And what happened then?"

"At some point, I couldn't hear him following me anymore. Maybe he tripped trying to keep up with me. I heard him shouting like he was mad, or in pain, but I couldn't hear what he was saying." The lies tumble out of my mouth. "All I wanted was to get away from him." That much, at least, was true.

"What happened next?"

"I kept running, all the way down, until I came to the parking lot at the trailhead. I got a few bars of service and called my mom to come pick me up."

"What did she say?"

"She said she'd be there as soon as she could. But we live nearly two hours away. It took a long time."

"Your wilderness group was looking for you the whole time."

"We—I—stayed out of their way."

"What happened when your mother arrived?"

"I got into the car. She was angry with me."

"Why?"

"She…she didn't believe me about Paul. She didn't believe he'd been…doing what he did." I blink back tears. Is that why the shadows came? Because I was vulnerable? Because I was mad at her?

I shake my head, trying to clear the guilt, the anger from my mind.

"What did you do?" Larsen asks.

"Nothing. I got into the car and my mom drove off. We were still arguing when she drove the car off the road."

"Where were you sitting?"

"In the passenger seat."

Officer Larsen stares at me, and then flips a paper over in the file in front of him. "Your mother was not intoxicated in any way when she drove off the road, but the initial forensic report indicates that the car flew off the road at approximately twenty-five miles per hour and collided head-on with a tree. Is this true?"

"Yes, we crashed into a tree," I whisper. "I don't know how fast we were going."

"From your vantage point in the passenger seat, did you see anything in the road that might have caused your mother to swerve?"

Just the shadows, I think, fighting back tears. But I can't tell them that.

"No. I didn't see anything."

"Can you tell us what happened right before the crash?"

"I…I think I was having a panic attack."

"And then what?"

"And then…and then she drove off the road."

He looks up at me. "You didn't grab the wheel at any point?"

"No."

"Did you touch her at any point?"

"No."

"Do anything that could have distracted her from the task of driving?"

"No."

"Miss Perez," the officer says, his voice taking on a formal tone. "This is the second time in under a month you have been involved in what could have been fatal incidents. In both cases, you were completely unharmed. In the first, you escaped from a massive fire at an abandoned barn. You emerged from this inferno with no clothes—" he glances up from his file and he looks at me in a way that makes my skin crawl "—but unhurt, though the barn and parts of the surrounding area were destroyed. In the second, which happened a few hours ago, your mother crashed her car into a tree and has been hospitalized in a medically-induced coma. Your sister was bruised and has whiplash. But you, again, are uninjured."

As the temperature rises, the radiation emitted from the body appears a blinding white. This indicates that the black body is now radiating light across every wavelength of the visible spectrum.

I can feel the heat rising in my face. The anger. At myself for failing to protect Ada and Mom. And at the officer for forcing me to relive these moments I want to forget.

"What are you saying?" I demand.

"In my experience," the officer says, "people don't usually turn up at the scene of a crime for no reason. Especially when they come out the other side unscathed. And especially—" he fixes me with that blank, empty stare "—not when it happens twice in a row."

"I get it," I say, too loudly. "You think I set that fire. You think I drove us off the road. You think I *want* to hurt people." I'm on the edge of my seat. "That I want to hurt myself so badly I'll destroy everyone around me."

"Miss Perez—"

"You think I'm trying to hurt my family?" I shout, my hands on the table. The officer pulls away. "You think I'd hurt

Ada? My mom? You think I'm crazy enough to do this shit on *purpose*? I don't want to hurt anyone, it just keeps happening!"

Larsen pushes back his chair, standing up, walking around to me, just as I realize what I've said. But it's too late, Larsen has a pair of handcuffs out and I might as well have said I did it, not intentionally but I did it. I might as well have handed him a confession.

An example of a nearly-ideal black body is a supermassive black hole, which forms when very massive stars can no longer sustain the energy they are expending and collapse onto themselves.

"No," I whisper. "No, this isn't real. This is just my imagination, this is just a dream, just like Silas, like the shadows, like the color world, like everything else." The world starts to spin, my head pounding, my skin feeling like it isn't a part of my body. I close my eyes, determined not to see, not to watch this happen.

"Noomi Perez, you are under arrest in connection with crimes of arson and assault." I lean over to the side of the chair and retch—empty of substance, it's just a dry heave—as he pulls my hands in front of me and clicks the cuffs closed. My breath catches and I swallow a sob. I open my eyes, watery from vomiting, and stare at the floor. Beige linoleum with crosshatching squares in a pattern that vaguely resembles the flooring in our school bathrooms, and a brief moment of clarity leaves me shocked by the banality of this observation. How can I think about something like that at a time like this?

And then Larsen's hand goes to my elbow and he jerks me up out of my seat, and I am thrown back into the moment. His palm digs into my back, pushing me forward. I close my eyes again as I walk into a future so real that I could never have imagined it.

Cigarette Burns

"People assume that time is a strict progression of cause to effect, but actually, from a non-linear, non-subjective viewpoint, it's more like a big ball of wibbly wobbly, timey-wimey... stuff."
—The BBC's Doctor Who, Episode 3.10, "Blink"

I stare at the ceiling, tracing an invisible pattern in the polished cement. The springs from the cot press through the thin mattress and into my back. I adjust my spine and shoulders for the hundredth time. It does no good. The springs dig into my skin, albeit at a slightly different angle, but the discomfort is no better or worse.

At least my eyes are finally dry.

In what world could I have predicted that I, a 4.0 student with honors in every class, would end up on a cold mattress in a cement box at four in the morning? What set of equations account for my arrival in this strange room with three walls and a set of iron bars? Surely Newton's equations could not have predicted this future. Einstein's relativity cannot explain the dramatic warping of spacetime in my world. The threads of the world cannot possibly have woven to create the reality I am currently living.

And yet, here I am.

I trace another spiral in the cement ceiling, radiating outwards from the dim lightbulb in the center of the room, curling around itself until it reaches the walls.

What will Kalifa say?

Claire?

I can't expect them to be friends with me after I've spent a night in jail. Who will want to be friends with the girl who can add *criminal* to the list of words that describe her?

What will I tell Ada?

It's been four hours since Officer Larsen walked me—dragged me—into this cell in the station and closed the door behind me. Four hours since I essentially admitted complicity to setting fire to the Morelands' barn and crashing my mother's car. Four hours since I thought I might escape this mess unscathed.

No one will escape unscathed, I've realized. Not me. Not Ada. Not my mother. Not my friends. Not Silas. We will all be irrevocably changed by my failure to fight the shadows—and myself.

"Silas," I whisper. The word slips out of my mouth, unintentional. I glance around, half-startled, wondering if I said it or if I imagined it. Imagined my lips moving, imagined the tremor in my vocal cords, imagined the waves of sound against my ears. Can I trust my senses? I no longer know.

But as I glance around the room, I realize that Silas is there. Sitting in the corner. In the jail cell. With me.

I sit up abruptly. He's on the floor, elbows resting on his knees. His head reclines gently against the wall. His eyes are closed.

I stare at him.

"Am I imagining you?"

"You've asked me that before, Noomi." He sounds exhausted. "I'm real. I promise." He inclines his head. "Paul's real, isn't he? And he could see me."

I look away, remembering just a few hours ago, embarrassed that I doubted him again. That I doubted myself.

"Of course," I say. "Sorry." It's been a wild night, I think, but I keep that to myself. "What are you doing here?"

"I said I'd check on you."

"Oh," I say. "Yeah." In the face of everything else, I'd forgotten that too.

Silas looks up and around, surprised to see where we are: in a prison cell.

Another fragmented vision bursts into my mind. Like earlier when I was sitting across from the officer and I felt like I was in a cave or a tunnel, a massive emptiness pressing down on me. But this time it's not that. It's a vision of *myself*. Sitting here exactly where I am, on this cot in this cinder block cell. I'm watching myself, like in a dream where you're both falling and watching yourself fall.

I close my eyes as the vision washes over me. Just like before, it's over as soon as it's begun. I press my fingertips to my temples, feeling Silas's eyes on me.

"What happened?" he asks. His voice carefully neutral. It sounds like it took a lot to keep his tone so even.

The thought of relaying the events of the evening to Silas makes me wonder if I'm going to cry again. But when I open my mouth, words arrive there intact. My voice hoarse but steady. My throat as dry as my eyes.

"I think…I told them I did it. They brought me here for questioning. I got angry. The officer didn't believe me. What I was telling him about Paul. I got angry and started shouting. I didn't mean to say what I did. It didn't come out right. But it sounded a lot like a confession."

"What did you say?"

Two hours ago, the memory would have been like a knife in the gut. Now, I just feel empty.

"I said, 'Do you think I'm trying to hurt my family?'" I emphasize the same word I did then, when I was facing the officer. "I said, 'I don't want to hurt anyone. It just keeps happening.'"

Silas holds my gaze a moment longer before letting his head slide back to the wall, closing his eyes again.

"I don't know much about the law, Noomi, but that doesn't sound like a confession to me. Especially considering you're a minor."

"I as good as told them I did it."

"You made some vague statements that could easily be misconstrued. You didn't admit to anything. I doubt they'll have much of a case, especially once you get a lawyer."

"A lawyer?"

Silas blinks at me. "They read you your Miranda rights, didn't they?"

"Well, yes, but—"

"You have the right to be represented by an attorney. The courts will appoint one, if your family doesn't hire one for you. Your attorney will argue that you were under undue stress while being questioned and that your statements shouldn't be permissible in court."

I consider this revelation. I didn't know any of this. Is it possible? Is it possible there's a way out? The hope is too tantalizing to consider, the future too inscrutable. I've gone over the memory of my interview with Larsen more times than I can count in the last four hours, and I don't have the energy to do it again.

I grip the sides of my cot and change the subject.

"You seem tired," I say, trying to make it sound less like an insult and more like a question.

He takes a deep breath. "I followed the Paths Paul was making for the shadows." He hesitates. "Or they made for him. I'm not sure which is which. At any rate, I followed them down."

"You went after the shadows? What did you find?"

"It's...difficult to describe. But you probably know better than anyone." There's a long silence. I assume he's searching for the right words. I wait, letting him gather his thoughts. "I followed their energy patterns. The shadows leave trails of nothingness behind them. Dead space. No energy. No movement. It's easy to follow once you can see them. I followed them down." He stares at the wall. "Down is maybe too simple. It's not down so much as it is *back through*."

"Back through time?"

He reaches into his pocket and pulls out a piece of stiff drawing paper, folded into quarters. He hands it to me, and I open it tentatively, unsure what to expect.

"More like…back toward the beginning. It's both temporal and spatial."

On the front of the paper is another of Silas's drawings. He has a distinct style, with vivid colors and structured shapes and an undercurrent of absurdist imagery that could only come from someone's wild imagination—or visits to other worlds. This piece looks like an optical illusion drawn by M. C. Escher with added details by Dr. Seuss. There are tunnels that look like cyclones connecting about fifteen globular, unbounded spaces. They burrow and twist through and around each other, and the spaces are color-coded by vibrant expressions of the colors of the rainbow. At the bottom of the drawing is a black hole that drains away off the page. At the top, the colors are brightest and most vibrant. As the drawing moves from top to bottom, the colors fade into black, white, and grey.

"It's the multiverse," he says. "As best I can understand it."

"Wow." I sit back, stunned. Not only by the quality of the drawing but also by the careless way he handles his work. The paper is crumpled and lined with creases from being folded over and over. Some of the ink is smudged, particularly at the corners. But the artistry shines through.

I point to the bottom of the page. "Is that where the shadows are coming from?"

"Yes."

"And this," I point to the top, "is where the color world is? Chroma?"

"I think so." He sighs. "It's hard to explain because I don't really understand it. We're three-dimensional creatures. I can't see all the dimensions of spacetime, so I can't imagine them. I followed them down, or back, whichever you want to call it."

I start to hand the drawing to him, but he waves me off. "Keep it," he says. "It's yours." I nod and fold it up, trying to do so more carefully than he did, but the paper is already so wrinkled, it doesn't matter. I slide it into my pocket.

"The gravedigger said the shadows would have to travel a long way to reach the color world."

"Who is this gravedigger you keep talking about? You mentioned him last night."

"I don't know." I shake my head. "I've seen him twice, but never in this world. Once in a dream, and once in Chroma."

"Did he say anything else about the shadows?"

I rack my brain. I was stressed and afraid when I was there. It's hard to remember everything. "He said they would have to eat their way through a lot of other worlds before they got to Chroma."

Silas nods. "I think that's what they're doing here too. They're growing. Gaining strength by feeding on other, weaker worlds." He fixes his gaze on me. "You're their only portal to this world, Noomi. You have to stop them."

"I'm trying." I sigh. "Isn't it a good thing, if they're not attacking me right now?"

He shrugs. "It could be. But it could mean that when the attack comes, it'll be a thousand times more powerful than before."

I shudder.

His eyes glaze over as he stares at the wall. "As I went back, I touched the edges of so many worlds that don't exist anymore. They're just… empty. Hollowed out."

"I know the feeling," I murmur.

His eyes are wide and unfocused, as if he's in a trance. "It was like cigarette burns on a blanket. Holes in the fabric of spacetime. Patches. Not like the Paths we use to travel—no, these were holes where there should have been worlds. The places where there should have been something were nothing. They were…zeroed out. Empty."

"Did you find them?" I ask. "The shadows?"

"No," he says. He shakes his head, as if to shake off the memories. "I couldn't continue. Following all those Paths was exhausting. I don't think the shadows see me as an energy source like they do you, but I could feel how draining they were. Every time I got close to them, I felt like I was falling asleep, or unconscious. I couldn't stay."

"Was it…hard? Being so close to them?"

"It was terrible," he admits. "I don't know how you handle it." He looks at me. "Close your eyes, Noomi."

I obey, and the familiar lines, the dim but colorful threads of the world, illuminate the backs of my eyelids.

"Keep your eyes closed and look at me."

When I turn to Silas, the lines around him are pulsing a low, reddish orange.

"Now look at yourself."

I hold my arms out. The lines around me are a rich blue, the color of a deep, crystal-clear ocean. Then I straighten my spine and look down at my legs, my torso. The energy there, in my chest and belly, is a deeper blue, pure and crystalline and dark.

"Look at all that energy. So bright." There's almost jealousy in his voice. "Getting so close to them…it sucked a lot of it out of me. My colors are usually a brighter green, higher up on the spectrum. Not today." The colored lines that make him up change shape as he presses his head back against the wall. "But even on my brightest days, I'm no match for you. This is how they find you, Noomi. You're the most powerful ball of energy walking around in this world. In most of the nearby worlds. And, like the shadows, your energy is growing."

"How do you know?" I ask, looking at myself in awe.

"I've watched it happen."

"You don't sound happy for me."

"I'm worried, Noomi. I'm worried about what's going to happen when the shadows try to come back. I'm worried that your energy is growing so strong that if they come through you again, they'll suck half the multiverse with you."

I push this dark thought away to ask the question that's been on my mind since Silas told me he followed the shadows down to wherever they came from. "Why?" I ask. "Why did you do it?"

"I need to know," he says. "You've been dealing with them for years, but I've only touched the edges of what they're capable of. If we're going to fight them, I need to know what we're up against."

I stare at him. The rush of emotion I feel when he says this is so overwhelming that first it registers as emptiness. Too much to process. Several seconds go by as I think about his words. Silas is the first person to take the shadows seriously. To truly understand what I'm fighting. And tonight, after helping me escape the man who was bringing the shadows to me, he voluntarily sought out them out—the devastating creatures that have been haunting me for almost a decade—chasing them through the fabric of the world so he could *learn* about them.

And he did it all to help me. To help me fight them off. Without prompting. Without demands. With no promises of safety or compensation.

When it finally registers, it hits me like a train. Like a vise clamping my chest so tightly it takes my breath away. I stand up and walk over to him, sit next to him, and take his hand in mine.

"Thank you."

He's watching me, surprised.

"For what?"

"For believing me. For caring. For trying to help. You're the first person in my life—aside from my sister—who's ever really done that."

He stares at me, his dark green eyes as inscrutable as ever, but this time, through the exhaustion and surprise, I get a glimpse of what's behind the mask.

"It's hard to explain," he says, "but I knew the moment I saw you, on top of that mountain, that I wanted to be around you. Like we were bound together somehow. Not just because we're both Pathfinders. Although that's part of it. But it's so much more than that too. And whatever I need to do to help you fight these things, I'll do without question."

I nod. Squeeze his hand back. Relish the feeling of his fingers in mine. I rub my fingertips over a callous on his thumb, put my head on his shoulder and close my eyes. He tips his head slightly so it rests against mine. He exhales. I hear it in his chest and feel his shoulders droop.

And finally, sitting there on the cold, concrete floor, our bodies pressed together, my head nestled into his shoulder and our fingers entwined, I find sleep.

74,280

((20 hours x 60 minutes/hour) + 38 minutes) x 60 seconds/ minute = 74,280 seconds

I jerk awake the next morning, my head still on Silas's shoulder, as I hear loud voices outside. Silas scrambles to his feet and I follow suit, our bodies falling apart from each other like leaves from a tree. He puts his hands on my shoulders.

"They're coming to get you out of here," he says. "I'm going to go to my world and rest. I'll be back soon."

When can I see where you live? I want to ask. *When can I see your world?* The words dance on the tip of my tongue, but my mouth won't comply, foggy from the haze of sleeping upright against a cement wall for not enough hours. All I do is nod.

He takes my hand and smiles, exhaustion present in his eyes as it surely is in mine. "Remember the color world. I'll see you soon."

I try to smile back, but my face feels broken. I squeeze his hand instead.

He closes his eyes and disappears.

The scientist in me observes this process with calculated interest. I've never seen him find a Path without taking me with him. His body seems to dissolve, fading into the colors of our surroundings. It only takes a second, and I wish I could record it on video and watch it again and again, slowing it down to catch the details. At the end, it looks like he's a three-dimensional outline in space, the shape of him there but none of the substance.

And then he's gone, and the wrought-iron door barring me from the outside world slides open. A kind-looking officer with deep wrinkles in his forehead and very little hair walks in.

"You okay, little lady?" he asks, and instantly I wonder where he was last night, why he wasn't the one to ask me questions, why it was Larsen the tree man instead of this gentleman with a generous smile.

"Noomi!"

My abuela throws her arms around me, sobbing openly. Everything is a blur. I get my things back. My phone, my keys, my wallet. There's an attorney with her who introduces himself as Daniel Hirata, shaking my hand. Says my mother called him weeks ago, after the barn fire, and how sorry he is he couldn't get here sooner. Something about *habeas corpus.* I recognize the words from my Latin class. He says the officers should never have brought me here after the crash. He'll review the interview transcripts today but he's certain my statement won't be allowed in court. We'll meet tomorrow morning to talk about next steps if the prosecutor decides to bring charges. Ada's small body, shaking uncontrollably, ends up in my arms, pressed against my hip. I kiss her on the cheek and she smiles but doesn't say a word.

On the way out, I see Officer Larsen through an open door. His face as wooden and expressionless as last night. I glare at him, wishing the shadows would attack him instead of me. He shuts the door, and I turn away.

It's 8:15 by the time I emerge into the chilly spring morning, the sky blue and the sun shining in a way I hadn't believed possible a few hours ago. My ears ring with the shock and confusion of it all.

On the sidewalk outside the station, I ask the question I've been dreading.

"How's Mom?"

Mr. Hirata glances down at Abuela, who frowns and refuses to meet my eyes. Ada's fingers tighten around mine. Mr. Hirata excuses himself, claiming he needs to retrieve some paperwork from inside.

When we're alone, I turn to Abuela and ask again.

"How is she?"

Abuela clears her throat. She looks me in the eyes. "*Gloria a Dios*, your mama is alive and stable," she says. "The doctors say she has a contusion and some internal bleeding. They don't know when she's going to wake up."

The fragile hope that had bloomed around me crumbles.

It doesn't matter that I'm out of prison. It doesn't matter that my late-night confession won't hold up in court. It doesn't matter that the sun is shining and the sky is blue.

The car crashed. My mother is in a coma. Ada is silent.

None of this would have happened if it weren't for me. If I hadn't called her to pick me up last night. If I had been able to fight off the shadows in the car while we drove. If I'd been stronger.

Or if I were dead.

I force my mind to go blank. I don't allow myself to think. I paint white walls in my head, over and over and over, as Abuela drives us away.

Later that evening, I'm eating dinner and staring at the clock on the wall in Abuela's kitchen, counting the seconds that have passed since I checked my mother's breathing in the car. Abuela is washing dishes and mumbling to herself about things that need to be done around the house.

The answer is 74,280.

74,280 seconds when my mother could have been conscious and healthy. 74,280 seconds when my sister could have been smiling and talking and learning. 74,280 seconds that would have been better if I didn't exist.

"*Más*?" Abuela says, pointing at the food she's cooked.

"No, *gracias, Abuela*. I'm very full." She frowns, displeased. Wielding her spatula like a weapon, she loads another tamale on my plate anyway.

"Noomi, you're so thin these days. A growing girl should eat more." She hands me a ramekin of my favorite *salsa de árbol* to smother the tamale.

"Where's Ada?" I ask, reluctantly taking up my fork again, using the edge to cut a tiny piece of masa and bring it to my mouth.

"She's playing outside. It will do her good."

"Any word from the hospital?"

Abuela clucks her tongue between her teeth. "No, Noomi, and there's no point in you asking me every fifteen minutes. The doctors say she needs time."

I suck at my teeth, biting back impatience as I stare at my plate, mushing my food around.

"Noomi," she says, reaching across the island to take the plate from me, "if you're going to play with your tamale instead of eating it, it would be better for you to go upstairs and study. Finals are coming up and your mother will be happy to hear you've been working hard when she sees you again."

When she sees you again. The words stab at me, corkscrewing in my ribs.

"Why should I study?" I whisper. "I'm worthless. All I've ever done is hurt my family."

Abuela freezes in the act of packing my uneaten tamal back into the Tupperware. She sets the plate and the fork on the island. She walks over and sits next to me.

"*Mírame*, Noomi." Look at me.

My head feels like a mountain, too heavy to move.

Papier-mâché fingers grasp mine where they sit uselessly in my lap. A light touch under my chin pulls my face in her direction. Compelled by her strong hands and the tone of her voice, I find the courage to look at her. The wrinkles around her brown eyes are soft with age. But now when she looks at me her eyes are fierce, though the heat is tempered by tenderness.

"Your father, too, wanted to leave this world when he was young. He had the same demons you have. *El miedo.*" The fear. "*Las sombras.*" The shadows. "Your papa had no siblings, you know, and his father abandoned us before Esteban was born. He had no one to teach him how to be a man." She squeezes my hands so tightly it hurts, so tightly I can feel her bones against my own. "Once, he tried to drown himself in the ocean when we were visiting the coast. Do you know this story? Do you know what happened?"

I shake my head, shutting my eyes to stop from crying. I remember what I saw while Pathfinding. I remember him collapsing on the ground. I remember *Abuela*, so much younger than she is now, crying as she ran to him, pleading with him to wake up.

"Open your eyes, Noomi," she says. "*Mírame.* You can't see the truth with your eyes closed." Tears drip down my cheeks, but I obey. I taste it at the edge of my mouth. Her shining skin, her almond eyes, swimming in my vision. "This is what happened. I dove into the ocean and swam after him. I dragged him out myself." She lets out a short laugh, and it startles me. "Imagine! Me, a small woman, dragging a seventeen-year-old boy from the depths of the ocean. And do you want to know the craziest part?"

I nod, staring at her wide-eyed, my tears drying as rapidly as they appeared.

She leans in and lowers her voice, "I didn't know how to swim."

"What?"

She lets go of my hands and leans back, laughing and smiling.

"*Si! Es verdad.*" It's true. She slaps one hand down on her knee. "I had only been in the ocean one time before, and I nearly drowned. But this time, God gave me the strength. He gave me the strength I needed to save my son. This is the power of love, Noomi. It is the love I gave to your papa and I give to you. It is the love your mother gives to you. It is the love God gives to us so we can share it with others. I loved my son enough to jump into an ocean that could have killed me too."

"But," I start, my voice in tremors, "were you able to cure him?"

"Cure him of what, *corazón*?"

"The shadows. The darkness that made him jump into the ocean in the first place."

Abuela shrugs. "Maybe. Maybe not. Some things are in God's hands, Noomi. After the miracle that day, Esteban decided to come to America to learn chemistry. He was happier. He met your mother. They had you. He got a good job. He learned to live with the shadows. I think they never truly went away, but he was happy enough."

I sigh, remembering the storms my dad brought home, the anger and rage he would take out on Mom in the privacy of our home, the shouting matches we could never predict, the terrors he inflicted, not often, but often enough. His anger wasn't directed at me, but I was precocious, and I listened, even when I didn't want to. I wonder how much my *abuela* knows of these—my father refused to talk about them after the clouds had passed. I very much doubt that my mother, with her penchant for privacy and terse acceptance of my father's flaws, would have shared those experiences with her mother-in-law.

But I don't want to dredge up those memories. Not now.

Not now when my *abuela* is enveloping me in a hug that feels like being wrapped into a swan's white wings, folded and tucked in close where everything is warm and feather-soft. Not now when tears are once again spilling hot onto my cheeks from the pain and sweetness of being held and loved when I still don't believe I deserve it. Not now when she's whispering over and over again *lo vales, lo vales.*

You are worth it. You are worth it.

BRANEWORLD

"A striking fact is that many of the major developments in fundamental theoretical physics—relativistic physics, quantum physics, cosmological physics, unified physics, computational physics—have led us to consider one or another variety of parallel universe." —Brian Greene, *The Hidden Reality: Parallel Universes and the Deep Laws of the Cosmos*

T*omorrow.*

"Too-mar-row."

"Okay, spell it."

"T-O-M-R-R—"

"I think you forgot a letter."

Pause. "Oh! I forgot the other 'oh.'"

"Good job. Want to start over?"

"T-O-M-O-R-R-O-W. That's a hard one."

"Why's it hard, little Peach?"

Ada frowns. "There should be an A in there somewhere."

I laugh. "Well, 'ay' or no 'ay', the doctors are going to wake Mama up tomorrow. Aren't you glad you know how to spell the word now?"

"I know!" she exclaims. "I can't wait."

"Okay. I need to get to my homework now. Can you ask Abuela to help you with your spelling?"

She nods and jumps off the bed and runs downstairs to where Abuela is making *papas y frijoles*, a simple but delicious dish she claims to have invented. I'm old enough to know that potatoes and beans have been prepared for centuries, but Ada still believes Abuela invented it. Our family's version of Santa Claus is the myth that Abuela invented every dish she's ever cooked. Kuri looks up as she leaves, perhaps debating whether to follow her but decides instead to nestle back under my side.

But instead of picking up my calculus textbook and going to work on this week's problem set, I turn to the stack of books Mr. Arcadio dropped off for me yesterday. I pick through them and find one on the bottom that looks interesting. *The Hidden Reality: Parallel Universes and the Deep Laws of the Cosmos*, by a physicist named Brian Greene. I've heard of him. My Dad used to talk about how his work on string theory was relevant to his own research on chemical valences. I open the cover to find a pink sticky note on the inside.

We found something that might be helpful! Look for our notes.—Claire & Kali

A grin slides across my face. They must have checked this out for me and passed it to Mr. Arcadio when he was dropping off his own selections. I flip through the pages, looking for the yellow arrow stickers Claire loves and Kalifa's pink thumb tabs.

Kuri sits up, his long snout disengaging from where it was pressed against my side. He sniffs the air, unsettled. I run my hands over his long, soft ears to calm him.

The doorbell rings. Kuri leaps off the bed and runs downstairs, barking madly. Adrenaline floods through me. I stand up and shut the door, walk back to my bed and bury myself in my pillows. Whoever it is, I don't want to see them. I can't face anyone from the real world. Not yet. Not while my mother is in the hospital, not after I've been held overnight in a holding cell, not when I still don't know for sure if the things I'm seeing are real.

But when I hear Abuela open the door and Claire and Kalifa's voices ring out from downstairs, I realize that the real world is coming back to me, whether I'm ready for it or not.

I unbury myself from my pillows, open the door, and lean on the railing that overlooks the foyer.

Kalifa and Claire are standing in the entrance hall.

"There you are!" Claire yells, using her theater voice and not her inside voice. Abuela winces.

Kalifa starts nodding to the music coming from my room. "Daft Punk? I thought you didn't like them."

"You got me into this album!"

Claire drops her backpack and charges up the stairs. She wraps me in a hug, and moments later, the cool silk of Kalifa's hijab is pressing against my cheek. There's a long silence while I let myself sink into the warmth of their presence.

Finally, they pull away. We all stare at each other.

"Did you hear–?" I start.

"Why haven't you been responding to our texts?" Kalifa demands.

"You haven't responded to any of our messages," Claire says. "So we decided to just...come over."

Kalifa puts a hand on my shoulder.

I hesitate. "What have you heard?"

"Nothing," Claire says. But she glances at Kali, and I know they've heard something.

"Rumors, that's all," Kalifa says. "But we want to hear everything. From you. Not anyone else."

"Did you get our books?" Claire asks. "Mr. Arcadio said he'd pass them along."

"I got them," I say. "Thank you."

I wave to Abuela and Ada from the balcony. "Will you call when dinner's ready?"

"Of course," Abuela says. "It's a good thing I made enough so your friends can eat too."

"Oh, that's okay," Claire says, using her theater voice again. "We ate already."

"Nonsense." Abuela waves her off. "There will be food for you when Noomi and Ada are ready to eat."

I beckon Claire and Kalifa into my room and close the door. The electronic music washes over us, and I sink into the swivel chair at my desk. Claire flops onto the bed, and Kali sits down in the old, worn leather armchair. The chair was my dad's. It used to sit in his study when we lived in the old house. A deep maroon, the color of red wine, adorned with simple brass fittings, it's the most comfortable chair in the house. My mother wanted to throw it away when we moved here a few months after he died, but I insisted we keep it.

"First things first," Kalifa says. "Why haven't you responded to our texts? Or called us back?"

"I..." I stare at the floor. "I didn't know what to say."

"We've been so worried," Claire says. "We heard your mom was in a car crash, and something happened at your wilderness group, but it was all just rumors—from school, from other students. We didn't know what was true."

"It's been a crazy few days," I admit. "I hardly know where to start."

"I can't believe this is all happening so soon after the fire," Kalifa says.

A new song comes on the playlist and Claire jumps up, holding her arms above her head as she bobs to the rhythm. "When did you get into electronic music, Noomi?" she asks.

"Around the same time I realized it's perfect for problem sets."

"Why don't you tell us everything—from the beginning," Kali says. "I want to hear how it all started. Don't leave anything out."

Claire stops dancing and sits down. I glance back and forth at them. They're watching me expectantly. I want to tell them everything. The shadows. The color world. Paul. Silas. Ada and her light. But will they believe me? No one from this world has. Can I trust them? They believed me when I told them that my panic attacks are more than that. But will they believe that Silas is real—that he comes from another world? Will they believe in the color world? Will they believe that I'm a Pathfinder, that I can visit other worlds?

Or will they think I'm crazy?

I think back to my realization last week—though now it feels like years ago. The realization that I have to try something different, something more. I have to find another way.

I have to trust them.

"This is going to be a long story," I say. "I've got to start at the beginning, right after my dad died. Are you ready?"

Kalifa uncrosses her legs and leans forward. "Are you kidding? I feel like I've been waiting years to hear this."

Claire nods. "Me too."

So I steel myself and start talking. I tell them everything. How the shadows started coming right after Dad died. How infrequent they were at first. How my therapists all thought they were anxiety attacks brought on by grief and horror and post-traumatic stress. How the medications never helped. I tell them about my suicide attempts—all eleven of them—and how they made the shadows worse, drew them to me, but I didn't realize it at the time. I tell them about my most recent attempt with the gasoline, and how Ada was always able to make the shadows go away until the dream I had when they spoke to me for the first time. I tell them about meeting Silas, and his drawings, and our trip to the desert world. I tell them what he told me I am—a Pathfinder—and what that means.

Claire and Kalifa look at each other briefly, skeptically, but I plow ahead, fully committed to the story now, uncaring whether they believe me or not. Caring only that I tell someone, anyone, everything that has happened, desperate for someone in this world to understand what I've been through. I tell them about seeing my father, and the fire in the barn, and how even the doctors agreed it was near-impossible I could have come out unscathed.

"Can we see?" Claire sits forward.

"See what?"

"How you…you know," Kalifa says.

"I can't hurt myself?"

"Yes."

I take out the knife Dad got me when I was little, the one he used to teach me how to whittle a stick to a point, and open the blade, dull from use and never very sharp to begin with. I pull a few tissues from a box on my desk and set them on my jeans to catch the blood, take a deep breath and hold the knife above my left arm. On the exhale, I jam the point through my forearm.

As usual, there's no pain.

To their credit, neither Claire nor Kalifa scream, though Claire does let out a low, theatrical gasp. When I pull the knife from my arm, a few drops of blood spill onto the tissues and the wound immediately begins to heal. When I look up, Kalifa is staring at the closing wound with the rapt attention of a scientist watching an experiment. Claire's jaw is slack, her eyes as round as her mouth. When I glance back at the wound, the skin is unblemished. There is no scar. There never is.

Claire looks up at me. "Does it hurt?"

"Never."

"That's incredible," Kalifa says. "We should tell your doctors. Maybe they can run some tests to find out how this is possible." When she looks up and sees me shaking my head vigorously, she holds her hands up. "Only if you want to. Okay, please continue. What happened next?"

I continue the story, telling them how the shadows started coming more frequently, and not just to me. Into the world.

How they visited Dr. Chase and Silas helped me flee. I tell them about sleepwalking and visiting the bioluminescent world, meeting the gravedigger, seeing a world where I had succeeded in killing myself. I tell them about Lefka, singing to us, and the holes in her sky she was able to close.

And then I tell them about Paul, how he touched me and the shadows appeared all around us. I tell them about the meditation session, my visit to Chroma, my flight with Silas through the woods, the car crash, my mother's injuries, and spending the night in a holding cell. By the time I come to the point where I explain that Silas went to find the shadows, I find I'm blinking too fast, and I reach my fingers up to touch my cheeks and find tears dripping down my face.

I take a deep breath. "I think that's everything."

"Praise Allah," Kalifa murmurs. "The Holy Book was right. Humans *can* travel to the heavens."

Against all odds, I laugh. "I'm hardly the next Muhammad. I can't even keep my family alive, let alone lead a nation."

"I've always known there had to be an explanation for everything the Qu'ran teaches," Kalifa says, the reverence fading as excitement pulses into her voice. "I bet Muhammad and Jesus were Pathfinders!"

"I didn't want to tell you," I say, my voice lower, "because I didn't think you'd believe me."

"If you hadn't shown us the thing with your arm, I might not have," Kalifa admits. "But now that I've seen that, I'll believe anything you tell me."

"I was terrified you'd never want to see me again. Especially after spending the night in prison."

Claire clucks sympathetically. "I can't imagine how terrible that was. But people go through so much worse. We wouldn't abandon you after a little thing like that." She crawls forward on the bed, reaching out to grab the book I had been reading before the doorbell rang. "Noomi, look. We found something in this book that backs up the things you've been experiencing. That's why we gave it to Mr. Arcadio to pass on to you." She opens to the introduction, where there's a passage underlined in thin pencil. Neither Claire nor Kali would mark in a library book. Not to mention the lines are wavy and uncertain; nothing like Claire's bold double-underlines or Kalifa's brackets around important passages. I wonder whose markings those are. Every time I see an anonymous mark in a library book, I feel a strange sense of connection with that distant, unknown reader.

"Those aren't our marks," Claire says. "Someone else underlined it. But it's incredible—read it."

So I do.

> *A striking fact is that many of the major developments in fundamental theoretical physics—relativistic physics, quantum physics, cosmological physics, unified physics, computational physics—have led us to consider one or another variety of parallel universe…in some, the parallel universes are separated from us by enormous stretches of space or time; in others, they're hovering millimeters away…A similar range of possibility is manifest in the laws governing the parallel universes. In some, the laws are the same as in ours; in others, they appear different but have a shared heritage; in others still, the laws are of a form and structure unlike anything we've ever encountered.*

My mind goes blank while I process this. I stare at the space between the lines, thinking hard. Then I read the passage again. *Many of the major developments in theoretical physics… have led us to consider one or another variety of parallel universe.*

"Holy shit," I whisper. So, it is possible. Influential scientists—scientists my father respected and admired—have acknowledged that parallel universes are a mathematical possibility.

I reread the last line, out loud. "In some, the laws are the same as in ours; in others, they appear different but have a shared heritage; in others still, the laws are of a form and structure unlike anything we've ever encountered."

"Doesn't that sound like your color world?" Claire jabs her finger at the page.

"It does," I acknowledge. "In fact…the gravedigger said something similar while I was there: is it so hard to believe, taking quantum unpredictability into account, that particles could behave slightly differently in different worlds, which could, throughout the expansion of time and space, build upon themselves to create vastly different outcomes and phenomena? That's what he said, more or less."

"Yes!" Claire exclaims. "Exactly!"

No, it's not so hard to believe, I think, responding to the gravedigger's question. Indeed, given everything I've seen and witnessed—from the state of Los Angeles seven hundred years into the future, to a feathered, singing dinosaur, to a world made entirely of liquified color—the only thing that seems impossible is that none of these things are real.

Ada can see Silas. Paul can see Silas. Silas is real.

The color world is real. Lefka is real. The gravedigger is real.

A rush of emotion floods over me. I feel sweet and cool and calm. Relief. It's relief that I don't have to doubt myself anymore. Relief that I can trust my experiences. Relief that I have some real-world grounding for the things that seem beyond comprehension. Not only do my friends believe me, they've helped validate my experiences.

"There's more," Kalifa says from her reading chair. "There's a thumb tab in there somewhere. It has a description of a multi-world hypothesis Claire and I found particularly compelling."

She doesn't sound like a high school student. She sounds like a researcher explaining a theory she wants to pursue.

I thumb through the pages, searching for her pink tabs. I find it in Chapter 5. The tab has an arrow on it, pointing to a paragraph that begins, *I've been focusing on the relationship between three-branes and three spatial dimensions because I wanted to make contact with the familiar domain of everyday reality.*

What's a brane? I flip back through the pages to a section titled *Branes*, and a passage that reads:

> *By the late 1990s, it was abundantly clear that string theory was not just a theory that contained strings. The analyses revealed objects, shaped like frisbees or flying carpets, with two spatial dimensions: membranes, also called two-branes. But there was more. The analyses revealed objects with three spatial dimensions, so-called three-branes; objects with four spatial dimensions, four-branes, and so on, all the way up to nine-branes.*

"Is brane just a shorter word for membrane?" I ask, looking at Kalifa.

"That's the way Greene uses it," she says. "It means dimension, too, or maybe universe. He uses it to mean a lot of things, but it mostly seems to be a spatial understanding of how different dimensions are connected."

I keep reading.

> *Let's suppress one spatial dimension in our visualizations and think about life on a giant two-brane. And for a definite mental image, think of the two-brane as a giant, extraordinarily thin slice of bread.*
>
> *To use this metaphor effectively, imagine that the slice of bread includes the entirety of what we've traditionally*

called the universe—the Orion, Horsehead, and Crab nebulae; the entire Milky Way; the Andromeda, Sombrero, and Whirlpool Galaxies; and so on—everything within our three-dimensional spatial expanse, however distant… to visualize a second three-brane we just need to picture a second enormous slice of bread. Where? Place it next to ours, just shifted slightly away in the extra dimensions. To visualize three or four or any other number of three-branes is equally easy. Just add slices to the cosmic loaf… the branes can be oriented any which way, and branes of any other dimensionality, higher or lower, can be included just the same.

I remember Silas's drawing, which I smuggled out of the police station with me, retrieve it from the drawer where I stored it and press it against the desk, attempting to smooth it out. I stare at the fuzzy worlds connected by wild, multicolored tunnels that zip every which way, the way the colors fade at the bottom and grow ever more brilliant toward the top.

"What's that?" Claire asks.

"Silas gave it to me. It's a drawing of the universe—the multiverse." I pass her the paper.

"Wow," she says. "This Silas guy is talented." She looks up at me. "Is he cute?"

Kalifa reaches across the armchair to smack Claire on the leg.

"Claire! Is now the time? Really?"

I grin at them. "He's really cute. Dark hair, long eyelashes, green eyes."

"Does he like you?" Claire asks.

"I think so," I say quietly. "I hope so."

There's a knock at the door. "Noomi?"

"Come in, Ada."

She pokes her little head in, big eyes wide as she stares at us, her hair falling messily in front of her face.

"Abuela says dinner's ready," she says. "Want to come eat?"

I look at Claire and Kali. "Surely you can't pass up Abuela's *papas y frijolas*."

"Definitely not," Kalifa says.

"Now that you mention it, I could eat," Claire says.

"Let's go!" Ada crows as if she's won a great battle.

As I stand up and lead my friends down the hall, I realize that I have won a great battle. The battle for my friends. And now I have a new weapon against the shadows.

Confidence.

ZALAAM

"The truth is the light and the light is the truth."
—Ralph Ellison, *Invisible Man*

We walk through the tiled hallways with bleached walls, the sanitized scent of rubbing alcohol in my nose. Ada bounds forward, clinging to my arm, pulling me like Kuri does in his evening walk before his little legs grow tired. Abuela walks close behind us, glancing around every few minutes as though men in blue are going to pounce on me at any moment and carry me away.

We got two phone calls this morning. The first was from the hospital, to say that the anesthesia to induce a coma had been pulled back and Mom would likely wake up in a few hours, and did we want to be there? The second, from Mr. Hirata, to let us know that the district attorney was likely to charge me with both assault against Paul and arson.

I'm as nervous as Abuela, but for different reasons. In some strange way, I've come to terms with the idea that they might lock me up. It might even be a good thing. Keep me from hurting anyone else. And besides, my Pathfinding means I would always have an escape. But if Mama's different…if her injury has caused lasting damage…the thought makes me sick.

We tried to explain to Ada that Mom might not be like she was before; that she had suffered a spinal cord injury that might affect her ability to walk and talk when she woke up. At the time, Ada seemed to understand. But now it seems she's completely forgotten.

I called Dr. Chase yesterday, seeking answers to more than just the question of Pathfinding. She had offered to write a letter of recommendation to the judge, assuring him of my character, academic potential, and good behavior. I thanked her, but couldn't resist asking why.

"In what world is this not my fault?" I asked. "How far do I have to travel to find a world where I didn't almost kill my mother?"

"It's not your fault," Dr. Chase soothed. "From what you've described, your mother took her eyes off the road. I don't want to shift the blame to your mother, here, but it's the responsibility of the person driving."

"But I'm the reason she couldn't see," I protested. "The shadows were bleeding out of me. Even Ada saw them."

"Ada's a child, Noomi. She doesn't know what she saw."

She does, I wanted to scream. She knows more than you do. Instead, I thanked her for her time and hung up the phone.

"Will Mama be happy to see us?" Ada asks, pulling my arm. "I brought all my spelling homework so I can show her when she wakes up. And I brought my art project too. Will she be hungry? Will she want to go get ice cream when the doctors let her out?"

Who gave Ada a triple-shot of espresso?

"Remember, Sweets, just because Mama will be awake doesn't mean the doctors are going to let her out today. They have a lot of tests to do."

Her room is halfway down a long hallway. The dull chatter of nurses, beeping medical instruments, and the pattering of feet down hallways form a stream of noise that babbles around us. As we approach her room, one voice crystallizes: it's my mother's.

"What street do you live on?"

"Lincoln Avenue."

"What year is it?"

"2017."

"Count to ten backward for me."

My mind translates so fast, it takes me a minute to realize that they're speaking in Arabic, not English.

As she too recognizes the voice, Ada freezes, listening. After not more than a second of standing stock-still, she sprints down the hall. I try to grab her hand but she's too fast. Her backpack flies from side to side as she hurtles across the tiles. I jog after her.

"Ada! *No corra en el pasillo!*" Abuela calls after her. Don't run in the hallway! But it's too late.

"Mom!" she shouts, bursting into my mother's room.

"Ada," I hear her say. "I'm fine, I'm—"

I round the corner to see a doctor with blond hair grabbing Ada's arm with one hand, pulling her back, defeating her attempt to leap onto my mother's bed with her. There's another doctor, a tall man with dark hair, sitting in the chair by the window. He has distinctive high, flat cheekbones and a narrowed chin. He looks like he could be my uncle. I recognize both men. They're my mother's co-workers at the hospital. Dr. Hassan and Dr. Sterner.

"Sorry, hon, you can't get on the bed with your mom right now," Dr. Sterner says as he grips Ada's wrist.

I swoop in and scoop her up. He meets my eyes with a look of gratitude. But his furrowed brows and thin-set lips tell of worry too. I look away.

"Hi, Mom," Ada says quietly. "Are you okay?"

I meet Mom's eyes. Tears are spilling down her cheeks.

"*Marhaban, sokar. Ana bikhair.*" Hello, Sweet One. I'm fine.

But the IV in her arm, the bruises on her neck and collarbone, and the pallor in her face tell a different story.

"Noomi, Ms. Perez," Dr. Sterner says quietly. "Can I speak to you outside?"

My heart races. I nod. Grab my grandmother's hand. We walk out together while Dr. Hassan stays with Ada and Mama.

Out in the hall, he shuts the door behind us and looks at us gravely. "As you know, when someone suffers from a traumatic brain injury, it's difficult to anticipate how they will function and how recovery will progress. All things considered, Saida's doing remarkably well. Her memory seems to be intact, and she's been able to answer all our questions up to a few minutes before the accident." He looks at me kindly. "She remembers picking you up. She remembers getting back in the car and driving off. But then, she says, everything is black."

I nod eagerly. "That doesn't mean she doesn't remember," I say, thinking of the shadows right before the crash, and wondering if this means Mama remembers them. "It just means..." I fumble for words. "It just means it was really dark."

His expression changes from consolation to confusion. "Well, yes, of course it was dark," he says. "It was nighttime. But that's not what's worrying."

"What is, then?" Abuela demands, clutching my fingers.

He inhales. "She won't speak in English."

"Won't?" I repeat. My breath is short. "Or can't?"

"We don't know yet. I had to bring Dr. Hassan up from ER because he's the only other physician at the hospital who speaks Arabic. She seems to be able to *understand* English just fine. But she's having problems saying the words back." Dr. Sterner sighs. "It's best to take immediate steps to rehabilitate, so we're going to begin speech therapy today."

Guilt settles over me like an iron blanket. "Will she recover?"

He looks me square in the eye. "Your mother is a very intelligent woman, Noomi. We can hope for a full and speedy recovery. But rehabilitation can take time in cases like this.

We don't really know what to expect." He reaches out, puts his hand on my shoulder. Grips it tightly. "Your mother is well regarded here, professionally as well as personally. She'll have a top-flight team of neurologists and speech therapists working with her. We'd all like Dr. Perez back at work as quickly as possible, and we're confident she'll get there."

"When?" I whisper.

He purses his lips. "That I can't say." He releases his grip on my shoulder. He turns to open the door to my mother's room, and walks back in.

Abuela squeezes my hand. "*No es tu culpa*." It's not your fault.

I don't respond. We go back into my mother's room. Inside, Ada is giggling at something Dr. Hassan said. Mama smiles.

"It's good to see you, Mom," I whisper, reaching out to take her hand. "How are you feeling?"

"*Ana motabah*," she says. I am tired. Then her eyes widen. She stares at me. Her mouth opens. She starts to say something but stops.

"Are you okay?" I ask.

She shakes her head. My heart races. Dr. Hassan stands up, leans forward.

"What's wrong?" he asks.

"*Zalaam. Shareer.*" I freeze. "*Shouar sayaa.*" The darkness, she said, using two distinct words for darkness. "Dark, night," and "black feelings, evil." Your eyes, she said.

My heart pounds in my chest. The shadows, here? Now? I scan the room. Searching for a trace of them. But there's no darkness, no shadows. None of the usual tiredness or emptiness that accompanies them. The sunlight through the window is yellow-white and clear. Ada's eyes are as green as ever. The shadows aren't here. What is she talking about?

"*Ma alkhataa*?" Dr. Hassan says. What's wrong?

She shakes her head. "Not here. The car," she says in Arabic.

"You saw them?" I whisper.

"*Osadekak.*"

I suck in a breath. Let it out slowly.

I believe you, she said.

Zalaam. The darkness.

She saw it too.

She knows.

She believes me.

The Torch

"The canoe, a dim shadowy thing,
moves across the black water,
Bearing a torch ablaze at the prow."
—Walt Whitman, "The Torch," *Leaves of Grass*

When we leave the hospital, it's getting dark outside and we're all tired. Abuela offers to stop at the library with us before it closes. She knows this will cheer both me and Ada—a visit to our favorite place. I want to do more research on the branes, on particle physics, on string theory, on quantum mechanics. I want to understand what's happening to me.

Urgency builds as we push open the double doors. I stand on my tiptoes, peering around for Mr. Arcadio. I want to find him, to ask him about some of the books he's left for me. Ada's hand is warm in mine as she babbles about the *Saddle Club* book she just finished and how excited she is to find out what happens in the next one. As we are enveloped in the warm interior of the library, it happens again.

A fleeting vision.

Rushing water over my face. My chest is tight, my eyes swimming. I can't breathe. My lungs are hot with need, but the water is frigid and my limbs are numb. I'm drowning.

But then it's over. I inhale sharply.

It's strange. The shadows haven't attacked since the night on the mountain. But the moments of darkness been replaced with visions, flashes of scenes I've never experienced and have no memory of.

"Noomi?" Ada leans into me. "Are you okay?"

I loop one arm around her. "It's nothing, Sweets. Just tired." It occurs to me that no one else has noticed these things happening to me. I squint at Ada. "You're very perceptive for an eight-year-old."

"I'm watching out for you," she replies. I recall the conversation I overheard between her and Mr. Arcadio. *I need to figure out how to shine my lantern at Noomi's shadows.*

I squeeze her shoulder. "You don't have to worry about me."

"Hmm," she says, doing her best imitation of a grown-up. She stares across the floor of the library. She doesn't believe me. But instead of arguing, she says, "Okay."

I focus on the mission at hand: finding Mr. Arcadio. He's nowhere in sight. But that doesn't mean anything. He could be in the back, going through books to reshelve and put back into circulation. He could be deep in the stacks, or up on the second floor. I follow Ada through the library to the children's section, where she plops her book bag down on her favorite table. While she starts going through the shelves to find her next read, I head out on a search mission.

But a deeper look through the library reveals nothing. Mr. Arcadio is nowhere to be found.

I'm reluctant to talk to any of the less-friendly staff for fear of critical looks and cold words, so I head upstairs and find one of my favorite librarians: an older woman with straight grey hair and round tortoise-shell glasses who speaks in hushed tones after three decades of working in the library and always has a kind word.

"Ms. Gunther, is Mr. Arcadio working today?"

"No, dear. He wasn't feeling well today so I'm covering for him. He should be back tomorrow." Before I can thank her and walk away, she reaches out to touch my arm. There's sympathy in her eyes. "I'm so happy to hear your mother's doing better." She lowers her voice more than usual. "And Noomi, that DA's a tremendous pain in everyone's ass." I turn an erupting laugh into a cough-snort. It's very unlike Ms. Gunther to use curse words. "I wouldn't worry about him at all. I'm sure Mr. Hirata will be able to get the charges dropped."

"Thank you," I say. "But how do you know so much about the case?"

She sighs. "I suppose young folks like yourself don't read the local papers."

My stomach drops into my boots. Wide-eyed, I blurt, "It's in the paper?"

"I'm sorry to be the one to tell you." She pulls out a rolled-up newspaper from behind the service desk. "But it's better that you know. Here you go." She opens the paper and places it in front of me.

I gasp. On page three, there's a half-page spread about the case. The headline reads *LOCAL GIRL TO BE CHARGED IN ARSON CASE*. There's a photo of me. My school photo from the beginning of this year. My hair a little shorter. Wearing the nice shirt my mom picked out for the photos.

"Don't worry, hon," she says. "No one thinks this is going to go far."

"My college applications," I whisper.

"Will not suffer unless you're convicted," she says firmly, "and that will never happen."

"But everyone knows."

She stares at me. "Everyone knows you had nothing to do with this." She emphasizes the last three words, enunciating and drawing them out.

"Noomi?" A tug at my sleeve and a high-pitched voice. My mouth still hanging open, I turn to see my sister, concern written all over her face. "Will you come read with me?"

I force my jaw to close. Reorient myself. Shake off the pall that threatens to settle over me.

"I'll be there in one minute."

She relents, letting go of my hand and pointing to a table in the corner, where I make out her brightly colored unicorn backpack. "I'm over there."

"What happened to your favorite table downstairs?" I ask, surprised.

"I wanted to sit up here with the adults," she says, a half-smile on her face. But it's a deceptive smile, not a playful one. She's watching me. I frown at her back as she walks away, and then turn back to Ms. Gunther. With a trembling hand, I push the paper back to her side of the desk.

"Thanks for your help, Ms. Gunther. I've got a lot of homework to catch up on."

"Sorry to give you a fright, Noomi," she says, a sad smile on her face, "but it's better that you know."

Is it?

I plant myself in the seat across from Ada and pull out my chemistry textbook. She smiles toothily at me as I sit and then returns to her book. I pull a piece of graph paper from a notebook and get out my calculator, prepared to work through a few practice problems before doing more research on quantum physics. Even after missing so much school, I'm determined to do well enough to get a perfect five on the AP test. I want to make it up to Mom. I want to make her proud.

Leafing through the pages, I arrive at the chapter we're working through. Elementary particles and how they influence chemical bonding properties. I already know the basics: protons, neutrons, electrons, and photons. Those particles, including electron valence and bond pairs, is most of what will be on the exam. But there might be a few questions about the particles that have been discovered or theorized in the last fifty years, and their roles in the four major physical forces. Gluons, for instance, are responsible for bringing about the strong force as they are constantly exchanged between the quark-bound triplets that make up protons.

Something about the phrase *quark-bound* strikes me. I ring it through my head a half-dozen times. *Quark-bound. Quark-bound. Quark-bound.*

It occurs to me that there might be something in my chemistry textbook that relates to what I'm experiencing. Maybe I don't need to dig through the stacks to find more information about Pathfinding. Maybe it's been right in front of me all along.

I squint at a large table in the book with descriptions of all the sub-subatomic particles. It lists the spin, mass, "color", and charge of each particle. *Up, down. Charm, strange. Top, bottom.* And every quark has an anti-quark. There's a sidebar that explains how quarks combine to create less-common particles, such as mesons, which are made up of a quark-anti-quark pair and only exist for the tiniest fraction of an instant, 10^-8 seconds. But what I find most interesting is a note in the main body of the text:

> *Everywhere in the universe, quark-anti-quark pairs are constantly popping in and out of existence, even in the midst of stable particles such as a bound triplet of up-up-down quarks in a proton configuration.*

What did the gravedigger say about Pathfinding? I rack my brain to remember his exact words, picturing us hovering, melting together in the strange, aqueous color world: *The energy that binds you in this world must ultimately be given back to the world it was taken from.*

That sounds suspiciously like quark-anti-quark pairs popping in and out of the universe. I turn the page, looking for more information about antimatter. There's not much in the main text, but a sidebar catches my attention.

> *One of the great unsolved mysteries of quantum physics is why matter so greatly outnumbers antimatter particles in our universe. Given that these particles are equal but opposite, one would assume they would exist in equal quantities. But on Earth and in our observable universe, matter vastly outnumbers antimatter. Astrophysicists have theorized the existence of antimatter clouds or galaxies, but these are so far only theoretical. No experimental confirmation of mass quantities of antimatter has been shown.*

"Noomi, look." Ada's voice tugs at me.

"Just a minute." I read the sidebar again, my mind racing. Could this be how we interact with other worlds? When I Pathfind, am I creating an anti-matter copy of myself in my world, but a real matter copy of myself in a different world?

"Noomi, look at me." Her voice is higher, more insistent. I tear my eyes away from the textbook to look up.

I am immediately bathed in warm, yellow-green light that radiates out from my sister like a cloud. My jaw drops. It's brilliantly colored, like the sunlight that filters down onto the forest floor, with ten times the radiance and intensity. She's smiling in her seat, enshrouded in the light like a queen, like a little goddess who wants nothing more than to revel and dance and play. The light behaves not like rays but like a gas, clustering around her, expanding slowly outward.

I chance a look around. The cloud of light is so visible to me, but no one has lifted their eyes from their books.

"What are you doing?" I ask in a hushed voice. "How are you doing that?"

"This is my torch," she says simply.

"Why—but this…why can't anyone else see it?"

Ada shrugs. "It's not for them. It's for you."

"But what…"

"I read in one of my books about an antidote. It's a medicine that works against poison. This is the antidote to your shadows." She smiles, illuminated by this joyful, otherworldly light.

I stare at her. Words refuse to form. My thoughts as scattered as the stars.

My salvation.

My sister.

Planck's Constant

"It is now a matter of finding the probability W so that the N resonators together possess the vibrational energy U_N. Moreover, it is necessary to interpret U_N not as a continuous, infinitely divisible quantity, but as a discrete quantity composed of an integral number of finite equal parts."—Max Planck, "On The Law of Distribution of Energy in the Normal Spectrum," *Annalen der Physik*

It's anxiety that opens my eyes at five in the morning. Instantly I'm awake and alert, blood thrumming through my veins like drums.

Today is the arraignment.

Mr. Hirata called yesterday to say that the district attorney plans to charge me with one felony count of arson and one felony count of assault. I thanked him and asked when and where we should meet. He said my grandmother would need to drive me to the courthouse an hour before the arraignment, where we would go over my responses and next steps.

"Really, Noomi, you shouldn't worry. They don't have a leg to stand on."

Except my confession.

"You sound very composed," he said, after reminding me of the time and room number where we were to meet.

Didn't he just tell me not to worry? I nodded wordlessly for several seconds before realizing he couldn't see me through the phone. "Yes," was all I managed. "See you tomorrow."

Even with Ada speaking again, Claire and Kalifa on my side, and my mother awake and recovering, it's hard not to feel overwhelmed by the forces against me.

I thought about Pathfinding a way out. Get out of Dodge. Only in my case it's the whole universe. But I remembered what the gravedigger said in Chroma, "Over a long enough timeline in any world other than your own, you will dissociate back into the fabric of the multiverse. The laws that bind you will eventually dissolve. The energy that allows you to Pathfind must ultimately be given back to the world it was taken from." Escape would be temporary. Eventually, I would have to return or die.

Once, death would have seemed like the right path. But now, with the taste of hope like honey on my tongue, I don't want to give up without a fight.

I rub my eyes, sitting up. It's dark as pitch but I'm wide awake. Rain pounds on our rooftop. Imagined scenes from the arraignment flash before me: the trial, dramatic testimony on the witness stand, a conviction, spending half my life in prison. How did I get here? It seems impossible. All I ever wanted was to escape the shadows.

I throw the covers off and stand, pulling on a long-sleeved shirt, jeans, and rain boots. It's cold and forbidding outside, but I don't care. I need to feel something other than this fear. The clockwork motion is moving against me from within my world and without. My sweatshirt and jacket are hanging by the door. I pad downstairs as quietly as I can, bundle up, stuff my feet in my boots, and step outside.

Rain taps at my hood. I zip my jacket as high as it will go, duck my chin, and start walking. With no direction in mind, no aim but escape, and nowhere to be for at least two hours, I might as well make it a long walk. I wander down the street, meandering under the streetlamps for several blocks. The trees hang low and I admire the way the rain drips off the leaves. Closer to the ground, the tulips have popped. Singular flowering units of yellow, red, and violet make their presence known in the pockets of light along the sidewalk, smiling gaily, undeterred by rain. The daffodils, by contrast, are slumped over and heavy, water dripping off their petals as they bow to the ground. On this soggy morning when I am preoccupied with my own fate, I find the dying daffodils morbidly fascinating. I pull out my phone, cover it with one hand, and bend to take a photo.

"Interesting how humans are so fascinated with death."

I glance up. A man in a bright yellow rain slicker and black work boots stands a few feet away. I squint at him, blinking rain from my lashes.

"Mr. Arcadio?"

He smiles, his expression warm as always. His white beard is scragglier than usual, and his eyes are bright and inquisitive. Despite his age, there's something that always makes him seem childlike.

"You're up awfully early, Noomi."

"I could say the same to you."

"All seasons but winter, and sometimes even then, I take a turn around the neighborhood every morning at this hour." He winks at me. "I've been an early riser since my college days."

I stand, abandoning my photo shoot. It was useless anyway—water has dripped all over my camera lens. Mr. Arcadio looks at me, his smile fading.

"Today's the arraignment, isn't it?"

"How did you know?"

"Noomi," he says with a hint of reproach, "I've been friends with your family since you were this high." He holds a flat palm to his knee.

There's a long pause, and I can feel his eyes on me. I try to think of something to say, some way to change the subject, but the trial is looming in front of me like the rain clouds overhead, and there hasn't been anything else in my thoughts since I woke up. I want to squirm away. I don't want his pity.

"Are you ready?"

"Ready for what?" I turn and close my eyes. Irritation flutters in my chest. I came out here to be distracted, not reminded.

"Ready to fight."

"Mr. Hirata said I don't have to do anything."

"I'm not talking about the courts."

"What are you talking about, then?" Frustration leaches into my voice.

Instead of answering, Mr. Arcadio turns to the flowers in front of us. "Often, when I see tulips, I think of Planck's constant and his theory of light quanta." I'm so surprised I can't think of a response. "Tulips comprise such a singular unit of color. Discrete quanta. Like Planck's theory of discrete, indivisible units of light. Tulips are units of color like photons are units of light."

He turns to meet my eyes. To my surprise, he offers me his hand. "Would you like to know the answers to your questions?"

I stare at him.

"Are we going somewhere?"

He smiles. "Yes."

This strange interaction reminds me of something. Silas. Holding his hand out to me, the campfire behind us. *Do you trust me?* he asked.

I glare at Mr. Arcadio. Suspicious, but tempted by curiosity, I reach for his hand. Our fingertips touch ever so gently. He closes his eyes. The realization hits me just as the world disappears.

Mr. Arcadio is a Pathfinder.

A soft *whoosh* as I fall backward. A whirlpool of shimmering multicolored feathers swirling around me—

Plummeting

Shrinking

Collapsing

Thunk

My feet hit solid ground and this time I swear I can feel my bones reconstituting, ligaments binding, fascia stretching throughout my skin. This world must be similar to mine. My physical makeup feels identical—not like in Chroma, where the liquefied color around me obeyed rules so very different from the ones I was accustomed to.

I stare around me, taking in my surroundings.

Green, fresh grass. A blanket of stars overhead so bright they light up the world. Tulips blooming everywhere, in every imaginable color. And two massive, looming grey walls ahead of me. They stretch into the distance, to the right and left, over the horizon, as far as I can see. Straight ahead, there's a gap between the walls. The implication seems to be that I should walk through.

Mr. Arcadio has disappeared.

Mr. Arcadio, the Pathfinder.

Or was that an impostor, another Pathfinder imitating Mr. Arcadio's form?

Suddenly afraid, I take a step back. Did Paul trick me? Am I in danger?

"Where am I?" I wonder.

"This place is for you," a voice booms out, coming from everywhere and nowhere, like the voice of God in movies, only the voice is feminine, a pretty alto that reminds me of Lefka's singing. The voice seems to beckon me forward. "I built this world."

"What is it? Who are you?"

"This is a labyrinth. And I am its creator."

The Kardashev Scale

"It will prove convenient to classify technologically developed civilizations in three types: I — technological level close to the level presently attained on earth, with energy consumption at ≈ 4 x 10^19 erg/sec. II — a civilization capable of harnessing the energy radiated by its own star (for example, the stage of successful construction of a "Dyson Sphere"); energy consumption at 4 x 10^33 erg/sec. III — a civilization in possession of energy on the scale of its own galaxy, with energy consumption at ≈ 4 x 10^44 erg/sec." —Nikolai Kardashev, "Transmission of Information by Extraterrestrial Civilizations," *Soviet Astronomy*

"You didn't answer my second question. Who are you?"

"You will meet me at the center of the labyrinth. The labyrinth will answer your questions."

I frown. "That could take ages. This place is *enormous.*"

"As am I," the voice says. "As are you."

Reluctantly, I start walking forward. Though the stone walls look miles away, within a few steps I've closed the distance. At the threshold, I hesitate.

What am I doing? Am I crazy? Listening to voices in the sky telling me to walk into this giant maze? I've listened to Kalifa's diatribes about mythology enough to know what happened to the innocent youths from Thebes sent into the labyrinth as a sacrifice to the Minotaur. I should Pathfind home and forget this ever happened.

But that seems as impossible as continuing forward. The answers I've sought for years are at my fingertips. Am I going to turn away?

No. I have to keep going.

Suddenly, I wish Silas were here.

I take a step forward, crossing the threshold. As I do, I glance behind me, half-expecting the gap to close, preventing me from moving any way but forward.

But nothing happens. The path back out is clear, available. I take another step forward, and still nothing happens. I'm free to turn back at any point. Relief washes over me, and now I step forward confidently. Tulips bloom around me, the stone walls bleak but the ground brilliant and colorful.

Soon, I see the walls loom sharply ahead of me, blocking the way forward. The passage turns to the left, and as I make the turn, the tulips begin to wilt and die. They blacken as if burned. A sharp wind picks up, blowing into my face, and I raise my forearm to shield my eyes. The ash from the tulips blows behind me, creating a vortex of shadow. The wind grows so strong I have to fight to keep moving forward.

What's happening?

Massive columns shoot up around me, growing impossibly tall and thin, blocking out the stone walls of the labyrinth, rising to the sky, so high I can't see the tops. Just like in my dream. The emptiness is coming. The fatigue. The apathy. It settles on my shoulders, bowing my neck. The shadows from the pillars expand, blooming, growing far beyond their purview.

They solidify, taking shape. This is new, I think distantly, my thoughts echoing as though from a mountaintop many miles away. My mind fogs up and all boundary between thoughts dissolves, dissociates. The shadows form the walls of my existence.

They look like shells, spiraling outwards according to the golden ratio, growing ever larger as they pinwheel through the sky.

We are not evil, little one, they say in my mind. *We are balance. We are a great race from an old universe. When the energy from our suns was expended, we learned to source energy from other worlds. Now, we are powerful. What the universe creates, we destroy. Our energy is growing, and you are our source.*

"No," I whisper. A memory curls around me, drifting like smoke. A deep green like pine trees.

Ada's eyes. Silas's eyes.

For dust you are, and unto dust you must return.

I grasp the memory and cling to it with everything I have.

We are the Harbingers. You are a wellspring, and we are thirsty.

"No," I say again, stronger this time. A new memory pops up. The tulips. Discrete quanta of color.

At my feet, the tulips begin to bloom. They pop like raindrops on the ground, replacing the ones swept to ash, bursting open with impossible vibrancy. The shells of darkness begin to fray. Their structure fades. The tulips are blooming everywhere. The apathy lifts and I find new strength.

Ada's eyes. Silas's eyes. Tulips. Chroma. Bioluminescence. The force of all these colors comes rushing back into my mind like a waterfall. Rushing in. Being filled. Resilient. The vacant feeling inside me disappears. I am strong.

"You can't have me," I shout. "Not now. Not ever."

And with that, they're gone.

The stone walls of the labyrinth are back, untouched, as grey and uncaring as ever. The tulips are everywhere, the grass fresh and deep. And the sky overhead is as brilliant and starry as before.

A deep tiredness rushes over me, the kind I can feel in my bones. I fall to my hands and knees, breathing hard. The grass is springy and damp and the tulips as soft as ever, so I roll onto my back and rest.

"What just happened?" I ask no one in particular.

"Have you not been seeking to know what are the things that haunt you?" the voice asks. "Now you have met them, and you know."

So the voice belongs to Mr. Arcadio? A million questions crowd my mind as my thoughts settle and reconstitute.

"I don't know anything more than I did before."

"They told you their name, and they told you where they are from. You think that is nothing?"

I nod, the grass soft against my cheek as I try to process all this. It's always hard to sort through memories after an attack. Everything is jumbled. I feel so tired, and it's hard to focus.

"They're called Harbingers," I say, "and they're from an old universe." I think of Silas's drawing, remembering how the worlds at the bottom were grey and black. *It's not so much* down *as it is back through,* he said. "Are they...aliens?"

"An interesting choice of word," the voice says, and I swear there's a touch of amusement there. "Yes, they are a different race than yours, and they do not come from your Earth, so in that sense, they are aliens. But this word is too limited, too small, to understand all the life in the multiverse. You will learn."

I nod, trying to understand, but my mind feels as cloudy as when the shadows—Harbingers?—were here.

"You are tired," the voice says, "and there is more to learn. Keep walking, and you will find a fountain in the walls of the labyrinth. The water will restore you."

"One more question, and then I'll move," I say. I'm enjoying lying here in the grass too much to leave. "Why did you let them come here? I thought you said you created this world. Surely you don't want them to destroy what you created."

"What you saw was an illusion. I created that interaction based on my own memories and experiences with the shadows, sharing it so you could learn. The labyrinth is full of such illusions. They will teach you, but they are not real."

My heart sinks.

"So, I didn't really fight off the shadows by myself?"

The voice is full of consolation. "No. But you did well. It is good to practice when you are not in real danger. Now you will be stronger."

Buoyed somewhat by this reassurance, I roll over and push myself to my feet. Still exhausted, my limbs are reluctant to obey. I look around and realize I was in a corner. There's another turn ahead. Nestled into the outside corner, where the stone walls meet to form a right angle, is a beautiful fountain, as promised. The fountain stands out in stark contrast to the grey walls of the labyrinth—tiled into a mosaic featuring a climbing vine, a blue sky, and a yellow sun, with water babbling from a bamboo pipe into a clear stone basin. I cup my hands and raise them to my mouth, eager to drink. But just as I bring the water to my mouth, I pause.

"There aren't any caveats here, are there?" I feel like I'm in some mythological tale, like Theseus and the Minotaur or Orpheus chasing his lover into the land of Hades. "Like, I can never return to the real world after I've eaten the food of the dead?"

When the voice is silent, and no answer is forthcoming, I shrug, and put my face in my palms, drinking deeply. The water tastes fresh and clear, as if from a mountain spring. As I drink, I can feel it cooling the back of my throat, the insides of my body—extinguishing a flame I didn't know was there. It runs like electricity through my skin, straightening my spine, renewing my tired muscles, infusing me with a vigor I haven't felt in ages. Desperate for more, I bend to drink directly from the basin. It's so delicious, it's almost sweet.

Sated, I straighten, and wipe my lips on the back of my hand. I turn to the corridor ahead of me, paved with tulips and green grass, and start walking. The labyrinth guides me in a straight line for what seems like miles before it finally bends back to the right.

"The reason Theseus needed string was so he wouldn't get lost in the maze." My voice echoes back to me as I think out loud. "But there are no dead ends or other pathways in this labyrinth."

I wait, hoping my ponderings will incite some response from the ethereal voice. But nothing comes.

"Maybe it's not a maze, then," I mutter. "But I sure wish I knew what was going on."

The path goes on and on, straight as an arrow, for so long I'm once again starting to grow tired, the effects of the clear water from the fountain wearing off, when I see another corner. There's another fountain here, and eagerly I run toward it for a drink, cupping my hands before I'm even there, prepared to catch the water as soon as I'm close.

But as I stretch out my hands in anticipation, a hot, dry wind blows from around the corner. Dust blows into my eyes. I hold up a forearm to shield my eyes and turn in the direction of the wind.

The formidable walls of the labyrinth are gone. In its place, a desert in bloom. Prickly pear cacti and saguaros blossom with yellow and pink flowers. Palo verde trees stand out in shades of yellow and green against the pale dust of the horizon. The oily smell of creosote is heavy in the air. Dust rolling across the valley floor reveals a town in the distance.

Steadily, surely, my feet carry me there.

Much more quickly, it seems, than I walked the corridors of the labyrinth, I've arrived at the edges of town. I walk the streets feeling out of place. There are people here, sitting, walking, selling fruit. A small church on the outskirts of town with fading white paint. Cars rumble by. I stare, looking at everyone, everything, wondering what I'm doing here, how I got here.

"*Hola*?" I say uncertainly to one of the passersby. But the woman—middle-aged, her hair tied in a high bun, wearing flip flips as she walks down the street—ignores me.

I try again with an old man sitting on a plastic chair outside a cafe, sipping a Coke. I walk right up to him and wave in his face.

"*Hola, señor*!" I shout. Still nothing.

I am invisible.

Emboldened, I run into the middle of the street, enjoying this jaunt with invisibility. A series of motorbikes roar past, and I jump out of the way. I'm not fast enough, and one rips right through me.

I feel nothing.

Not even the wind from their passing.

I take a moment and stare at myself, how intact I am. This is more than my usual ability to heal. This is more than invisibility. I am *not present*. I am *not here*.

I'm still in the labyrinth," I say, wonderingly. This is another vision. So what am I supposed to see?

I continue, trusting my feet to carry me where I need to be. They carry me left, and then right, and then straight for several blocks, meandering through the outskirts of town. I watch the people go by, listening to their gossip, their complaints about work, their questions about the rain and when it will come, and how much there will be this year. They talk about fish, visiting the coast, going to school, moving to the city, moving home. They cart around groceries, share sips of soda, drink espresso, open bottles of beer.

"Esteban, *levántate ya!*"

That's my father's name.

Instinct tells me to follow the voice. I duck into an open doorway, adorned by what was once a brightly colored mat, now faded from years of dust and wear. Inside is a little foyer and a much larger kitchen, with a broad wooden table, a four-ring gas stove, and an assortment of pots and pans hanging from the walls. Feeling like an intruder, I look down the hall, where a much younger version of Abuela Mariana is wielding a broom and knocking violently on an inner door.

"If you forget your chores again, you won't get your allowance!" she shouts in Spanish.

I walk past my grandmother, marveling at the youth in her face, the lines that are only just beginning to show. Her hair is lustrous and black, pulled half-back with a clasp, shining like mine. I raise a hand to her cheek, wanting to feel how soft her skin is, wanting to hug her to me and tell her who I am. But my hand passes clean through. Not even a whisper of feeling. The only sensation aside from the pounding of my heart and the rhythm of my breath is the wind, dusty and hot, blowing right through the walls of the house, right through me.

I turn away and walk through the door to a bedroom. My heart stops when I see my father passed out on the floor.

I freeze, taking in the scene. The bed is messy, the sheets twisted on top of a colorful wool blanket. Dad's face is pointed upward, his eyes closed, his expression vacant, deathly. He's lanky, his limbs angular and awkward. He doesn't look like a big teenager—but then, he will never be a big man. My mother is relatively small at five foot two, and he only had six inches or so on her.

He gasps as he wakes up, his head lifting from the ground, his eyes wide and terrified.

And then he looks at me.

"You," he says in English, his voice low and urgent. The bones of the handsome face and sharp jaw line he will have ten years from now when he marries my mother are beginning to emerge. The same shockingly black hair. The same green eyes Ada inherited. "I saw you before. Years ago. They came then too." He pushes himself to his feet and stares at me, holding a hand in front of him as if to ward off some demon. "Are you helping them?"

My heart breaks.

"Dad," I whisper. "You don't know me yet, but you will."

He hesitates, confused. "Who are you?"

"I'm your daughter." My voice cracks. "I…I don't know why I'm here, or how, but I'm glad…I got to see you."

He stares at me, his expression guarded.

"I think I'm here to learn something about you and the shadows," I whisper. "Can you tell me about them?"

"You know them?" Shock in his eyes. "*Las sombras?*"

"*Yo también los tengo.*" I have them too.

"I've had them since I was a kid," he says, in English again. "I don't know why. But I can go to crazy places too. None of my friends believe me when I tell them." Hope flares in his green eyes. "Can you travel?"

"Yes," I reply. "I just learned how. That's how I came to be…here. Can you help me fight the shadows?"

He shrugs. He still looks confused, and a little scared. I try to put myself in his shoes. How would I feel if I'd been passed out from an attack and someone I'd never met showed up in my room, claiming to be my child from the future? I'd be scared and confused, too.

"I haven't figured it out yet," he says. "I can only tell you what I've learned about them."

"Please," I say.

"Have you ever heard of the Kardashev Scale?" I shake my head. "The Kardashev Scale was conceived of by a Russian astrophysicist in the '60s. It offers categorizations for possible alien civilizations that might exist elsewhere in the universe. The first level, Type I, encompasses civilizations who have learned to harness and store all the energy that reaches their planet from their parent star. In some sense, this would include plant life on Earth, but humans aren't even at this level yet, as we can't harness the totality of energy from the sun without the millennia-long cycles of plant life and decay that create coal, natural gas, and oil, and our solar capacities aren't yet efficient enough." His tone is analytical, talking like the professor he will be one day.

"The second tier, Type II, planetary civilizations, includes beings that can harness and store *all* of the energy emitted from their parent sun, not just the energy that reaches the civilization's native planet. The third tier, a galactic civilization, includes civilizations that can harness and store energy from their entire galaxy. At present, all of these civilizations are hypothetical only to Earth-bound humans, but—" he gives me a knowing glance "—if you've traveled to other worlds, I'm sure you've encountered alien races who fit these criteria."

"Well…" I search for the right way to explain my limited experience with Pathfinding, but I'm still tongue-tied, trying to process these revelations.

"But Kardashev had no concept of civilizations from *parallel* worlds, or that there might be infinite parallel worlds from which to draw energy. My theory is that Kardashev needed to envisage a *fourth* tier, which is what the shadows have attained, which might be called *universal* civilizations. These civilizations—of which the shadows seem to be one—would be advanced enough to have drained their entire universe of energy through planetary and galactic means and have now turned to the Pathfinders in their bid to siphon energy from neighboring universes as well."

"That makes perfect sense," I exclaim. "It's what they told me: 'We are a great race from an old universe. When the energy from our suns was—'"

But he cuts me off, carrying on as though I weren't speaking. "Keep in mind, though, this is only a theory. I still need to actually find one of them, or someone who knows them, to test my theory."

Abuela pounds on the door again.

"Esteban, *por el amor de Dios!* If you don't open this door, I'm going to break it down!"

"You need to go," he says. "Mama will kill me if she sees you in here."

"Please," I say, "one more question. How do you cope? How do you deal with them?"

He looks me straight in the eye, and once again I feel fully in the presence of my father. I want to run to him, to press myself into his arms, to hug him and hold him and tell him I love him and one day he'll know and love me too. But there's that hard edge of tension in him, the rigidity with which he holds his body, and I can tell he's sensitive and tired after fighting them off, and uncertain, still, about who I am.

"I don't know," he says quietly. "Sometimes I'm okay with it. I accept this as a part of my life." He stares at the ground. "But other times…it gets so bad, it makes me want to die."

"I know," I whisper. "Me too."

He nods unhappily and takes a step toward me, holding his hand out. I offer mine as well, hope blooming in my chest, and suddenly I am desperate to feel his warm hands again, to touch the skin of the man who will be my father. But Abuela pounds on the door again, and the warm wind picks up, impossibly blowing from *inside* the house, and my father's hand passes through me as everything around me crumbles, turning to dust, my dad's youthful face withering and fraying and dissipating, and the tulips are back in bloom at my knees and the sharp walls of the labyrinth are towering above me and the grass is green and wet and no longer welcoming—I'd give anything to be back in the dust with him—as I collapse into it, sobbing, wanting more than anything in all the worlds to hold his hand one last time.

1 X 10^9 JOULES

"Data from ground-based and balloon-borne electric field meters are used in conjunction with lightning mapping array data to estimate the amount of charge transferred and energy liberated by 40 lightning flashes in four New Mexico mountain thunderstorms...Using average charge and potential values for the group of storms yields lightning energy estimates of 2 x 10^8 to 7 x 10^9 J, depending on flash type and storm stage."—Maggio, Christopher R.; Marshall, Thomas C.; Stolzenburg, Maribeth. "Estimations of charge transferred and energy released by lightning flashes." *Journal of Geophysical Research: Atmospheres*

"Why?" I shout into the cold stone corridor, unsure whether the voice will even respond. "Why didn't you let me be with him? Why didn't you let me touch him?"

"I could no more have let you touch him than I could put the moon in the palm of my hand." The voice, feminine and godlike, rings clearly and calmly through the walls of the labyrinth, through the corridors of my mind.

"But I was right there. He *saw* me."

"What you saw was nothing more than a memory."

"I was talking to him!" I shout angrily. "It's not fair to take that from me!" But there's a quiet, nagging voice at the back of my head. He cut me off mid-sentence. Dad would never have done that. We weren't participating in a conversation—I was filling in gaps where I wanted to see them.

"You were talking to a ghost," the voice says. "Truth is not so sentimental as justice, Noomi. I told you during your encounter with the shadows that I built this world and all you encounter within it. I cannot be blamed if you, in your haste to raise the dead and blur the lines between past and present, forgot what I told you about the rules of this place."

I have no response to this, so I bury my head in my forearms and cry.

It's a long time before the voice speaks again, more quietly this time. "You might think it unfair that I would refuse to let you speak with your father after so many years of longing, and I sympathize, which is why I was careful to warn you that everything you would encounter here is a part of my memory. What you just saw is a record of the first and only time I visited your father in his home in Sonora. I could no more alter that memory to accommodate your desires than I could change the Paths that brought the shadows to you."

This is comforting, although I can't help but feel the hurt. He was so close. So close I could have touched him. Held him. Pressed my cheek to his chest like I did when I was little. To learn it was all an illusion, that he wasn't even talking to me, is a knife in the gut.

"I still don't understand," I say. "How I got the shadows too. Is it inherited? Like a disease?"

"The labyrinth is large. There is more to see."

"I don't know how much more I can handle."

"The water will revive you."

I don't want to be revived. I want to travel to a world where my father never died, the shadows never existed, and our family is intact.

But that world doesn't exist outside my mind, so I push myself to my feet and totter to the fountain in the corner. The water sings against the stone, light and airy, and I drink, slaking my thirst, before washing my face and my hands in the basin.

As I raise my face from the cold water, I find myself face-to-face with another colorful mosaic in the wall. But this one is different from the landscape at the previous fountain. Here, the mosaic depicts the Minotaur, the mythological half-bull and half-man that haunted the Cretan labyrinth, eating the innocents from Thebes who were sacrificed there every year. His horns are starkly blue, his face contorted in a snarl, his teeth reminiscent of a saber-toothed tiger. He glares at me, and I jerk away, stumbling backward, slamming into the stone walls of the labyrinth, unable to tear my eyes from the Minotaur.

"I thought this wasn't that kind of a labyrinth?" I mutter. The voice does not respond.

But despite my fear, the Minotaur seems to have no intention of leaping from his tiled form and stalking me like prey through the corridors.

I tear my eyes from the image and turn away. I keep walking.

This time, the labyrinth bends and turns many times, always in a similar pattern. Right, left, right, left. The halls are growing shorter now. It's hundreds of steps between each turn, but there are no choices, no alternative turns, no decisions to make; I have no choice but to go forward or go back.

Then, at last, there's another fountain, tucked into a corridor that's roughly a third the size of the first two massive hallways I walked down at the exterior of the maze. I break into a jog and run toward it, eager to see what knowledge or information will be imparted here—eager, perhaps, for another look at my father. But this time, nothing happens. No warm wind blows. No blooming shadows taking form. No vision, no experience.

Disappointed, I dip my hands into the fountain, hoping for another refreshing drink. But as soon as my fingers make contact, I jerk them back—shocked, literally, by an electrical current flowing through the water.

What the hell?

Tentatively, I try again, dropping my index finger to the surface of the water. Again, a jolt of electricity runs through me. As usual, there's no pain, but the sensation is startling.

Confused, I look up and around, but nothing has changed. The labyrinth is as stark as ever. Then I look at the mosaic. This one is different again. Neither a peaceful setting sun nor a dangerous Minotaur look back at me, but a child, a boy, holding his arm up to a stormy, chaotic sky as a bolt of lightning sears through him. I stare at it, remembering something I haven't remembered in a long time…

And as I stare and think and remember, the wind whips up around me, and raindrops are pattering against my jacket like they were back at home in Oregon. The boy in the mosaic is standing about three hundred feet from me, on a small butte surrounded by palo verde trees and saguaros in the distance. The sky above us is ripping itself apart as clouds tatter and roll and electricity crinkles like gunshots through the atmosphere. But it's not just in the sky, it's on the ground too, leaping down like the hand of God outstretched to touch Adam's, and the boy in the distance is alight, aflame, lit up by the crackling through him, and we're living out the moment immortalized in the mosaic, and he screams so loudly it makes a counterpoint to the thunder rolling across the valley. I run toward him, remembering the knotted skin that rippled across my father's back from his shoulder blades to his hip bones, the scars he never liked to show us, the reason he always wore a tee shirt even in the dead heat of the summer, even at the swimming pool or in the lake or in the river, the knotted, winding, gnarled tree trunk of a scar that curled around his back like a cat's tail, the skin he wouldn't let me touch unless I begged, the scar he got from a lightning strike when he was five years old, Abuela told me one time, another sign God had protected him, for the only way a child could have survived such a thing was by a miracle.

And I think: Now I know why he has storms inside him.

I watch with a mix of horror and revelation as my father, a little boy, collapses under the pressure and power of a billion joules, crumpling like burned paper. I run to him, arms outstretched, as he falls, but already the vision is fading, the tall stone of the labyrinth coming back into view, and the last thing I see is darkness bursting around my father, splattering like black paint through the desert and the saguaros, and then I am pounding my fists on cold stone and shouting at nothing.

I take a deep breath to calm myself. I should know not to get attached to the visions by now. But it's so hard. I want to help. I want to see. I want to participate, not as a witness but as a player in the game.

I straighten and turn away from the walls. The fountain, babbling peacefully, is back in its place, and I wonder if, now that the vision has played out, I might be able to drink. Cupping my hands, I dip them into the stream, and this time I'm rewarded. I raise my hands to my mouth, drinking thirstily, staring at the mosaic, which has returned to tiles and stone.

I keep walking, heading deeper into the labyrinth, muttering aloud as I process all I've seen so far.

"Dad was a Pathfinder. But was he always a portal for the shadows? Did he always have them, or did they come after he was struck by lightning? Did he become a Pathfinder in the same moment as the shadows found him? Or did they find him because he was already a Pathfinder?"

And then, a different question. "And why did they find me in the moment when he died?"

The omnipresent voice returns no answer, no clarity, no thoughts, so I continue in silence, my mind running in circles as I move through the halls. Distantly, another question chimes in the back of my mind: If everything in here is a memory from whoever built this world, does that mean she witnessed the lightning strike, too?

How?

I spend some minutes pondering this question but come to no answers. Finally, after what seems like days of walking, the walls peel back and open, revealing a small chamber, an inner sanctum. There's a fountain there, too, not built into the walls like the others but circular, standing in the center of the chamber, with an elevated basin like a birdbath and a larger stone pool below. Amazed and excited—ready to have finally reached the center—I break into a jog, running toward the fountain, steeling myself for whatever I'm about to see.

As I enter the sanctum, the high walls dissolve, the fountain disappears, and for a second I'm floating in an empty, horizonless sea of tulips and green grass.

And then a crib materializes.

I gasp, and my hand goes to my mouth.

Ada's crib. I'd know it anywhere.

A scream pierces the air. A child crying. The rest of the room takes shape—the wallpaper, the pink paint, the door slightly ajar, the wooden blocks sprawled across the ground, the changing station. But the grass and the tulips are ever-present. A reminder that this isn't real.

But it is.

I remember it too.

Ada cries, standing at the edge of her crib, grasping at the bars as she wakes up from her nap, and my father comes in to shush her. Mom was at the hospital, I remember. It was her first year after residency.

I remember everything from that day. Things I shouldn't remember. Details that should have faded with time are instead burned into my brain like the scar on Dad's shoulders.

He picks her up, lifting under her arms, and nestles her against his hip. Oh, Dad. You had storms in your soul and darkness in your mind but you were so good with your girls. Almost immediately, she stops crying, and he bounces her up and down gently, until he puts his nose to her belly and inhales. He wrinkles his nose, but smiles.

"Lucky enough to poop and sleep at the same time, aren't you?" he says, and bops her nose with his finger, resulting in a cascade of giggles. I watch in awe, fighting back the tears. I've never seen this part—the tenderness, the intimacy. I didn't see it from this angle. I didn't see this *much*.

I only saw the aftermath.

"Quite the smelly one you are today," he says, setting her down at the changing station. "Let's get you cleaned up, and then we can have a snack."

He turns to pull a diaper from the drawer, and that's when it happens. But it's not what I thought it would be.

A man materializes next to him. A tall, willowy man with blond hair and handsome but angular features. A sharp jawline, round lips, and high cheekbones.

A man I'd recognize anywhere.

It's Paul.

He looks younger, but intangibly so. The youth shows more in his eyes than in his skin. There's a pride there, a haughtiness I haven't seen in him before.

My father freezes. "What are *you* doing here?" he says contemptuously.

In my mind, I'm screaming the same question. What are you doing here?

I suck in a breath, trying to process this. My dad knew Paul? And that he was a Pathfinder? How?

Paul says nothing. He simply reaches out and touches my father. Though he tries to recoil, there's nowhere to go. He's backed up against the wall.

And then there is something that can only be described as an explosion.

There's no sound, no fire, but more like a supernova, the dying of a star right here in Ada's nursery. A tunnel of blinding white light that comes from everywhere and nowhere, so brilliant I have to cover my eyes. When I open them again, trying to see everything, the light has been separated into every imaginable color of the rainbow. Then it dissolves, frays into dust.

The nursery is back. Paul has vanished as quickly as he came. My father is frozen. Ada is wailing.

And the shadows are everywhere. Dripping. Popping. Curling like smoke. Eviscerating the room. Drowning out everything.

My father stutters, blinking his eyes rapidly, as though trying to clear the shadows away like cobwebs. His hand goes to his heart. He leans on the changing station for stability. I can see him trying to stop them. But inside his chest, his heart is stopping.

The same electricity that brought the shadows down on him thirty years ago now cripples him from the inside out.

He chokes, sputters.

Tears drip down my face. The inky black is everywhere. I can't feel the sensations of apathy and fatigue like I would in a real attack, but still it's enough to cut to my bones.

And then he falls.

In my memory, it's a massive sound. The sound of a redwood tumbling from hundreds of feet, the mass and momentum of the trunk, the snapping of branches as it falls, the careening to the ground and the final echoing *whump* at the end.

But it turns out it isn't actually like that at all.

He falls in a stagger to his knees—that's the first sound. And then, more solidly, he collapses to his side. The noise echoes more through the bones of the house than it does in the air, but I know that just down the hall in the kitchen, ten-year-old Noomi can hear it. Her eyes widen in surprise. She walks down the hall while my father stares at the wall, trying to get up, willing himself to get up.

All around him, shadows are bleeding through the wall, dripping over everything, into everything, staining the world an inky, oily black, the kind no soap will wash off, the kind no light can banish.

And into this chaos walks my younger self, her hair in a short bob, her newest book clutched to her chest. She's staring around in fear and awe, looking at the shadows, uncertain of what she's seeing as she watches her father die.

Bravely, little Noomi walks toward him. She looks around at the shadows everywhere and refocuses on Dad.

"Dad?" I say. "Are you okay?"

He looks up at me. Stretches out a fingertip, hand trembling, shadows everywhere. He's crying, but there's nothing he can do.

I go to him. I take his hand. A shock runs through my ten-year-old body. From my vantage point as a witness, I can see little Noomi's body jump from the shock.

And somehow, without reason or logic or sense, the shadows screech to a halt. My father inhales sharply—it will be his last breath.

And the shadows, howling in anger and pain and the sense that they've been robbed of something long promised, liquefy, coalesce, condense, get sucked into my tiny body.

"*Lo siento, mi amor*," are my dad's last words.

I'm sorry, my love.

THE MINOTAUR

"Within this labyrinth Minos shut fast the beast, half bull, half man, and fed him twice on Attic blood, lot-chosen each nine years, until the third choice mastered him."—Ovid, *The Metamorphoses*

The vision dissipates, fading like mist.

The labyrinth returns.

The tulips bloom.

The grass is soft and springy at my feet.

Sitting on the edge of the fountain, letting the water in the basin wash over his hands, is Mr. Arcadio. Wearing the same yellow slicker he had on when I met him on the sidewalk this morning. Surrounded by yellow tulips, he looks like one of them.

He looks at me and smiles.

Rage lights up in me like a wildfire.

"You," I spit. I want to howl and cry and tear him apart limb by limb all at the same time. "You knew? All this time? You knew everything about me, my dad, the shadows, and you never said anything?"

"A labyrinth, Noomi, is not a necessarily a maze," he says calmly, as though I hadn't spoken.

I gape. He's still speaking in riddles? After everything he's put me through?

"Though a maze is always a labyrinth. A maze is a puzzle. A riddle. A problem to be solved. But a labyrinth, particularly in a unicursal pattern like this one, meaning that there is only one path available to the entrant—is not a puzzle. It's a meditation."

"I didn't need a fucking meditation!" I explode.

Mr. Arcadio shakes the water off his hands and wipes them on his pants. He doesn't even look at me as he continues.

"Unicursal labyrinths have been used not just in human symbolism, but in many civilizations across the multiverse to calm the mind via ritualistic walking. Similar to chanting, sitting meditation, or prayer, walking a unicursal labyrinth is a way to access the deepest corners of your mind while achieving outer stillness and focus. It is also relevant," and here he finally looks up, "that there is only one way in and one way out. There are no other paths. Only one future. Only one past."

"I could have turned around and walked out at any point," I say, angry at myself for buying into his games instead of just spitting in his face and leaving like I should.

"You also could have found a Path to your home world," he points out, as though trying to be helpful, "but you did not. You chose to stay. Why, Noomi? Why did you continue to walk the path even after your confrontation with the shadows and your emotional encounter with your father?"

I glare at him, but I can't help but fall into his trap. I'm engaged, caught up in the question. If he's withheld this information from me my whole life, now I have to know why.

"Because I wanted to know. Because you told me you would show me."

He nods. "And so you walked the only path that was available to you."

"What does that have to do with why you kept this information from me my whole life?"

"Think back to the days before you met your friend Silas, before you knew what Pathfinding was or what it means. Remember how you felt then. Put yourself in your own shoes.

Remember how uncertain you were of your own clarity, your strength. Remember the helplessness, the despair that drove you to so many attempts at ending your life. Now imagine that into that chaos, that desperation, I came with these memories of your father, disturbing images of pain and anguish and death. And ask yourself—would you have been able to process and understand all that I've shown you here without first walking the path you've been on since you met Silas?"

I shake my head. "I might have changed my mind sooner. I might have started trying to survive earlier, in earnest."

"Would you have understood everything I've shown you when you were ten in the year after your father died?" he asks. "Or when you were thirteen, and the shadows still seemed like a bad dream and a harrowing memory?" Reluctantly I shake my head. "You cannot face the answers until you understand the questions. Only recently have you begun to ask the right questions."

"Then answer my questions," I say. "I still have so many."

"I will try," he says with a nod.

"Who are you? Really, who are you? I've known you my whole life and I know nothing about you. You saw all these moments in my father's life—how?"

"Has Silas described to you how proficient Pathfinders can see the lines of energy in and around the multiverse? I took an early interest in your father's life, as Pathfinders are astonishingly rare, and I saw his energy from afar when traveling to this world several years after he was born. His journey and growth as a Pathfinder was unusual, like yours. I started watching him. In moments when great power seemed to coalesce around him, I visited him. I was able to bear witness to two crucial moments in his life—the moment when he was struck by lightning, and the Harbingers took note of him and began attempting to destroy him so they might tunnel into this world. But he resisted, so they enlisted the help of another talented Pathfinder—who later began to dog you as well."

"Paul."

He nods. "Because of the concentration of energy bound up inside Pathfinders, we are only vulnerable to biological death while in a world not our own. However, we are extremely vulnerable while in a Path. Traveling. Your father, like you, could not have killed himself—not in his own world—no matter how hard he tried. In a foreign world, maybe, though it would have taken great effort. But when Paul touched him, he forced your father into a Path along with him. As best I can understand, it was there that he dealt the killing blow, before returning him to his own world, ripe for the Harbingers to destroy both him and the world around him. That was the second moment I witnessed.

"Paul succeeded in killing your father, and the shadows would have destroyed your entire world in that moment, if not for the final action your father took—passing both his abilities and his curse onto you. No longer a Pathfinder, relieved of the burden he'd spent most of his life fighting, your father died, and the shadows began pursuing you as a new target."

I nod, processing, fitting these explanations into the images Mr. Arcadio showed me and my own memories. "That's why he said, 'I'm sorry.' He wasn't apologizing for dying. He was apologizing for passing the shadows to me. But he had no choice. It was me or the whole world."

"Exactly." Mr. Arcadio takes a deep, heaving breath, his chest swelling with emotion. "It must have cost him so much, those last moments, knowing what he'd done to you."

I nod. My whole body feels heavy with the weight of this knowledge. And yet, I'm grateful to finally know, after all these years, why the shadows have been haunting me.

"I still don't know who you really are. And how do you know Silas?"

"Ah."

He shifts, his absurd slicker crinkling as he does. The crinkling sound grows, turning to static, blurring the outlines of Mr. Arcadio's form. I squint, unsure what's happening, but the static is growing, taking over his whole body as he turns to face me. I take a step back. His body is changing. The slicker dissolving. The yellow growing brighter, even more vibrant—golden, shiny and metallic. The back of his body extends, growing, shifting, folding outward. There's a light emerging from behind him, so bright it's hard to look at, and I shield my eyes with my hand, taking another step back, my heart pounding.

"I am very old," the voice says, and this time it's not Mr. Arcadio, but the ringing, imperious female voice I heard as I walked the labyrinth. "And I am certainly not human." The static form begins to stabilize, from the inside out, and I can see magnificent blue, red, and yellow splashes on the collarbone of an emerging female body, the rest of which is shining, glimmering gold. "Your civilization first knew me as Isis, goddess of magic, but I have many names, many bodies, and many meanings," she says. "I am one of the original Pathfinders of my civilization, from a star that died long ago. My true name is unpronounceable in your human mouth, so I have many, in all the languages and cultures I visit." A pair of wings unfolds behind her as she opens her arms, majestic and gleaming.

The transformation complete, she stills. Nude and poised, she stares at me.

"Wow," is all I can manage. "I had no idea Mr. Arcadio was a woman."

She laughs, lowering her arms, and her wings fold gently behind her.

"Humans are so foolish," she says. I lower my eyes, chastised. "Even you, for all your intelligence, still attempt to classify me according to such illogical rules as gender. My true gender is something you would not recognize or understand," she says. "I am neither woman nor man, nor anything worthy of wonder or curiosity." She looks at her long limbs, her shining body. "This is just a form I took when it impressed the humans I met five thousand years ago on the banks of the Nile. They liked it, so I kept it. Silas met me in this body years ago while Pathfinding, and he has come to know me this way."

"I imagine he likes it quite a bit," I murmur, feeling a twinge of jealousy. How can I compete with the supernatural goddess standing in front of me?

The lines blur, and once again the figure shifts. The edges go jagged and the gold fades into a hue I recognize as more human. Brilliant color gives way to grizzled grey, and in a moment, I am standing face-to-face with the gravedigger from my dreams, leaning on his shovel.

"I presented this form to you when you were dreamwalking because I wanted you to understand that death is final, fatal, and there can be no return. I don't want to dig your grave, Noomi. I want to help you live a life free of the things that haunt you. But in some worlds, as possibilities split and diverge, that possibility of dying becomes reality. I am determined to ensure that in yours, it stays forever a possibility."

"The cat is alive," I say, my mind foggy. "The cat is dead."

"Yes. But the time has come to open the box. Your fight with the shadows will lead you to the center of your own personal labyrinth. And when it does, I want you to remember: even when it feels like a maze, a puzzle to be solved with myriad possibilities , that is not the reality. There is only one path in, and one path out."

I shake my head. "I still don't understand."

"You will. It's time for you to go. Time has passed in your world, and soon your abuela will be looking for you."

"I have one more question."

He nods, his grey eyes filled with clouds. I meet his gaze in wonder. Mr. Arcadio, this man I've known all my life, contains so many secrets, so many questions. And he's not even human.

"On the mosaic in the fountain...after the memory with Dad, when he was talking about the Kardashev Scale."

"Yes?"

"Why did the mosaic show an image of the minotaur? There were no monsters in this labyrinth."

The gravedigger cocks an eyebrow at me, as if surprised by this question. "No monsters?" he says. "Can you tell me honestly you saw no monsters in this labyrinth?"

The question stops me. I hesitate before answering. "Not like evil beasts or demons..." I reply, thinking out loud. "But I did see things that haunt me. The shadows. The memory of Dad dying."

"The most fearsome demons we encounter are the ones that lurk within us. Our memories. Our fears and insecurities. What frightens you more, Noomi? The shadows? Or the fear that you won't be able to overcome them?"

I nod, understanding. "This isn't just a labyrinth. It's also a mirror."

His eyes gleam, and for a moment I wonder if there isn't something demonic within him too.

"Within every one of us is both the Minotaur and the hero. Theseus went willingly into the labyrinth where the monster waited. Armed with nothing but his wits, a sword, and Ariadne's string, he defeated the Minotaur and liberated Thebes. But when he set sail, he kidnapped Ariadne and dragged her from her home, only to abandon her at the next port. One moment, a hero. The next, a monster. At every moment, it is up to us to decide: which will I be? The Minotaur? Or the hero?"

THE CAVE

"To begin with, tell me do you think that these men would have seen anything of themselves or of one another except the shadows cast from the fire on the wall of the cave?" —Plato, *The Republic*

By the time I walk through the front door, it's seven-thirty in the morning, and I manage to sneak in just as Abuela emerges from the guest bedroom to make coffee. Padding upstairs, I sneak back into bed, pretending to have been asleep as Abuela knocks on my door to tell me it's time to get ready to go.

I bumble through the rest of the day, dizzy, like a bird who's lost her sense of direction.

Abuela drives me to the courthouse and sits with me in a small, stuffy room that smells like old dust while Daniel Hirata explains patiently that the only words I have to say are *not guilty*. We go into a courtroom and the judge calls my name. Says something about the D.A. dropping charges. Someone mentions Dr. Chase's recommendation letter. I hear words like *indictment* and *arson* and *civil claims* like the gentle humming of bees. Background noise. I smile, nod, and say the words out loud: *not guilty*. Everyone is impressed with my composure. I am asked to promise to appear in court. When I make this promise, the judge tells me I may go.

The humming grows louder. My mind is full of memories. Was I in the labyrinth for an hour or a year? Words and images echo and resound, bumping into each other, careening around like particles zipping through an accelerator.

Does anything in this world, this mundane world of courtrooms and civil claims matter when I can travel to another universe in the blink of an eye?

I spend the day pondering this question, anxious and on edge, wondering where Silas is and why I haven't heard from him since the night we spent in a holding cell. Wondering if the things he said were true: that he cares about me, that he's been drawn to me since the beginning. Are those things still true? Why haven't I heard from him?

I haven't been visited by the shadows, either.

Nor have I seen Paul.

Are these things related? I wonder. But I have no answers, no way to find out.

After the courthouse, we go to the hospital to visit my mother, picking Ada up from school on the way. We stay there with her for a few hours. The doctors say she will be discharged tomorrow. Her speech is improving. Words in English are coming back. I smile and laugh with Ada when they tell us the news, but inside, I am as far from that hospital room as it is possible to be.

In the afternoon, I have an appointment with Dr. Chase.

It's too much to happen in one day.

Spending the morning out of time and space with Mr. Arcadio's strange series of alter egos.

Then the courthouse.

Then the hospital.

Being in Dr. Chase's office is the most normal thing that's happened all day, and it still doesn't feel real.

Now, sitting in the waiting room, staring at the ficus tree in the corner, I realize the answer to the question I've been pondering all day. The answer is, yes, this world matters. Because my family is here. Because my future is here. Because everything I've ever known centers and grounds here. Because here is where the shadows want to find me. Here is where I must defeat them.

Dr. Chase made a special appointment to meet with me later in the afternoon. Her personal assistant has left, and Dr. Chase asked for a few minutes to write an email before we start our appointment. I brought a book to read while I wait, but there's no point in opening a book only to be cut off moments later. Sure enough, as my eyes begin to glaze over and I'm sliding into a dazed nap, a voice rings out:

"Ready?"

I straighten and nod. Push myself out of my chair. Smile. It's a genuine smile, and that feels good.

I'm armed, now. With knowledge, with confidence, with the trust and surety of my friends and family. Mama is getting better. She saw the shadows too. Ada has her lantern. My friends believe me. Mr. Arcadio is a Pathfinder.

I know what I have to do.

"Yes, I'm ready."

She leads me back into the private room. I take my usual seat on the red couch and she settles into her black chair.

"How are you, Noomi?"

"I'm good. I'm well. Thanks."

"How are you holding up under the stress of everything?"

"Things are looking up. This morning at the arraignment they didn't announce charges for arson. Which means it's just assault I have to worry about. The only reason they're going for the assault charge is because they actually have a witness for that." I pause. Look her straight in the eyes. I want her to feel these next words. "Mr. Hirata said it was most likely because of the glowing reference letter you wrote for me. I want to thank you for that."

Her face lights up. "Everything I wrote was true."

"Thank you anyway."

"Do you want to talk about what's happening in the case?"

"No. I don't want to, but I should. I'm afraid. And I shouldn't be dealing with this at all."

"Why do you say that?"

"Because I didn't do it. Silas did."

"Silas was the one who hit Paul?"

I'm on shaky grounds here. I trust her more than I ever have after she wrote me that glowing testimonial for the judge. But if I continue, she might trust me less than she ever has.

"I know it sounds crazy."

She meets my eyes. Nods. "It doesn't sound *crazy*, Noomi. But it does sound like you might be trying to pass accountability for something you did on to someone who exists only in your mind."

"I'm willing to accept the punishment if the judge finds me guilty. But obviously that's not what I want."

"How does Silas feel about all this?"

Is she taking me seriously? I can never quite tell.

"We haven't really talked about it. I think he just wanted us to escape a bad situation. I don't think he meant to hurt him."

She nods, unsmiling.

"Do you want to tell me what Paul was doing that created this fear in you?"

"He brought the shadows to me."

"You mean he triggered a panic or anxiety attack?"

I stare at her. "No. I mean he brought the shadows to me."

"Noomi…" Her expression is pained. "Can you explain how?"

"I'm not really sure. Part of it was this dark story about the myth of an oak tree from Norse mythology that some Christian missionaries chopped down. He called it Donar's Oak. But the other part was…it's hard to explain. He was looking at me, and then he touched me, and the shadows were there. Generally, the shadows are a slow build. They creep up, like a fever or a head cold. But this was an ambush. One minute I was fine. The next minute everything was black."

"Stories have power, Noomi. I read the myth of Yggdrasil in college, and I remember being horrified too, as I always am when I hear about the destruction of ancient and sacred things. It's no wonder it affected you." She pauses. "Have you considered the possibility that Paul didn't know what he was doing?"

"Yes." My voice is flat. "He knew."

She folds her wrists delicately atop her crossed legs, a blonde pretzel. "How can you be sure?"

I look her in the eyes. "I know because he touched me and the shadows came," I say. "I know because he brought them to me, and he did so without hesitation, without question, without fear. He wanted it to happen. He made it happen."

"No one can make you have a panic attack, Noomi."

What a perfectly reasonable thing to say if you still believe the shadows are nothing more than the conjurings of an irrational mind.

Everyone else believes me. Silas, Ada, Mama, even Claire and Kalifa. Why don't I prove it to her?

"Dr. Chase," I say, pulling a pen from my pocket, "do you remember a few weeks ago when I was in your office and the shadows started appearing?"

She stares at me blankly.

"What are you talking about?"

"The shadows appeared. Here, in your office, while we were talking." I twirl the pen between my fingers. "Your eyes were so black it was like looking into space. Do you remember that?"

"Have you been experiencing things no one else can remember?" Her voice is low. "Memories of things no one else can verify?"

"You don't remember because that's what happens when the shadows come," I say. "I've been telling you this for two years. It's why I wake up passed out in the park after walking Kuri or asleep in the car. It's why I try never to go anywhere alone, because when I do, they find me and they obliterate me. I pass out. I lose time. I lose my memories. You don't remember me being in your office one minute, and then gone the next?"

"Noomi," she says carefully, "are you feeling all right?"

I click the button on the pen that pops out the sharp, inky tip. And I jam it two inches deep into my thigh like a shot of adrenaline.

Dr. Chase leaps from her chair. She stares at me wild-eyed. "Why did you do that? Why would you hurt yourself like that?"

I pull the pen out and the wound heals behind it. There's blood on the pen, but not on my body. When I don't move, she stops moving too. Watching my face. Her gaze drops to my thigh. She stares. Her mouth hangs open. Her face turns white.

"I've been telling you for a long time that I'm not normal, Dr. Chase. Remember the incident in the barn? How the doctors all said it was a miracle I was unhurt? It's not a miracle."

I search her face, scrutinizing her, but she looks as blank as a stone wall. Unable to process. In denial. She sinks back into her chair as if gravity has suddenly taken hold again. Weightless before, now she drops like a stone.

"That's not possible," she mutters.

"You saw it with your own eyes."

"Is this some kind of joke? A magic trick? An illusion?" She lunges forward, snatching the pen out of my hand. She presses it into her palm, shakes it, rattles it against her ear.

I cock my head to the side, watching her. Something strange is going on. "It's not a joke, Dr. Chase. It's what's been happening to me for the last seven years. Just like the shadows."

"No." The hardness in her voice frightens me. "This isn't real. This is crazy."

The calm I felt moments ago evaporates. "How can you say that? You saw it happen."

She's staring at the pen, her eyes round. Abruptly she looks up at me. There's a fanaticism there. "You're doing something. You're lying. You're having a psychotic break."

"You...you saw the medical reports," I stutter. "The doctors—"

"No one knows what happened the night of the fire," she snaps. "Why would the doctors believe you?"

She's not making any sense. I shiver. "Dr. Chase, I—"

"You crazy girl." Her voice is low. I recoil, pressing myself into the couch. "I've been trying for years to help you, and nothing has worked. You're insane. And now you're trying to make me think I'm the crazy one."

My heart feels like a piston in my chest but there's a steadiness in my mind I didn't expect. She's never really believed me. Even when I trusted her, she still acted like I was a disease she could cure. Why would now be any different? I take a deep breath, put my hands in front of me, and stand as calmly as can.

"I think I'm upsetting you, so I'm going to leave now."

I sidestep in front of the couch, heading for the door. But before I can make it, she flips open a panel on the arm of her chair—a panel I never knew existed—and presses a button. I freeze, staring at her. I half-expect an alarm to start blaring, lights to flash, and metal sheets to slide into place over the doors and windows. But for a long, unsteady second, nothing happens.

We stare at each other before I find words.

"What did you just do?"

"The police will be here any minute."

I feel electrified. Every nerve in my body is alive and tingling. "What are you going to tell them? There's no wound. There's no evidence I tried to hurt myself or you."

She holds up the pen. Unsmiling. Still covered in my blood. I shudder violently.

"I have this."

Castor and Pollux

"There are darknesses in life and there are lights, and you are one of the lights, the light of all lights." —Bram Stoker, *Dracula*

In the eternity that passes while Dr. Chase watches me like a rabid animal who's just infected another host, I make a decision: I'm not going to stay here. I'm not going to wait for the officers to drag me away and lock me up or commit me to a mental hospital. As hard as it will be to explain my sudden disappearance from Dr. Chase's office, it will be easier than being walked out in handcuffs.

I close my eyes and the world shifts from the crisp, vivid colors of everyday life to the porous threads that make up the worlds. Empty of feeling, I watch Dr. Chase stand there, waiting for me to do something. I search for a thread to pull me to another world.

I find a Path that looks promising. It feels as dark as I am. But not as empty. There's something glimmering there. Something light and bright, singing to me. With no energy left to care if anyone sees me Pathfinding, I step into the black and the image of Dr. Chase splinters before me, replaced by the *whooshing* vertiginous falling that is the space between worlds. A second and a thousand years later, I open my eyes in my chosen world.

I am standing in the sky. I have been transported to the empty blackness of space. Curious what form my body takes here, I glance down. There's nothing to see. I extend an arm out and feel my limb stretching. Move my legs and feel them moving. But there's nothing. I am as empty as the vacuum around me.

But it's not entirely black. In every direction there is a sea of stars. Pinpricks of light that decorate every inch of surrounding space. No wonder it felt glimmering.

"How am I alive?" I murmur to myself. "How is this possible?" No sound emerges, but I can hear my voice in my head.

I find I can glide through the vacant space with movements like swimming. I stop swimming and learn that I can do the same by walking. I spend a few minutes walking around, feeling my body moving but invisible, shocked by the strangeness of it. But none of it matters. The stars don't grow closer or further. My body is moving, my muscles engaging, but nothing changes in this vast desert of stars. So I stop and look around. I lie on my back, as if I'm lying on the grass in a park to gaze up at a clear night sky. I take a breath and smile. It's deeply relaxing here.

I could stay here. Stay here and never leave.

Constellations form out of the blackness. The Big Dipper, Ursa Major, is always the first one I see. Then Cassiopeia. I must be close to Earth if the constellations look the same. If I were far away, the stars wouldn't arrange themselves in the same pattern in the sky. Everything would look different. I must at least be in a similar area within our galaxy. But Earth, the moon, and any other planets are far enough away to be mere pinpricks along with the rest.

In this void, it's easy to get disoriented, so I find a star—the North Star—and use it as my center. It's strangely grounding, out here in space, to find a navigational point in common with explorers from the past.

From the north star I branch out, naming every constellation I can remember and identify. It's always hard to pick out the individual stars that make up the constellations and string them together. I think back to the origin stories of many of these constellations in Greek and Roman mythology. The legends say that Zeus hung the images of great heroes or demons in the sky so that even in death, they wouldn't be forgotten. There's Orion, the hunter who was killed by a scorpion, whose image also hangs in the sky, and became my zodiac sign, Scorpio.

I search for the other constellations. I don't know them very well, but out here, with nothing in the way, they're easy to find. Libra, the scales. Leo, the lion. Gemini, the twins. Gemini is a nondescript constellation: essentially just two lines of stars, connected at the top by an imaginary line.

Zeus must not have been much of an artist.

"Do you know the myth?"

I jerk upright—whatever that means in this directionless space—backing away from the voice. But my fright only lasts an instant. It's Silas, of course. Though I can't see him, I can tell by his voice.

"Silas, I have so much to—" *to tell you*, I finish in my head, trailing off as I wonder what he's talking about. "What myth?"

"The myth of Gemini. The twins."

"I used to," I say. "I can't remember now. Why?"

"Castor and Pollux are twins," Silas says. "But not really. Both were born to Leda, a mortal woman. Castor was the son of a mortal man, but Pollux was the son of Zeus, who appeared to Leda as a swan and seduced her. Along with Helen of Troy, the siblings were born together out of an egg."

Something is ringing in the back of my mind. An echo, a memory, an idea. The flashes I've been experiencing over the last few weeks, since the crash. The visions.

"You've been seeing things, haven't you? Strange images at sudden moments. I have too. We've been watching each other travel, Noomi. Every time you take a Path, I feel it.

And every time I travel, I see you wherever you are in that moment."

A word floats up at me from my research into Pathfinding. "Quantum entanglement," I whisper. "Is that how you always know how to find me?"

"I think so," he says. "I get flashes of you in my mind. I didn't know they were you, either. Not until today when I got a flash of you at Dr. Chase's office. Then I knew, because I've been there before. I was able to tune into those visions more clearly to follow you here."

My head spins. "I didn't know I was watching you."

"We're connected. Like Castor and Pollux. We're bound together somehow."

A thought occurs to me. "Silas, when were you born?"

"November 11, 2001," he replies. "Eleven in the morning."

I nod, awed. "Me too."

"What are the odds that two Pathfinders, both human, would be born at the exact same time in different universes?"

"Astronomical." I glance at the stars around us.

"It's funny," he says. "We're like Castor and Pollux. But our zodiac sign is Scorpio, not Gemini."

I laugh. "Who said the zodiac is accurate? My friend Kalifa says it's more important for the stories we tell ourselves than for the truth of the predictions or personalities."

"Kalifa sounds smart," Silas says.

I pause, thinking. "Something about the coincidence of our birth has bound us together. Our timelines—past, present, and future—are tied up together. Quantum entanglement. It's why we can feel each other travel."

"What does that mean?"

"I'm not sure, but I read about the concept recently. I was trying to make sense of Pathfinding. I think it means the particles that make us up are connected somehow. That because we're...we're kind of twins, in a cosmic sense, the matter that makes us up is subject to quantum entanglement. You can't do something to one of us without doing it to both of us."

"That's not any clearer than what you said before," he says.

The thoughts are coming together more quickly now, and my words come out in a rush. "Quantum entanglement is what happens when two particles are created that have equal but opposite properties. Such as spin. Say you generate two particles simultaneously; one whose spin is negative and the other whose spin is positive. If you try to measure something about one of those two particles, it will affect the properties of the other. The particles are *entangled*, and doing or recording something to one means you necessarily change the other. And no matter how far apart the particles are, changing one inevitably and instantaneously alters the other. Does that make sense?"

Silas is quiet. I wait as patiently as I can.

Finally, he responds. "I think so. Keep going."

Breathless, I continue. "I think our entire selves are entangled. The systems that make us up are bound together. When your body is annihilated in one world and recreated in another—which is what Pathfinding is—I see it. I *feel* it. And when I travel, you do the same."

"How is it possible for that to happen on a macro, biological level?"

"I don't know," I reply. "But scientists have proved that it happens in chlorophyll production in plants. Within a plant cell, photons create quantum entanglement between light-receptors and energy generator systems. I read about it in biology class."

There's a long silence. "I don't understand it. But it explains why I've always been drawn to you. Even before I saw you the first time, I felt...pulled to you."

Something else dawns on me. "You started this conversation talking about Castor and Pollux. But they had a sister."

"Yes. Helen of Troy."

"Doesn't that..." I dig around in my head for Kalifa's extensive knowledge of mythology. "Doesn't Helen mean light in Greek?"

"Not exactly," he replies. "It could derive from torch—" chills run up and down my spine "—or from moon."

"That explains Ada's lantern," I say, remembering the vibrant green in the car the night of the crash, and at the library, the light that only I could see. I pause, looking at the outlines of Silas's body in space, made up of a thousand brilliant stars. "How do you know so much ancient Greek?"

"I used to draw scenes from old stories," he says, a little bashful. "I went through a phase when I was really interested in *The Iliad*."

There's a long silence. This new understanding of the connection I've felt to Silas since the day he offered me a handful of peanuts on the mountaintop—it feels like a revelation. Like the fulfillment of a promise.

It feels like permission.

For what?

"Noomi," he says. I shiver at the tension in his voice. "Come here."

Ah, I think. That's what.

And I do.

I fall into his arms. His body. His essence. We are incorporeal but I can feel every inch of him. The tension, the intensity, the desire. It's like holding starlight, the way the softness of pale rays iluminates my skin. Like the softest silk; like flower petals against my skin. It's like holding my hands beneath a fountain and letting the water run over me, and the water is light washing through the darkest places in me.

"Let's go back," I say. I am thirsty for so much more.

He nods, and I close my eyes, seeking the right threads. When I find them, I reach for his hand. I grasp for the light, feeling it, pulling, opening—

I fall into the Path.

The soft *whoosh.*

Feathers against my back.

Falling into a void. Being compressed, tightened, shrunk to nothing.

And blooming again, fully human, mass, weight, and pressure, on the banks of the river.

I meet his eyes. Dark green and mossy, rich with life and wildness. He crosses the space between us in a heartbeat. Bends to me like a willow to the wind.

Lips, touch.

Pressure, warmth.

Sweet, soft.

I kiss back in earnest, and he presses his body to mine. I lean back as he wraps his arms around me and runs his hands up the blades of my shoulders. My hands go to his hips, my fingertips dig into his spine.

How long have I wanted this?

"Since the first time you saw me," he whispers in my ear.

How do you know what I'm thinking?

"I feel like I know everything about you." He smiles and I can feel it even with my eyes closed, his lips changing shape as he kisses me again, the warmth and excitement curling inside him. "And what I don't know, I want to learn."

His hands wrap around my hips as he pulls me toward him, and I can see the hunger in his eyes. It feels so good to be wanted—and to want him in return. I bite his lip, pulling it with my teeth as his tongue rakes across mine. His fingers press into my sides and run up my body, tracing my hips, the outlines of my ribs, my navel, my spine. I dig my fingers into his shoulders, kissing my way down his jaw and to his neck, desperate to taste every inch of him. His fingers go up, under my shirt, and I shiver from the contrast of his warm fingers against my skin, and the chill from the late afternoon air.

Behind us, the river rushes on, the sweet sound of running water carrying across the grass and through the trees as evening mist settles around us.

But then he stops.

Pulls away.

Meets my eyes.

My stomach does a backflip, and I search his face, his mind, for some understanding of what's happening, why the magic is ending.

"Noomi," he says. "I need to tell you something."

I lean into him again, pressing forward, tilting my head upward for another kiss. "Can it wait?"

He shakes his head. "It's about the shadows. And Paul."

I freeze.

"Tell me."

"I figured out why they haven't been coming recently. I think Paul is setting a trap. Remember how I told you it's possible to stumble into a Path if you're not careful? You need to watch your movements, watch yourself. They're trying to destroy you."

"I've known that for a long time." I curl against him, pressing into his chest, letting him wrap his arms around me. Even after everything that's happened. All I've learned in the last few days. Kalifa, Claire, and my mother all believe me. This new wonder standing in front of me. Even after everything, the battle isn't over. "I don't want to fight anymore." The words come out unbidden.

"Don't say that, Noomi. We're in this together. And we're going to win."

"How did you find out about Paul?"

"I followed him. He was meeting with someone. I don't know who. They talked about you. About how there's a Path inside you that makes you the perfect entry point for the shadows. And they talked about trying to lure you into a Path, and the shadows will be waiting there to kill you and swallow your world."

My heart aches. Just when I've discovered how sweet life can be, someone is so eager to take it away from me. I wrap my arms around Silas. Press my cheek to his shoulder. I can no longer wish none of this had happened. If none of this had happened, I would never have met him.

My phone rings in my pocket, vibrating against my hip. Silas glances down, and reluctantly I reach for it. I pull it out and swipe across the screen to open, reading the message there. It's from Abuela. The message is in Spanish, but I translate in my head: *Noomi, where are you? I've been calling and calling. Dr. Chase said you vanished from her office?? Call me back!!*

I check my phone for missed calls, but there are none. Of course. I wouldn't have been able to receive calls while I was in another universe. But then the phone vibrates again. *New voice mail*, the alert reads.

Regretfully, I peel away from Silas and let him wrap his arms around me from behind. I dial Abuela's number and press the phone to my ear. It only takes a second for her to pick up.

"Noomi, where are you? What happened at the doctor's?" she asks in Spanish.

"I'm fine, Abuela. I had to leave the office."

"Por qué? Qué opasó?"

I search for the word. "Dr. Chase threatened me." A lie? To your grandmother? No, not a lie. This is true. Dr. Chase did threaten me. She threatened to tell other people I'm dangerous. To tell the police I tried to hurt myself. This is no lie. "She said things that weren't true."

There's a long pause on the other end. I suck in a breath. "*Lo siento, mi amor. Eso es terrible.*" I'm sorry, my love. That is terrible. I exhale with relief. "Come home, Noomi," she says. "I need you to help me find your sister."

Behind me, Silas freezes. Every muscle in his body tenses. I can feel his breath stop, the tiniest movements of his body cease.

"Ada is missing?" he asks, his voice low. Panic rises into my belly as I repeat his question into the phone.

"*Si*," Abuela says. "Ada was playing in the yard. I called her in to do her homework, but she was gone. Nowhere to be found."

"I'm sure she just wandered down the street," I say, placating. Inside, my nerves are on fire. Ada, missing? Now?

"*Ven rápido,*" Abuela says. Come quickly.

The line goes dead.

"Paul," Silas says into my ear, that single word full of anger. "It must be him."

"Do you think he…" I can't bring myself to say it.

"Do I think he kidnapped her? I wouldn't put it past him."

I take a deep breath, trying to clear my head. Think rationally, Noomi. Stay calm. What's going on here? "What does he want with Ada?"

"She's bait," Silas says grimly. "He took her to another world to try to lure you into a Path where the shadows are waiting."

"How could Paul take Ada into another world? Wouldn't that kill her?"

Silas looks at me like this is a silly question. "Ada's a Pathfinder too. You didn't know?"

I gape at him. "I didn't know. How did you find out?"

He gives me a little smile. "She waved at me, that day she was in the car with your mother after the concert. She could see me. I already knew about you, of course. That's when I realized Ada was too." Of course. It explains so much. How much she understands of what I'm going through. The mysterious light she shined at the shadows. "The lines of power around her are faint and hard to see. She's still so young."

The implication settles on me like a weight. Ada's a Pathfinder. That means Paul could take her anywhere.

"We don't know if Ada's really missing," I say, as much to calm myself as to offer a rational perspective. "Maybe we're making this out to be more than it is."

"Still," he says, "we need to be careful."

"Let's go to the house. We can talk to Abuela, find Ada if she's there. And if she isn't—"

Silas doesn't say anything. When I look up at him, his mouth is set in a thin line, his jaw hard from clenching his teeth.

"If she isn't," he says, "we're going to get her back."

WEAVING

"So by day she'd weave at her great and growing web—By night, by the light of torches set beside her, She would unravel all she'd done." — Homer, *The Odyssey*

We're not far from my house, so instead of Pathfinding, we walk. Hand-in-hand, I lead Silas through the trees and grass and out onto the streets. It takes about ten minutes. Kuri is barking furiously, yapping as I run up the stairs to the front door. Out of breath and sweaty, I put my hand on the doorknob and start to twist.

But Silas pulls me back. "I shouldn't come in."

"Yes, you should." I grab his hand and pull him with me, torn by conflicting emotions. I need to find Ada. I need to reassure Abuela that Ada will be okay. But I wish I could savor this moment. I'm leading this human from another world, to whom I am mysteriously connected, to my home, the place I grew up. I want to show him who I am.

"I already know who you are," he says quietly. And I get an echo of his thoughts too. A swirling cloud of words and images that culminates in: *And you know me better than you think you do*. And then, almost shyly, "But I don't know your grandmother. Would you like to introduce me?"

I pull up short, shocked. "I thought she couldn't see you?"

Silas laughs. The sound strikes me as odd given the gravity of the situation. But I let myself smile back.

"I can choose how I present myself in your world, Noomi. Most of the time, I choose to be invisible. Only other Pathfinders can see me. But I can choose to be visible, too, although I'll never be quite as solid as I am in my home world."

"That explains Mr. Arcadio," I say. "He can change forms too."

But Silas shakes his head. "Only very experienced Pathfinders can shapeshift." There's a note of regret in his voice. "I can't do that yet. I can choose to be visible or invisible, but I don't know how to be anything other than myself."

I squeeze his hand. "I want you exactly as you are."

I turn the handle. Kuri starts barking again. Silas gives himself a little shake. I can't explain it, but he seems to solidify. The distinction between him and the lilacs behind him becomes clearer, as if before he was ephemeral, intransient. As if he's only now fully realizing his physical form.

I open the front door.

"Noomi!" Abuela comes running in from the kitchen, cell phone in hand. "*Gracias a Dios*, you're here."

"Has Ada turned up?" I ask. Kuri runs in circles at my feet, but for once, I don't pick him up. I'm not ready to let go of Silas. Not yet.

"*Aún no...*" Her voice shakes. "You don't know where she—"

She stops, looking Silas up and down.

"*Quién es este hombre guapo?*" Abuela asks, smiling. Her eyes stray to our hands, fingers entwined.

"Abuela, this is Silas. He's a new friend." I take a breath, forcing myself to focus. "Did you call Elizabeth or Maria's family? Is Ada with one of them?"

"Yes, I called. She isn't with them."

Silas and I exchange glances.

Paul, he says to me. I nod.

"Don't worry, Mrs. Perez. I'm sure she wandered off. Noomi and I will find her."

She nods. Silas squeezes my hand, once again the picture of steadiness. He turns to walk out the door, and I follow. It's not confidence in his movements, it's surety. Reliability.

"Where do we go?" I ask. "How do we find her?"

Silas closes his eyes, and I do the same. A long moment passes. The threads materialize before me. I can see Silas, composed of hundreds of millions of tiny, tightly wrapped lines, pulsing a dark but vibrant green. A Path appears a hundred feet in front of us. I watch it carefully, my eyes closed. It fades away. The moment has gone.

"Paths are as much about time as they are about space," Silas says quietly. "You can see their past and future if you're in the right place, and you can see their movements if you're in the right time. They slide, like everything else, through the dimensions of the world. I need you to focus on your sister. You know her better than anyone. What color is her energy?"

"Green," I respond immediately.

"Okay," he says "Let's go out back to where she was playing. If we're lucky, we'll be able to see traces of that energy behind her. It might give us a clue to where she went."

We walk around the side of the house. I open the gate to the back yard and push through the hedges my mother has so carefully pruned along the pathway. There's a wooden playhouse out back where Ada loves to hide. Mama bought it for us right after we moved here, to this house, in the year after my father's death. It was an attempt to give me back a shred of the innocence I'd lost overnight. The irony is that I rarely touched the thing. It felt too fake, too silly. The gesture was too clearly an attempt to return something I'd lost. But I already knew the thing I'd lost was irretrievable. At ten years old, after facing death in my own house, in my father's eyes, it felt like a terrible joke, a vicious prank the world was playing on me. I was an adult, I told myself at the time. I didn't need a playhouse. Much less one that could stand in for my dad. Even then, I knew better than to blame Mom. She was just trying to help. But she had no idea how poor a replacement a stolid, wooden playhouse was for a living, breathing father—even one who occasionally breathed fire.

But Ada loved it. She'd drag me out to play on the monkey bars, to climb the fireman's pole, to romp around in the "tree house." She used my pocketknife to make carvings in the walls and drew all over the thing in chalk, to be redone every time it rained. Which, in the Pacific Northwest, was frequently. I'm convinced it was the urgency of that fresh, blank canvas every couple of days that gave her the art skills she took with her to kindergarten.

Now, even with my eyes open, I can feel the traces of her in it. I close my eyes and the dust of her is all over it, threads that lead nowhere, like white lint on a black dress.

"She was here," I say to Silas.

"And Paul, too," he responds.

I glare at the playhouse, twice betrayed by this obscene monument. You tried to replace my father, and now you take my sister?

"Where are they?"

Silas watches the wooden structure with the air of a scientist observing a creature from behind a two-way mirror. His eyes flit from one side of the playhouse to the other, then he closes his eyes, like he's contemplating a deep problem.

"They're in a world close to this one," he says. "I can feel it. It's not far."

"Is there a Path?"

"Yes." He takes a deep breath and squeezes his eyes shut, like a child hiding from something frightening on the television. Then reaches out, his fingertips feeling at the gaps between worlds, peeling back the layers, searching for something close.

I feel the moment of tension, like a fish on a hook. He jerks forward slightly, pulled by something intangible, and sucks in a deep breath. His fingers delve into the lines. I shut my eyes so I can watch more closely.

One time, when I was a child and my father had just been awarded tenure at the university, we went to visit my mother's extended family in Jordan. There was an ancient woman at one of the hand looms in the market who looked like she'd walked out of the Stone Age. Her face was as impassive as a cliffside, but her hands were making magic, as delicate as any harpist's as they flew across the loom.

Standing there, watching Silas search for that opening, his hands remind me of the weaver's. Delicate, precise, unafraid.

He turns to me and opens his eyes.

"I'm sorry, Noomi, but I can't take you with me."

I stare at him blankly.

"Paul could be waiting for you on the other side," he says. "I can't let him hurt you."

His eyes are as iridescent as the rainbow.

I try to speak but the words die on my tongue.

"I'll be back soon. With Ada. I promise."

His hand in mine evaporates.

His outline crumbles and dissipates.

His silhouette in the setting sun vanishes.

I am clutching a ghost.

Silas is gone.

KERBEROS

"And before them a dreaded hound on watch, Kerberos, who has no pity, but a vile stratagem : as people go in he fawns on all, with actions of his tail and both ears, but he will not let them go back out, but lies in wait for them and eats them up, when he catches any going back through the gates."—Hesiod, *Theogony*

A guttural growl escapes my throat as my fingers clench around the air that was Silas. In my mind I can feel his regret, the sense of betrayal, the wondering if he's doing the right thing. I can feel him feeling *my* anger, reacting to it, pulling away, his intentions solidifying. My fingernails dig into my palms. Teeth grind in my jaw. Fury ripples through me like a breaking wave. In it I can taste my father—the rage that defined him, the uncontrollable anger that led him to throw pots at the wall and once to break a chair on the lawn when he thought I wasn't watching.

I will not be left out of this. The thought runs through my head a thousand times in the few seconds since Silas has been gone and I've stood staring at the outlines of the space he left behind. This is my fight. No one can win it but me.

And in the dark space of that thought, the battle comes to me.

The shadows, blooming as day fades to dusk, begin to grow. Expanding like the space of an inhale—waiting for an exhale that never comes. In the corners of my vision, they creep like spindly fingers, waiting to wrap their hands around my throat. They grow. They flower. They poison.

I suck in a breath, summoning all my energy for this fight. I close my eyes and imagine the tulips blooming everywhere in Mr. Arcadio's labyrinth. I remember the gravedigger liquefied in colors so wild and brilliant I could never have imagined them. I push aside my anger at Silas and think of the green in his eyes, the iridescence whenever he takes a Path.

The shadows are outside me, I tell myself over and over again. They have no power over my mind. I fought them off once before. On the mountain, facing Paul. Then it was anger that nourished me. Can I use that again?

I try to harness the anger. To let the sense of betrayal thrum through my veins. It strengthens me, and I nourish that seed.

But still, they're powerful.

The weights settle on my shoulders. Darkness clouds my vision and my mind grows empty. The colors in my memory begin to fade.

Buy time…find a Path…

I close my eyes. Distantly, a thought occurs to me. *You weren't supposed to Pathfind*, a low, echoing voice says, as if from far away. *That's what Paul wants. What the shadows want.*

I know, says the part of me drowning in apathy. But I don't have a choice. My vision blurred and my mind foggy, I feel around, waiting for an opening, a place where I can peel back the layers to fall into a Path to another world. I touch the edges of nearby worlds and find one that feels fresh, warm, and familiar. Dazed and sleepy, I step forward, conscious only of my need to get away, just for a few moments. I need more time…more time to fight them…

As I fall into the Path, I can feel Silas from somewhere in the multiverse, shouting, screaming at me not to do it. Angry, I ignore him, pitching myself voluntarily into the Path. With the familiar *whoosh* and the feeling of collapsing into myself and being reassembled on the other side, I arrive.

Ha. No Paul lying in wait for me here.

Somewhere, I swear I can feel Silas glaring at me.

I look around at my surroundings. My feet are anchored on the ground—I'm not in space or floating in a miasma of color. The ground is dense and wet. The air is humid and heavy, and I can taste water on the air. The treads of my sneakers dig into rich mud, fertile soil. I take a step and the ground squishes beneath my feet. Plant life abounds. There are massive trees with elongated leaves, their boughs so heavy they drip down like palm fronds. Ferns are everywhere. Little green things spring up at my feet, packed into small spaces, competing for attention. I glance up, past the tree limbs and overhanging fronds. The sky beyond is stormy, and the clouds are blue and grey, edged in purple and green, rolling, shifting, changing. Lightning flashes overhead.

I sigh in happiness, delighted that I'm lucky enough to visit these places, forgetting for a moment that I came here to escape the trailing darkness of the shadows, that Ada is in grave danger, that Silas left me behind.

"I think I went back in time," I whisper. "I thought Silas said we couldn't time travel?"

But then I remember his illustration, the way worlds expanded moving forward through time and contracted moving back. I recall the gravedigger's description of the laws of physics diverging as the worlds separate, and I recall how very little physicists understand about time, anyway. And I remember that I'm not in my own world. I'm *somewhere else*. I didn't travel back in time in my world, although this one may be similar to—it may even be an ancestor of—my own.

But already, the strange apathy is settling on my shoulders.

The clouds are darker than they should be. Purple fades to blue. Blue fades to black. Greys grow darker. The misty gloom, the heaviness of the air, seems to coalesce, solidify, settle around me, bowing my head, crumbling my shoulders.

Already? The question emerges like a sigh. They're here again, already?

Distant, echoing: They're following me.

Strength leaves my muscles. My bones feel loose and tired. A skeleton assembled improperly. Joints that refuse to bend. Tendons that can't pull.

Bioluminescence, I tell myself, trying to recall the blue. Chroma, I tell myself, trying to recall the swirling pinks and oranges. Here, now, I tell myself, looking skyward for the dark, intense colors on the clouds overhead. But the lights are fading. The colors sliding to grey.

I collapse. My hands hit the ground and are caked in mud. Water seeps in through my jeans. My vision has been reduced to my immediate surroundings. Green palm fronds. Dark earth. I close my eyes, pressing into the dirt, using my fingers to find a snag to another world.

They'll follow me anywhere. But I can't let them drown me.

I search for a new world. Somewhere distant, different. Somewhere far away from the shadows. I find one that feels so foreign I assume it must be very different from my own. The greens on the fronds around me fade to grey, then black. I pull at the tiny fibers of the world and carve out a new Path. So nice…so relaxing…to lie down…to fall into it.…

Noomi, stop! Silas's voice, enraged and afraid, pounds against the walls of my skull.

But it's too late. I'm falling into the vortex. Not just the pillowesque feeling of being enveloped by soft down, but the sudden realization that the Paths I'm following are leading me further and further away from where I need to be: with Silas, looking for Ada, protecting her from Paul. But this thought is too quickly forgotten as the Path consumes me, the crushing demolition of self and then the rebuilding, restructuring, recreating.

Here I am. That first thought feels clear and rejuvenated, like a drink of water after a hot day. The shadows are gone. Coherency and energy return.

But this world is different. Very different.

The air is smoky and hot. Too hot. I'm sweating, already. Where am I? I inhale and cough. Pull my shirt up over my nose. Hold my hands out and thick grey dust settles on them. Ash? None of this can hurt me, I remind myself, not really. Everything around me is dark, but there's pale white light from overhead. No sunlight touches this place, at least not now, but there's a canopy of stars above. The ground is rocky. I can feel it, hard and crumbling, under my feet. I turn around, scanning the horizon. In the distance is a massive mountain range, the peaks burning red-hot. A plume of smoke ten times the height of the mountain pillars into the sky. Lava? A volcano?

The ground starts to shake, throwing me to the side. The land cracks. The shaking intensifies, vibrating so hard my teeth are rattling in my jaw, my bones unsettled. The dirt liquefies. I stumble back, away from the mud, rolling tumultuously. Then the rumbling stops.

I stand, hands at my sides, unsure whether the quake will continue or not.

This isn't where I meant to go. I wanted something vibrant and welcoming. This is about as far from that as I can imagine.

In the distance, the molten rock, glowing fiery through the plumes of ash, begins to fade.

At first I think it's just the smoke and ash. But then the shadows start to bloom in midair, popping into existence, blacking out my vision. They seem stronger, here. Like little vortexes of emptiness sucking everything out of my surroundings, to the point where I can see nothing and feel nothing.

Can I go back? The shadows are already draining the spirit from my veins. Can I find Silas and follow him back to safety?

Again that thrum of rage through me. But it's anger that doesn't belong to me. It's Silas. He doesn't want me to follow him.

The foreign anger gives me a momentary burst of energy, even as the shadows cloud around, seeking to drown me. This barren land shines through the shadows. The magma, again bright and hot in the distance. The ash cloud, grim and foreboding but present, real, full. Not empty. Not vacant like the shadows.

The anger also gives me clarity of thought. I pause, reflecting, weighing my next move. The shadows are chasing me forward. But Silas says not to go back.

One path in. One path out.

The gravedigger's words: "Your fight will lead you to the center of your own labyrinth."

What if he meant that literally?

I close my eyes and the threads of the universe burst into life, stronger, undiluted by the shadows. Where are they taking me? I have to know. This time, I let my fingers find the Path by instinct, rather than by intent, blindly, like a harpist who knows exactly where her strings are, like the pianist who can play Rachmananov with his eyes closed. And sure enough, the Path opens. The hole gapes before me, like a wound in the fabric of spacetime. I leap into it.

I ignore the rush of Silas's fear. His fear doesn't have to be mine.

I let the Path crush and rebuild me.

On the other side, I am floating in a supernova.

Dust and gas swirl on all sides, three hundred and sixty degrees above and below me, in lights and colors and patterns unimaginable. They have coalesced into clouds of matter, vague shapes with blurred boundaries that morph and shift as

I watch. I am no longer composed of biological matter, but of the same stuff around me: I glance down at my hands, my legs, only to find that I am as unformed as the material I float in.

This must be like Chroma.

Something else Silas said jogs at my memory. What was it?

The memory triggers. I remember cold cement against my back, the stiff mattress beneath my legs. Down is too simple, he said. It's not down so much as it is *back through.*

I'm moving back through worlds, back to the genesis of the multiverse. That's where the shadows want me. I'm diving back into their realm—into the worlds they've already devoured, the spaces already swallowed.

I'm heading into the mouth of the underworld.

One by one, the glimmering stars in the distance are swallowed by darkness.

At last, comes a voice in my head. I shiver as ice and lead envelop my limbs. *Our portal has come to us. And now your world will end.*

"No," I whisper. "You can't."

We can do anything, the voice says, *now that we have you.*

THE LABYRINTH

"Damn it," he sighed. "How will I ever get out of this labyrinth!"
—Gabriel Garcia Marquez, *The General in his Labyrinth*

I scream my anger and fear to the blackened stars as the darkness rains across my vision. I throw my hands out, searching for a Path, but the threads are gone. I clench my fists and dig my fingers into my palms, bite my cheek with my teeth, desperate to feel pain, to feel anything, as every last sensation is erased.

Thank you, the voice says.

It sounds like echoes from the bottom of the ocean.

We have been hungry for a long, long time.

Silas! I scream, desperate to be heard one last time before I'm swallowed along with everything I've ever known.

Words ring up to me from the darkness. They sound cold and distant, but discernable. *One path in*, the voice says. *One path out.*

Suddenly, I know what I have to do.

I've never made a Path before. But I don't have the energy to fight what I know is right. Now or never. Now or everyone I love dies without trace or memory.

With the last of my strength, I reach out. My senses are fading to black, taste and touch and hearing dulled almost to nothing, but as I stretch out my fingers I sense what I'm looking for. The taste of ash on my tongue. A world of endless nothing. A grey so monotone it's worse than darkness.

Stop, says the voice of the shadows in my mind. But it's too late. I know the one place they can't find me. The one place they can't follow.

It's a world they've already destroyed.

I find the threads to the world I seek and pull, ripping the Path open. I take a deep breath and prepare to dive in.

And then I see a flash of color in the darkness. Oil-slick colors like a rainbow cut through the emptiness. A palm, not my own, pressing against my fingertips.

It's Silas. His touch electrifying. His words searing. His eyes so afraid.

"Noomi, *no*—"

But it's too late.

I'm already falling. I let him go.

"I'm sorry," I whisper. "This is the only way."

There's a ringing in my ears, a scream of anguish and power like nothing I've ever known. For a split second every sensation returns in the form of pain, pain I haven't felt since I became a Pathfinder, pain drawn to unimaginable intensity because I haven't felt real pain, physical pain, in so long I've forgotten what it feels like. Every nerve ending in my body is pulled in opposite directions. Every fiber of skin, every organ, every cell alight with flame.

It's the cry of the shadows, anguished and hungry, realizing their prey has escaped.

And then the Path crushes me. Silas's iridescent eyes flash one last time before mine, and then he, too is gone. The pain is gone. Just the sense of crushing weight of demolition, of collapsing into myself.

When I am rebuilt, I open my eyes in the world I tore into. Immediately I close the gash behind me. There are no other Paths—they were all destroyed when the shadows ate this world. Now, no one can follow. There's no one here. No Paths through which to chase me. No way to find me.

One Path in. One Path out. The center of my labyrinth. Where no one—not even the shadows—can find me.

The world I stand in is the grey of unpolished steel. The scorched color of ash. I look around, searching for more. But I already know what I'll find: nothing. A world as empty as the shadows.

I walk. My feet work, my legs work. My eyes are still wet and itchy. Some semblance of me remains.

I walk a thousand steps but nothing changes. Like being in the sky except there are no stars.

Cold.

Grey.

Empty.

And all around me, there's nothing to see.

EPILOGUE

CRYSTALLIZATION

"Nucleation, the initial process that occurs in the formation of a crystal from a solution, a liquid, or a vapour, in which a small number of ions, atoms, or molecules become arranged in a pattern characteristic of a crystalline solid, forming a site upon which additional particles are deposited as the crystal grows."
—Encyclopaedia Brittanica, "Nucleation"

With the force of an explosion, I'm thrown back onto the grassy lawn behind Noomi's grandmother's house. My head spins; my ears ring with the echoes of that anguished sound, the last thing I heard before my tenuous hold on Noomi's hand slipped and I was sucked bodily back through the Path I had built from Noomi's world to the earliest seconds of the multiverse.

My vision blurs as pain rushes through my body. I inhale; the breath comes hard. There's a pressure on my lower left abdomen that makes me think I might have cracked a rib. Ada's face swims before mine. She reaches out tentatively and puts her hand on my shoulder.

"Silas?" she says. "Are you okay?"

I push myself up onto my elbows. Blinding pain sears through my chest, but I fight the temptation to lie down again.

"I'm not sure," I reply.

"Where's Noomi? Did you find her?"

I focus on Ada's face, trying to solidify my vision, to stop the world from swimming. I wonder at her courage. Just moments ago she was with Paul in a desert world not far from Noomi's where I found them together. He had slung her across his shoulders like a slain deer as he ran through the dunes. When I shouted her name and she lifted her head and saw me, she started screaming, punching his back and kicking violently. Surprised by this ferocity, Paul dropped her, and she came sprinting toward me. The instant our hands connected, I closed my eyes, found a Path, and took us back to her home world.

I still didn't understand Paul's plan, how or why he was working with the shadows.

Not until I heard Noomi's silent scream in my head did I understand.

Ada was a distraction. Paul wanted to separate me from Noomi. Somehow—*how?*—he knew I wouldn't let Noomi come with me.

But he also knew Noomi would never sit idly by, waiting for me to return with her sister.

We'd played right into his hands. Damned if you do. Damned if you don't.

I felt every Path she took. I knew how far she was from her home world. But I had no idea how close she was to the shadows. They must have been pulling her further back, enticing her every step of the way.

When I heard her cry, I realized what I'd done.

I left Ada in the playhouse. Paul wouldn't be after her anymore, now he'd accomplished what he set out to do. But Noomi needed me. The shadows were drowning her, and she was too close to their world. There would be nowhere for her to turn.

By the time I got there, it was too late.

She'd already opened the Path and stepped into it.

I felt it when she closed the Path behind her.

I was thrown back into the Path I'd taken. Back here, onto the grass in Noomi's grandmother's backyard.

Despite the pain in my chest and the bruises already blooming on my back, I have the strangest feeling of crystallizing. Solidifying. The outlines of my body, normally faded and indistinct in Noomi's world, becoming clear and defined. The hair on my skin prickles.

I studied crystallization in grade school. Crystallization happens when dissolved molecules within a liquid or gas cluster together to form stable, microscopically solid structures that build outward in patterns.

Crystallizing. Solidifying. The molecules that make up my body are stabilizing and building outward. I feel solid in a way normally reserved for my home world.

Tentatively, I close my eyes, hoping to see the threads that bind the world the same way I always did. Hoping to reach out and find a Path. A way home. A lifeline to Noomi. But I already suspect what's happened. The threads are gone. The Paths are gone. There's nothing but darkness behind my eyes.

Noomi locked herself in a destroyed world—the only place the shadows can't get to her. But in the process, she bound me here, to this world. The last place I was before she closed the Path behind her.

If you can't travel, I can't either, I think, wondering if she can hear me. We are, after all, entangled.

Ada's face swims before my eyes.

"Yes," I say. "I found her."

"Where is she? Is she coming back?"

I wrap my arms around the little girl and pull her close.

"No," I say. "She's not coming back. Not for a long time." Maybe not ever. But I don't say that.

Ada presses her cheek into my shoulder.

"Why not? Where is she?"

I don't know how to tell her the truth. All I know is that my life has crystallized around one goal.

Find Noomi.

And bring her back.

~ fin ~

The next part of the story belongs to Silas.
Look out for book two,

Coming soon.

THANK YOU

Thank you for reading THE PATHS BETWEEN THE STARS. If you enjoyed this book, please consider leaving a review. Reviews help other readers find great books and are the best way to support independent authors.

Sign up for Amira K. Makansi's author newsletter to be the first to hear about THE WORLDS BETWEEN OUR DREAMS, Book Two of the Many Skies Series, and other books by Amira

LINKS TO OTHER BOOKS BY AMIRA K. MAKANSI

The Seeds Trilogy, including
The Prelude
The Sowing
The Reaping
The Harvest

Literary Libations: What to Drink With What You Read

ACKNOWLEDGEMENTS

This book has been a work in progress since 2014, when it was first birthed as an experiment on my blog. I am forever indebted to the readers who followed along with the earliest versions of the story and offered comments, insight, and their own creative spin, creating an organic storytelling process that felt revolutionary. These readers (many of whom are writers in their own right) include Daryl Rothman, Nillu Stelter, Jessica West, Rachael Spellman, J. Edward Paul, Graham Milne, Peter Samet, and many more. They helped guide the basic premise, the bones of the story, which gave me the fuel to keep moving forward.

The story did not end there, and for many years this novel was a quiet labor of love seen only by a few, who are responsible for motivating me to continue working. These individuals include my closest friends and family members: my cousin Rayan who reviewed and offered insight into the Arabic passages, my uncle Tarek Makansi, my dad Jason Makansi, my sister Elena Makansi, and my mom Kristy Blank Makansi, who did the stunning layout for this novel and to whom I will forever be indebted for all the hard (and free) work she does for her daughters. Other early readers who helped me with the first and most significant revision process include Nillu Stelter, Taylor Zajonc, and my agent, Andrea Somberg, all of whom read and offered feedback that helped this book become what it is today.

I owe a huge debt of gratitude to my editor, Debi Alper, whose comments provided both the confidence I needed to take this book to publication and the feedback required to make it a quality, well-written novel. I am also grateful to my proofreader, Shuna Meade, and my cover design team, James Egan and Kira Rubenthaler at Bookfly Design, for giving this book a beautiful face to present to the world.

I am thankful to all my friends for their support and encouragement throughout the process of creating this book, and a few deserve particular mention: Sky Evans, Eva Ford, Kristen Scheitler-Ring, Ava Derosier, and Cassie Spiker. Some friends offered consultation on some of the more technical parts of the book, such as Prashant Parmar, Maria Phyllis, and Hawk Dykes, and I will forever be grateful to them for sharing their valuable time and expertise with me.

It is no understatement to say that I don't know how I would have survived the last few years without my dog Alder. Although she will never read this book, I will always be grateful to her little soul for comforting me through hard times and celebrating with me in the good.

ABOUT THE AUTHOR

Amira K. Makansi got into writing accidentally, when her mother had a crazy dream and wanted to turn it into a book. That book became THE SOWING, the first book in the young adult dystopian SEEDS series, which has been optioned for a Hollywood production. She is also the author of LITERARY LIBATIONS: *What to Drink With What You Read*, an informal guide to pairing great drinks with famous books. After graduating from the University of Chicago with a degree in history, Amira quickly abandoned her quest to become a lawyer in favor of all things beverage-related. She spent her first few years out of college climbing around in stacks of wine barrels and hoeing weeds out of vineyards in France. She has served cocktails at a Michelin-starred restaurant in Chicago and cleaned hundred-year-old foudres at an Alsatian winery whose first vintage predates the French revolution. Now, Amira is delighted to spend her days promoting fine wines, writing, reading, drinking, cooking and exploring the great outdoors with her furry, four-legged sidekick, Alder.